THE DAY
THE THAMES
CAUGHT FIRE

PETER CHAMBERS

ST. MARTIN'S PRESS
NEW YORK

Library of Congress Cataloging-in-Publication Data

Chambers, Peter,
      The day the Thames caught fire / Peter Chambers.
         p.   cm.
   "A Tom Dunne Book"
   ISBN 0-312-04294-9
   I. Title.
   PR6066.H463D39   1990
   823'.914—dc20   89-77924
                                             CIP

First published in Great Britain by Chivers Press

First U.S. Edition

10 9 8 7 6 5 4 3 2 1

THE DAY THE THAMES CAUGHT FIRE

CHAPTER ONE

Baxter placed both hands at the edge of the pool, steadying himself. Then, in one clean movement, he heaved himself clear of the water and climbed out, scorning the submerged steps which stood ten feet away. He stood for a moment in the pale morning light, taking deep breaths, while water ran down his tanned and muscular frame to form small pools around his feet. He had swum his routine ten lengths, and was now ready to leave. There were other people using the pool, mainly members of the local swimming club, together with a few keep-fit enthusiasts, but he paid them no attention. One or two of them had tried to exchange pleasantries with him when he first appeared at the early morning sessions, but found it an unrewarding experience. Baxter was not by nature a sociable man, and he picked with care the few people with whom he chose to mix. Certainly he had no intention of becoming familiar with any of these soft-bellied City business types, with their rolled umbrellas waiting in the changing rooms.

He set off at a brisk pace to the far end of the pool, where he pushed his way through the clanking iron turnstile and headed for the lockers. Peeling the thick rubber band from his broad wrist he handed it to the sleepy attendant, who read the stencilled number and passed over the appropriate key. Strange sort of man, reflected the attendant. Same time every day, Sundays and all, and never said a word. Most people at least said good morning, or nice day, or something. Not him. Just walked in as if he owned the bleeding place, did his little swim, then pushed off. Not to catch a train though, like most. He didn't get that rich golden tan sitting behind any desk, and the muscles were used to something a bit more strenuous than picking up telephones. The attendant often wondered about him, but there was a chilling detachment about the man which discouraged even normal courtesies. It seemed to come from his eyes, which were pale and remote, and gave the feeling of seeing right through a man. He was one to stay away

1

from, you could be sure of that.

Baxter had no idea of what was going on in the attendant's mind, and he wouldn't have been in the slightest bit interested. A quick rub with a large rough towel, and he dressed swiftly. Casual slacks, a zip-fronted ski-jacket, and rubber-soled canvas shoes. Unwrapping the large handkerchief he checked methodically at the contents. Comb, car keys, a pound in loose change. Transferring these to his pockets, he walked out into the car park. At the far end he noticed a man sitting on a wooden bench, reading a newspaper. Lazy sod, he reflected. He'd probably kidded his wife he was having a morning dip, and now had to fill in time until the train went. Baxter unlocked the door on his two-year-old Cortina, and was about to get in when he noticed the envelope on the seat. How the devil did that get there? There could be no possibility that he'd done anything so careless as to leave any of the doors unlocked, but he checked nevertheless. Each door in turn resisted his touch. Whoever had left the envelope had been careful to lock up behind himself. He stared at the white oblong, not touching it. It was addressed, in large clear capitals, to 'MAJOR BAXTER'. It couldn't be a letter-bomb, it was too flat. Most people, in Baxter's position, would not even contemplate the possibility, but then, most people had not spent half a lifetime acquiring enemies in strange parts of the globe.

He picked up the envelope, examined it all over, then got behind the driving wheel, and opened it carefully. There was a single folded sheet of paper with a typed message.

'If you are available, be at the Lord Nelson in Oxshott at twelve noon, lounge bar. The enclosed will cover expenses.'

There were five brand new twenty pound notes inside. He looked at the money, then read the note again. Available. That was the key word. To the majority of people the word would have been innocuous. They would have taken it to mean that he could have had some earlier commitment at lunchtime, but that was not what it meant to Baxter. It meant that if he was currently open to job offers, it would pay him to be at this public house at the stated time.

And a hundred pounds for expenses.

That was a nice touch. It indicated that a hundred one way or the other was of little importance to whoever wrote the note. If Baxter chose not to keep the appointment, that would be the end of the matter. He smiled thinly. Somebody seemed to have his measure. He was not the man to hang on to the money, and forgo the satisfaction of facing whoever sent it. Curiosity would take him to Oxshott at lunchtime. Curiosity about his correspondent, and also about the proposition which would certainly be put to him.

He placed message and money carefully into the breast pocket of his jacket, and turned the ignition key. Then he drove slowly away, stopping at the exit-barrier to press three ten pence coins into the slot. The metal arm rose, and he moved out, pausing at the T-junction for a suitable break in the traffic. A bus stopped to pick up passengers further along the road, holding up the stream, and Baxter eased the Cortina onto the highway and was gone.

The man on the bench folded up his newspaper with great care. Then he stood up, smoothed his jacket, and walked across to a telephone box.

*   *   *

At five minutes to twelve that day, a blue Cortina turned into the narrow opening leading to the car park at the rear of the Lord Nelson. A tall, sunburned man climbed out, locking up with great care. Then he walked, with free-swinging steps, to the gaily painted door marked Lounge Bar, and stepped inside. It was a largish room, but low and raftered. A ship's wheel was embedded in the ceiling, and there was sea-faring bric-à-brac dotted around the walls. At that hour on a Monday trade was slack, and the florid-faced man behind the bar was waiting for his order as he crossed the carpeted floor.

'Good morning sir.'

'Morning. Scotch please. Bell's.'

'Anything with it, sir?'

'No.'

3

Baxter paid for his drink and looked around for somewhere to sit. There was an empty table in one corner, below a window, and it commanded a good view of both doors. It also had the advantage of being the furthest seat away from the gaudy juke-box, which was all lit up, but fortunately not at the moment in action. Settled in his new vantage point, he studied the other customers. A man and woman were deeply engaged in conversation in another window-seat. The man was doing most of the talking, keeping his voice low, and seemed to be trying to convince the woman about something. She was looking strained, and interrupted him from time to time. They had quite enough to occupy them without the added complication of anyone named Baxter. At one end of the bar stood three men, obviously local business types, who all knew each other, and chattered inconsequentially about the weekend's football. An elderly man and his wife sat primly, not speaking, with drinks on the table in front of them which were hardly touched. A bit of shopping, as evidenced by the plastic bags which rested on the floor between them, then a drink in the pub, and home for lunch. There was only one man who was unaccompanied, and he was perched on a stool at the opposite end of the bar from the football enthusiasts. This man watched the barman anxiously, eager to engage him in conversation whenever he came within talking distance. He was a familiar type, and there was usually one like him in most public houses. He would spend hours on his stool, spinning out his drinks, and ready to talk to anyone who would listen.

Baxter looked at his watch.

It was twelve noon precisely, and he frowned slightly. An appointment was an appointment, and inattention to the demands of the clock was to him an indication of a sloppy approach. It did not bode well for whatever was to follow. If people could not be bothered—

The rear door opened and a newcomer appeared. He was a man of medium height, with heavy tortoiseshell spectacles dominating his thick features, and a luxuriant crop of black curly hair, well-trimmed. He wore a dark grey business suit, with white shirt and a navy blue organisation tie.

4

He stood inside the door, looking around, then saw Baxter and came across to greet him.

'Afternoon,' he greeted, as though they were old friends, 'can I get you a drink?'

Baxter nodded, emptying his glass and handing it over. 'Bell's,' he replied.

The new arrival was a few years younger than himself, about thirty-five or so. His voice was gently cultured, without being aggressively so, and the hand which had removed the empty glass had been large and soft. Soft, thought Baxter. Yes, that just about summed up his new acquaintance. In the physical sense, at least. He would reserve judgement about the man's inner qualities until he'd had a proper opportunity to assess them.

'One Bell's.'

The stranger parked himself in the wooden chair opposite Baxter. In his hand was a half-pint mug of beer, and Baxter knew it would be bitter.

'Cheers.'

They sipped at their drinks, inspecting each other.

'You had no trouble in finding the place?'

Baxter shook his head.

'No. Not much traffic about today.'

The other man nodded, as though he'd said something of vital importance.

'That's why we suggested the Nelson. Usually pretty quiet on a Monday. My name is Halloran, by the way. George Halloran.'

He made no offer to shake hands. Baxter nodded, and waited for him to carry on. Halloran smiled briefly, and the waiting man wished he could have seen his eyes better.

'Are we to take it that you could be interested in what we have to say?'

Baxter stared at him coolly.

'You are to take it that I'm here,' he replied. 'You paid my fare, after all. It seemed only civil. And who's we? I don't recall seeing you in any royal photographs.'

Halloran smiled briefly.

'It's almost two months since you got back from Nawabia. Rather a messy business, that, and you needed a little time

to relax. Eight weeks seemed about right, and you're probably open to offers now. You're quite right, incidentally, I
claim no royal blood. I speak for others.'

He knew about Nawabia, then. Baxter's face expressed
no reaction to this news, but these people obviously knew a
lot about him.

'I'm listening,' he confirmed.

Halloran leaned forward slightly. Although his words
carried clearly over the table, the tone was so low that
no-one else could possibly overhear.

'You've always been a military man,' he began. 'This little
undertaking of ours is not strictly a military or political
matter. However, it is a complex business, and requires a
military approach if it is to succeed. We need someone like
yourself, with experience of personnel and tactics, someone
who understands the need for proper planning, rehearsal
and so forth. Do you think you might be interested?'

Baxter shrugged.

'How can I say? You haven't told me anything yet.'

'Ah no, so I haven't.' Halloran smiled, and took a brief sip
at his glass. 'I have a rather cautious nature, you see.'

At least he hadn't said 'we'.

'I like people to be cautious,' Baxter assured him. 'At the
same time, you can't expect me to buy a pig in a poke. Try a
little vulgarity, Mr. Halloran. Talk about unspeakable
things. Start with money.'

If he had been hoping to shock his listener, he was to be
disappointed. The only reaction was the pleasant sound of a
low, throaty chuckle.

'Very well. We are talking of large amounts. I believe, for
instance, that the little affair in Nawabia was to have paid
you thirty thousand pounds? In the event, you were never
paid the full amount, and were lucky to escape with your
life. The venture we are now considering would involve no
such risk, I can promise you, and the rewards would be
substantially greater.'

Nothing wrong with this chap's staff work, reflected
Baxter, with some bitterness. He had only just recovered
from that ill-fated expedition, and was still smarting from
the way he'd been cheated out of his money.

'You seem to know a hell of a lot,' he grunted. 'Go on then, let's hear about this substantial reward.'

Halloran nodded, almost as if to himself, and when he next spoke it was in little more than a whisper.

'We are talking in terms of a quarter of a million pounds.'

A quarter of a million? That was a great deal of money, by any yardstick, and was far more than Baxter had received in total for twenty years of fighting, with his life at risk more times than he could remember.

'Am I required to rob the Bank of England?' he queried.

There was no smile on the other man's face.

'No. We are not quite that ambitious.'

'How many of us will there be to share this windfall?'

George Halloran removed the heavy spectacles, and began to polish idly at the lenses. This man Baxter was definitely interested, despite his poker face and unrevealing eyes. It was time to be hauling him in.

'Share?' he echoed. 'Why no-one, my dear sir. The sum mentioned is your personal fee. Other—um—salary commitments will be our problem.'

Baxter knew that he would never get another opportunity like this. He would need to know a lot more about it, before final commitment, but a man would be a fool not to take it further.

'All right,' he conceded. 'I'm definitely interested. What happens now?'

His prospective employer replaced his glasses, pressing them into position with a final push at the bridge.

'Why, nothing,' he explained. 'The purpose of our little chat today was simply to establish whether you are to be considered as a serious recruit, and I think we've achieved that. I shall now report back to that effect, and you will be hearing from us further in due course.'

He stood up, with the evident intention of leaving. Baxter stared up at him.

'You mean that's it?' he demanded.

'For the present, yes.'

'Well, I want to know a hell of a lot more than I've been told so far,' he stated flatly.

Halloran bent down, his hands resting on the table.

'Of course you do, my dear fellow, and so you shall. But you must appreciate that this is a matter of some importance. You are the last person to wish to involve himself in a scheme which is not planned down to the last detail. Our little chat today is part of that planning. You will be hearing from us again within a week at most. For now, I wish you good day.'

He straightened up and nodded. Baxter made no move as George Halloran turned away and went out. As the door closed, he rose and looked out of the window into the car park. Halloran went straight to a gleaming red MG and began to unlock the door. Baxter twitched his lips. They seemed to think they were dealing with some amateur, he reflected. He didn't like the position he was in, one of waiting for unknown people to contact him when the fancy took them. It was too one-sided altogether. The more he knew about them the better, and his projected role of docile puppet, waiting for someone to pull a string, held no appeal. They'd made their first bloomer with the MG. It would be difficult to lose such a distinctive hare. He waited until the car was on the move, then left the public house and walked quickly to the Cortina.

The front tyres were flat.

CHAPTER TWO

Baxter was no stranger to Heathrow Airport, but it was his first experience of Terminal One. This was the point for departures on short-haul flights, mainly in Europe, whereas his normal destinations were much further afield. He strolled, fascinated, among the jostling busy crowds, soaking up the atmosphere of what the pilots referred to dismissively as the 'bucket and spade' runs. Although it was only mid-April, there was an air of holiday about the place, and there were a number of children in the queue he joined at the British Airways desk.

'No luggage, sir?'

The trim attractive girl behind the desk looked at him enquiringly.

'No. Just this.'

He held up his small leather handgrip for her to see. She nodded and smiled, handing over his boarding-pass, and gave her attention to the next passenger.

Baxter checked the details out of habit. He always checked everything, even his change at the supermarket. How did the phrase go? Mistakes Cannot Afterwards Be Rectified, that was it. Satisfied, he walked to the nearest bookstall to buy a newspaper.

His ticket was a first-class return to Palma, Majorca. It had arrived by registered post the previous day, together with five hundred pounds. There was no accompanying note. Five days had passed since his meeting with George Halloran, and he had found himself becoming increasingly impatient to learn more about this venture, with its stated promise of a quarter of a million pounds in his pocket. Baxter was very sceptical about that part. It was too much, vastly more than he had ever been offered previously, and he simply did not believe it. He was a man with long experience of optimistic promises, and had developed an attitude of wary mistrust, which had frequently stood him in good stead.

Later, as he took his seat in the first-class cabin, he

9

thought briefly about his last trip out of the U.K. At least, on this occasion, he had a return ticket.

*   *   *

Philip Ralph Baxter had been born on September 15, 1940. It was a day which would pass into history for quite other reasons, since it was the day on which the Battle of Britain was won. On that glorious day, while Moira Baxter threshed and suffered in a small London nursing home, the Royal Air Force was busy decimating the attacking Luftwaffe waves over Southern England. Baxter's father was himself an R.A.F. man, but, at that stage of the war, was less gloriously engaged in pilot-training. Lucky enough to obtain a forty-eight-hour pass, following the birth of his son, Philip Baxter hurried home. The capital was agog with the famous air victory, and both parents felt it was fitting that their son's name should mark the splendid coincidence. The vicar, however, patriotic as the next man, could not be persuaded that Raf was an acceptable baptismal offering, and the nearest they could manage was Ralph.

The small Baxter never really knew his father, who died in a blazing Hurricane when the boy was four years old. All he knew was that his father had been killed by the enemy, and the enemy were foreigners. A deep hatred of all things foreign was bred in the childish mind, and was in no way dispelled as he grew. He was an odd little fellow, rather small for his age, and very introspective. He would join in with organised games, and acquit himself well enough, but he showed, early on, some undesirable quirks of character. At football, for example, he was told that the object of the game was to get the ball somehow into the net at the opposite end of the field. There were a number of other boys who seemed determined to prevent him, and many of them were inches taller and pounds heavier. But the small Baxter was not to be deterred. He had been given clear instructions and an objective, towards which he proceeded, using feet, fists and even once his teeth, to discourage those who wanted to deprive him of the ball. Rescued finally from beneath a heap of enraged opponents, he was astonished to find himself

10

not praised, but berated by a furious sports master, and ostracised, not only by opponents, but also members of his own team. This episode led to one of the many meetings between his parents—Moira having married again—and the headmaster. Indeed, more than one headmaster, since the boy changed schools several times, but always with the same result. 'Lacks the team spirit', was one verdict, 'Considers himself above the rules' was another. There was one occasion when a master's car was set on fire. No-one ever traced the culprit, but it was noteworthy that the master concerned had recently had occasion to punish a certain P. R. Baxter.

At fourteen, the hitherto under-sized boy suddenly began to grow, and the next two years were a nightmare of let-down jackets and trousers, as his mother strove to keep pace with the advancing inches. At a height of six feet he ceased to grow upwards and began instead to fill out. By the time he was seventeen, he was a young bull, with strongly developed muscles and an ever-present willingness to exercise them, preferably on other people. Academically, he was of average ability and well able to pass the examinations which were thrust in front of him at monotonously regular intervals. At eighteen he went into the army, where he was an instant success. The various dramas which had punctuated his life up to that point had bred in him a certain awareness. Although his inclinations remained the same, he had learned that there were times when it was prudent to restrain them. He saw very quickly how unprofitable it was to thwart the instructors, and so he decided to keep a low profile on public occasions. The N.C.O.s were quick to mark him out as an unusual prospect. He excelled at everything physical and seemed to have a natural affinity with weapons. It was the boxing contest which finally put the seal of approval on Private Baxter's military career. He went for his opponents hammer and tongs, with no finesse and little skill, but he reached the semi-finals after four straight knock-outs. Now he met his match, in a regimental title-holder with much experience and ringcraft behind him. Against such opposition, Baxter's crude tactics could not prevail, but he left the other man with a number of painful blows to remember before he finally succumbed. A year later, the *London Gazette* noted the advent of a certain Second-Lieutenant Baxter, P. R., and it seemed the young man had at last found his niche. Overseas duty followed, and in 1960 he found himself in West Berlin as part of the peace-keeping presence. In the course of his duties, he encountered a black-market operation. Instead of processing his information through channels, he decided to deal with the matter himself, questioning the suspects with a degree of ferocity which would in no way have been countenanced by the constituted authorities. Nevertheless, he got results, and that small operation was brought to an end. There were a few raised eyebrows at the broken and bleeding condition of several of the guilty parties, but since they all admitted having resisted arrest, no further enquiries were made. Towards the end of his tour of duty, there was another incident which caused a flutter of concern among his superiors. Lieutenant Baxter was the driver of a jeep which ran down a young West German girl one dark wet night. The girl had been pregnant, but lost the child as a result of the accident. In her initial hysteria she had claimed that Baxter was the father of the child, but later retracted the statement, saying that she had been confused by the pain and the various drugs administered. Baxter's concern had done him credit, and he had made regular visits to the patient until she was safely out of danger. Little account was taken of the report by one nurse, who had entered the sick-room to find Baxter standing over the terrified girl with a hypodermic syringe in his hand. He explained that he had considered it a dangerous article to be within reach of anyone in a confused state of mind, and was simply moving it to a safe distance. It was shortly after this incident that the girl changed her original statement.

On his return to the U.K., Baxter fretted. There was no peace to be kept there, and indeed little soldiering of any kind. Fortunately for him, the stay was brief. It was a time of sporadic outbursts of unrest all over the globe, with consequent threats to expatriate British life and property. He soon found himself overseas again, and this time he was in his element. Unusually for a fair-skinned man, Baxter thrived

12

in the hot tropic sun, and he adapted with relish to the new conditions, weather and duty alike. He actually enjoyed the patrols, seeking out the roving bands of marksmen in the scrubby hill-country, and engaging them wherever possible. The streets of the city, too, held no terror for him. He would lead his men into the darkest by-ways, challenging anyone whom he considered to be in the least suspicious, and showing no mercy. It was inevitable, in such troubled times, that a percentage of innocent people should suffer, and Baxter's activities made a heavy contribution to those statistics. He neither showed nor felt any remorse, when it was demonstrated that the prisoner was entirely free of blame, and had his own formula for such cases. If the accused man was still alive, damaged and broken but still alive, then he was lucky. If, as was more likely, he was dead, then it didn't matter. They were all bloody foreigners anyway. You couldn't trust any of them further than you could see them, and all he had done had been to forestall some future treachery.

It was in 'Nam that he finally overstepped the mark, although, as usual, nothing against him could be proved. But the authorities finally realised that Baxter was becoming a liability. His superiors wanted him out of the way and it fell to his colonel to suggest a complete change of duty. Not merely a shifting from one theatre to another, but a different branch of the army altogether. There were a number of alternatives open, Signals perhaps, or the Engineers, several others. Wherever the choice lay, the receiving unit would be getting a damned fine officer, and he'd see they were aware of the fact.

Baxter listened to his colonel as he bumbled away, clearly as embarrassed as hell about the whole business. As well he might be, he thought savagely. They were suggesting that he'd be better off burying himself alive, that's what they were doing. Well, the hell with them. He was a fighting soldier, not a bloody mechanic or a clerk. If the British Army wouldn't let him fight, there were plenty of people who would, and he would go to them.

Three months later, Mr. Baxter spent half an hour drinking with some rather suave characters in a private room at a large hotel in the West End. When he left, he was Major Baxter in the glorious army of the revolution, with a fat retainer in his pocket. Thus began the career which he was to follow in a dozen different deserts, jungles and swamp-lands across the face of the globe, a fifteen-year span of blood-letting which had earned him the soubriquet of the Bad Major, or sometimes merely Bad Baxter.

Nawabia had been the scene of his most recent operation, and this chap Halloran seemed to know all about that. His thoughts were interrupted by the sudden crackle of the tannoy.

'We are approaching Palma Airport. Please fasten your seat-belts.'

CHAPTER THREE

As the bus slowed down to negotiate the busy corner, Hardcastle jumped off, narrowly dodged a following taxi, and reached the pavement. The bus conductor shouted an obscene forecast as to his longevity prospects, but he ignored it, along with a stream of abuse from the startled cab-driver.

The one-time cinema was now a bingo-hall, and he walked past the glaring posters, with their promises of huge sums waiting to be won, and turned into an alleyway at the side of the building. There was a small news kiosk which partly obstructed the access, and the proprietor watched as the newcomer made his way to an iron exit door, opened it and went inside. The man in the kiosk knelt down to undo a parcel of magazines, and spoke quietly into a small microphone.

Hardcastle shut the door behind him. He was now standing on a four-foot concrete square, completely sealed off from the main building except for a narrow flight of stone steps, which led down to a second steel door. There were no handles or locks on this door, which could only be opened from inside. Producing a plastic card from his pocket, he stretched up and inserted it into a narrow slot in the wall. There was a pause, then a faint humming sound as the door swung inwards. Hardcastle went through into the familiar corridor, and walked past several doors before reaching the room he wanted. Then he knocked briefly and entered.

'Ah, Hardcastle, we meet again.'

The mocking greeting came from a girl who had turned her chair to watch his entrance. Surrounding her on three sides was a complex of computerised gadgetry, but Hardcastle paid it no attention. His interest in the microchip, as he was fond of saying, was approximately equal to his understanding of it, which was nil. The girl was a different matter altogether. In her late twenties, she had ash-blonde hair which was pulled tight into an old-fashioned bun at the back of her head. Her face was long and narrow behind the saucer-shaped spectacles, which obscured about forty per cent of it. The mobile mouth, which could look so disapproving, was at that moment parted in a half-smile.

'Hallo Fiske,' he returned, annoyed to hear that his tone was much softer than he had intended. Jennifer Fiske always had the same unmanning effect on him, and he resented it.

Until two years before, when he first joined this strange organisation, he had been more than content with his own conception of himself as a macho combination of brains and physical prowess. The professorship which he held at a small northern university gave him ample scope for demonstration of his sharp intellect, while at the same time affording him sufficient freedom to carry on with his considerable sporting activities. A fearsome opponent in a rugby scrimmage, he was also a swimmer of note, and had at one time been a serious contender in the triple A decathlon events. Women had never been a problem, since he could meet most of them on at least equal terms whatever their interests. Indeed, life in general was decidedly pleasant, and he often wondered how he had come to permit himself to be seduced away from his comfortable niche. The people in Whitehall had been very persuasive, with their high-sounding talk of national security, debt to his country, and all the rest of it.

In his mind's eye, he had had some conception of his new role as being a kind of James Bond with extra added intellect. He would be privy to the innermost councils of political thought, making his modest but sound contribution to the furtherance of the democratic principle. In practice, he had found himself parked in a small office in a section which processed information connected with the progress of under-developed peoples. He had just begun to fret at the seeming pointlessness of his new role, when he found himself posted on a course described as Development Training. In the weeks which followed, he learned many things essential to his new existence, things far removed from the processing of paper, and which strained both his intellect and his physique to the limit. Since then, he had been sent to various parts of the globe to learn at first hand how best to serve the interests of under-developed peoples. There were others in the field, from different ideological backgrounds, whose plans for the less fortunate were markedly different from those of H.M. Government. Such people had to be countered and dissuaded, by whatever means came to hand, and Ben Hardcastle had proved himself a natural choice for the work.

Nowadays, he visited his office once a week only, in order to ensure that there was no paperwork jamming the system. His real base was this curious underground labyrinth, where Jennifer Fiske did magical things with what he called her 'mission control' equipment, and the strangely cold man called Jameson held sway.

'He wants you to wait five minutes,' announced the girl. 'Coffee?'

'Thanks.'

Hardcastle sat on a hard plastic chair, as she poured from the glass jug which never seemed to empty. Like that character in Greek mythology, who tried to drink the sea, he reflected. It was always good coffee, too, none of your instant granules. It was a pity they had to drink it from disposable plastic containers.

'Here.'

She placed the drink beside him, and at the same time put down a five penny piece.

'Thanks. What's that, a tip?'

'That's for your thoughts,' she replied, returning to her chair.

He stared at the coin, frowning.

'I thought the going rate was one penny.'

'For ordinary people's thoughts, yes,' she confirmed. 'I fancy your actual university professor's inner mind is worth rather more.'

There she was again, mocking him, eyes unfathomable behind the giant lenses. Hardcastle nodded.

'You're quite right, it is,' he agreed. 'One of the advantages of higher learning is that one's erotic fantasies are so much in advance of other people's.'

Jennifer Fiske grinned.

'And do these lewd imaginings concern me?'

17

'Exclusively.'

'Don't waste your time,' she advised. 'Stick to your sweaty little fans. They're so much easier to programme.'

A green light glowed on the desk. She jerked a thumb towards the inner door, and revolved her chair so that her back was to him. Hardcastle swallowed the last of his coffee, shrugged, and went into the inner sanctum, where a man sat watching his entrance.

Hector Jameson, for all his dandified appearance and occasional affectations of speech and manner, was a very tough nut. That was Hardcastle's private summation of him, an assessment which would have found favour in other quarters, although it would have been more elegantly expressed.

'Sit down, Hardcastle. It begins to look as though things are moving at last.'

The newcomer perched on another uncomfortable chair, the twin of the one he'd vacated in the computer room.

'Are they? I wouldn't know.'

There was no bitterness in the words. Hardcastle had long learned to accept that he only dealt with isolated pieces of a jigsaw puzzle. It was frequently the case that he never saw the completed picture. In the present instance, he had no idea of why the man Baxter should be of any importance. He simply monitored his movements, and reported. When the man finally did something interesting, by leaving for Majorca, he had fully expected to be told to follow him. Instead, he had been instructed to get back to base, and quickly. It made little sense to him, but then, that could be said of so much of his new work.

Jameson lit one of his Turkish cigarettes, and beamed.

'Interesting chap, your man Baxter. I think it's time you knew a bit more about him.' He opened a file on his desk, but scarcely glanced at it during the next few minutes. It was obvious that he knew the contents by heart. 'You recall all that fuss and palaver in Nawabia two months ago? Usual gang of roughnecks tried to take over the government. It was only because the Americans and ourselves were half-expecting it that they didn't pull it off. Baxter and his cronies got out by the skin of their teeth. We were really rather

18

upset with him at the time. Bad for the old image, to have Englishmen cavorting around the world like a bunch of international Al Capones. Still, he managed to get away. And it suited our purpose, as it happened.'

'Oh yes?' Hardcastle made no attempt to conceal his interest.

'Absolutely. Any theories about what was behind the Nawabia business?'

'The usual, I fancy. We found a lot of Russian equipment, if I remember rightly. And our old friends, the advisers, were on hand from Cuba. East meets West, with the usual half-starved bunch in the middle.'

Jameson narrowed his eyes and squinted disapproval.

'Note of political comment creeping into your tone, Hardcastle. Drop it. Last thing we want around here. Nasty shifty crowd, politicians. Remind me too much of dandelion seeds, blowing wherever the wind happens to take them. We can't afford to bugger about like that. Straight down the line, that's our game. Right and wrong is none of our concern, as you should know by this time. Get in, do the job, and get out quick. No time for speechifying. Don't want to have to remind you again.'

The offending man squirmed on his chair, nodding.

'Good. Now then, back to Nawabia. You obviously read the papers at the time. What you say is quite true, but it's only half the story. If our intelligence is to be believed, and I rather fancy it is, the glorious revolution was well on the way before the Russkis knew much about it. In short, they came in halfway through the picture. Not the first time it's happened, either. The view is held, and I'm bound to tell you I agree with it, that the opposition are being manipulated, and we can't have that, now can we?'

'I should have thought they were big enough to look after themselves,' Hardcastle replied. 'Why should we run round after them?'

His instructor nodded with enthusiasm.

'Oh quite, absolutely. Very capable chap, Ivan. Only trouble is, he lacks our breadth of vision, you see. Can't stand back and look at things objectively. Not like us in that respect. Show him something he doesn't like, and he starts to dash about shouting capitalists. To him that means Washington and us, and we really can't allow it. Trouble is, he's probably right about capitalists being responsible, but they're not official you see. Not at all.'

Hardcastle screwed up his forehead, clearly losing the thread.

'I'm sorry, but you're going to have to spell that out. Is it us, or isn't it?'

He was rewarded with a somewhat beady smile.

'Don't expect to have to explain too much, you know. Specially to an intellectual type like yourself. Still, you must be clear about this one, so I'll spell it out. We're not dealing here with governments, much less with ideologies. The people we're talking about are the money-boys. They're not concerned with boundaries and geography, still less with politics, except as tools. The concepts are too narrow and local, and worst of all, emotional. For a long time, these things were useful, because the money-men could operate under national flags, manipulating everyone else to achieve their ends. In the old days, it was easier than now. They could call it building the British Empire, developing the American West, any old tag would do. Out went the soldiers and the frontiersmen, and everyone was happy, but those days are over. A man's religion, or the colour of his skin, are no longer sufficient excuse for butchery and exploitation. There is only one major frontier left, and that is this nonsensical East and West division, so they have to do what they can with that. Life has become more complicated, even for the money-men. It was so much simpler in the old days. A few quick millions from armaments or trade goods were to be had for the asking. Child's play, by comparison. The only remaining target is the control of the resources of the planet itself.'

Jameson paused, and waited for Hardcastle to say something.

'The international conspiracy theory is not new to me,' said the listener stiffly. 'It's been mooted often enough.'

'Tchah,' exclaimed his senior dismissively. 'That's old hat, too. There might have been some kind of alliance between these chaps in the past, but we think it no longer applies. Ordinary men think only of money, but in the end it becomes meaningless. A man worth one hundred million is not going to exert himself to make it a hundred and ten. What would be the point? No, the real goal is power, and power has to be personal and individual. That's why we want to know who's behind these wars. That half-baked revolution in Nawabia was only a take-over attempt for its plutonium. No more, no less. Whoever sent Baxter on that little trip is likely to provide us with a lead to the real king-pin. Now do you see why we're so interested in this man? It wasn't his fault the thing came unstuck. He did his damnedest, and he's a good man. We think they'll use him again. That's why you're here.'

Hardcastle nodded uncomfortably.

'In that case, I don't see why you didn't send me after him.'

Jameson frowned at the shirtcuff on his right sleeve, then edged it carefully forward until it matched the exposure on his left.

'That would have put you at risk,' he explained. 'No fool, our friend Baxter. It won't suit our game to have the same face turn up in his vicinity very often. Someone else will pick him up at the other end, never fear. We shall know every move he makes. I rather fancy we already know one person he's liable to contact. Remember this chap?'

He held out a photograph. Hardcastle took it, staring at the face, and frowning.

'Why yes,' he confirmed. 'This is the man Baxter met in the pub at Oxshott, but this isn't the photograph I took at the time. This is much better. Do we know him, then?'

Jameson retrieved the glossy picture, smiling.

'Oh yes, an old friend. Not this department's, as it happens, but the Intelligence boys know him, and so do Interpol. Name is Halloran, mostly, George Halloran.'

The listener recalled once more the confident, prosperous-looking man with the red MG.

'Mostly?' he echoed. 'Has he another name, then?'

'Several,' confirmed the instructor. 'Among other things, he's a director of some broken-down shipping company out Panama-way. In that role he calls himself Charles

21

Cartwright. There's a hotel chain in India, where he's known as the Honourable Augustus de Vere Castleford. Chap changes his name the way you and I change shirts.'

'Interesting man. Does that mean he's one of these giant capitalists you've been on about?'

There were times when Hardcastle's turn of phrase offended the precise ears of his superior, and this was one of them. He resented the suggestion that he had been 'on' about anything. However, experience had taught him that the fellow's speech-patterns were too deeply embedded to be corrected now. Jameson contented himself with a slight wince.

'Not at all,' he demurred. 'My information is that Halloran, for all his outward trappings, is really a sort of glorified personal representative. The top man, the one who matters, is a far less accessible character, by the name of Ryder, Gregory Ryder. Now, there is a chap who really interests us. He heads up a most amazing network of companies, all over the world, and yet we know very little about him. Do you know, no-one can even say for certain what his nationality is?'

It was evident, from the warmth of his tone, that the man from Whitehall had a healthy regard for the mysterious Ryder. Hardcastle, having made one incorrect assessment, was emboldened to try again.

'Could he be our man, then?'

'It's possible,' returned Jameson shortly. He was rather annoyed at having his eulogy abbreviated. 'These money things are so damnably complicated that we can't actually work out where Ryder fits in, in league table terms.'

'League table?'

'Yes, you know the sort of thing. World's richest men, all that nonsense. He could be in the top ten, but on the other hand, he might not be in the top hundred. We just don't know. When I say the chap holds his cards up close, I mean really close.'

'Was there anything to connect him with the Nawabia affair?'

'Nothing,' came the terse reply. 'Not a single damned thing. Nor Halloran, for that matter, although that isn't

22

especially significant. There's more than one Halloran on Mr. Ryder's payroll. In fact, it would make good sense to use a different recruiting officer each time, wouldn't you say?'

Hardcastle nodded.

'That's what I'd do, in his place,' he agreed. 'Well then, what happens now?'

Jameson drummed lightly on the table top. The man had the delicate tapering hands of a violinist, thought his observer, not for the first time.

'A lot depends on what we hear from Majorca. You'd better be prepared to shove off at a moment's notice. There's nothing to say Baxter isn't already on his way. If he is, our man will tell us his next destination, and we'll get you there p.d.q.'

'On his way? Then why the return ticket?'

'Oh really, Hardcastle, sometimes your provincial mind puts rather a strain on my patience. A man has a return ticket, therefore he has to come back, otherwise he could have saved himself x pounds on the fare. We are talking here in terms of war, and you're worried about our suspect getting a bloody refund on his ticket.'

The rebuke was justified, and the sudden dull red on his visitor's face signalled that it had gone home.

'However, I rather think that he will come back,' continued Jameson, 'because he hasn't contacted any of his chums. I suggest you find a quiet chair somewhere, and start to familiarise yourself with the people on this list.'

He passed over a folder. Hardcastle opened it, to find half-a-dozen index cards, each with the photograph of a man, together with details of his physical description and recent history.

'These are his team?'

'Some of them, at least. There are probably others, but that is what we regard as his hard core. Pay special attention to the American, Mallory. He has been Baxter's number two in the past, and he's proved his worth. Luckily for us, he lives in London. Some of the others are scattered all over the place.'

Mallory was a reckless-looking man, with a devil-may-care look beneath the dark curly hair. He looked like the type a man would want beside him in a tight corner, reflected Hardcastle. He looked quickly at the other names, but none of them meant anything to him at that stage.

'Try to fix the faces in your mind,' came the instruction. 'If Baxter does come back here, and starts gathering up his team, he won't be putting a notice in *The Times*. A few phone calls, a quick word in a pub or a railway station, that's all the contact he needs. It's an odd thing about the man, that these people will go anywhere with him. He's as big a bastard as you could find in a month of Sundays, and yet the same names turn up around him time and again. Less the dead, of course. He always manages to lose a few.'

'And yet they still come?'

Jameson shrugged.

'No use asking me to explain it. Who knows what it is that rallies people? Look at Hitler. Anyway, buzz off and soak up that stuff. Tell Fiske where you're hiding. I'll give you a shout when there's any development.'

Hardcastle went back outside, where Jennifer Fiske was busily pressing buttons.

'Ah,' she greeted, eyeing the file, 'got some homework?'

'No,' he countered, 'it's prep. I have to stay in the building. Can you tell me where there's an empty desk?'

He was staring hopefully at an empty table in the corner of the room as he spoke. Jennifer shook her head.

'Not in here,' she dismissed, 'I'm not in the mood for your primitive mating calls. There's room next door for you, and you could try the blonde. She's very partial to what she calls the atherletic type. More your level altogether.'

He went out, smouldering. Some day—

But meantime, he had some work to do. He'd start with the American.

CHAPTER FOUR

Baxter restored his passport carefully to an inside pocket, and walked out into the sunshine. It was warm for April, even by Balearic standards, and his skin tingled with pleasure at the familiar sensation. All round him there was a jumble of activity, and he picked his way carefully through, fastidious in his desire not to be confused with these holiday-makers. He had a great contempt for the package-tour mentality, and grouped all participants under the dismissive heading of 'Blackpool-on-the-Med'. Most of them would spend the next two weeks bringing disgrace to the country of their birth, alternating their time between fornication and drunkenness, and all the while being ripped off mercilessly by experts. Serve 'em right, too. People who behaved like animals deserved all they got.

Although he had been given no instructions as to procedure, Baxter had no intention of standing around looking helpless. He would take a taxi to the best hotel in the capital, and leave it to his new employers to find him.

A man emerged from the throng, and stood before him, smiling.

'Mr. Baxter? My name is Williams. There is a car waiting.'

Williams was short and round, with a cherubic expression on his pudgy features which exuded good humour. Without waiting for an acknowledgement, he turned on his heels and led the way. Baxter followed, narrowly avoiding knocking over a small child who darted suddenly in front of him, to the accompaniment of a thin wail of despair from his mother. There was a black limousine waiting, and Williams waved him cheerfully into the rear sear, getting in beside him.

'You picked a good day. We've been having quite a bit of cloud these last weeks. Perhaps it's an omen, eh?'

'Perhaps,' grunted Baxter. 'Where are we going?'

'Not far. It's a forty-minute drive, once we get clear of this mob. Unfortunately we have to go through the city first.'

The peaked-capped chauffeur negotiated the busy

streets, and eventually turned north, pointing towards a line of hills. There were few signs of the tourist industry now, which was a coastal phenomenon. Here, the view was unspoiled by the hideous concrete hotels, and there were not many signs of life at all. They could easily have been in certain areas of Africa, or even India, reflected Baxter as he stared out of the window. He had never taken any interest in his surroundings, other than as possible cover or survival territory, but he recognised the bushes and the shrubbery which covered the hard earth. The few stunted trees, too, presented a familiar forlornness.

After about half an hour, they turned off the main highway and onto a narrow, dirt road.

'Nearly there. You'll be able to see the house a couple of miles along here.'

There had been no attempt at conversation on the drive, which suited Baxter very well. These people had simply been sent to collect him, not to perform some phoney welcoming charade, and it kept things on a business-like basis.

'There we are look, can you see?' Williams pointed out of the window, and upwards. 'Side of the hill. That's us.'

Baxter looked in the direction indicated, and made out the white walls of a building which was perched half-way up one of the hills, seemingly occupying a commanding view of the surrounding countryside.

'A bit remote, isn't it?' he commented.

'Suits the purpose,' was the laconic response. 'We shan't get there for five minutes yet.'

The road began to turn and twist as it negotiated the increasing elevation. Sometimes the house was in sight, and more often lost to view, as the approach took another direction. Finally, the chauffeur made a sharp turn to the right, and they were approaching the place head-on. It was a large house, abutted by several outbuildings to which it was joined by a high wall, eight feet at least, which in turn was broken up by graceful curved archways with black ironwork gates. Only a very wealthy man could have afforded either to buy such a property, or live in it. The upkeep would be enormous, reflected Baxter, as he made his habitual quick survey. Easy to defend. A machine-gun

on that roof there, another to the left, on top of that—
'Ah, there you are, Baxter. So glad you could come.'

His tactical appreciation was cut short by the rich voice of
George Halloran, who stood, beaming, in the open main
doorway. Halloran was wearing a white tropical suit, but
that was the end of his concession to local requirements. He
still wore a proper shirt and a club tie. From behind him, a
little swarthy man darted out, clearly a manservant, and
tried to take Baxter's handgrip. Baxter shook his head, and
held on. The newcomer looked anxiously at Halloran, who
waved him away. The car was gone, driven into one of the
low buildings at the far end of the courtyard, leaving Williams and Baxter to their devices.

Williams walked towards the waiting man, and Baxter fell
in beside him.

'That's the idea, come on in.' Halloran turned in to the
cool dark interior. 'I expect you'd like a drink after the
journey, eh? Or some iced coffee perhaps? I can thoroughly
recommend it. Little Pedro has a wonderful touch with the
stuff.'

'Nothing, thanks. Perhaps later.'

'Just as you will. There's someone who wants to meet
you, so I'd better make the introductions.'

They passed from the hall and into a large room which ran
from front to back of the house, and was at least forty feet in
length. It was unoccupied, and Baxter noted the rich furnishings as they proceeded through, towards the french
windows which stood open at the end. Williams, ever polite, had ushered Baxter forward, and was now bringing up
the rear. Halloran stepped out into the sun at the rear of the
house, where a marble terrace led to a shimmering pool.
There was cane furniture dotted around—none of your
striped awnings, noted Baxter—and there were two people
out there.

The first was a man. Even seated, it was plain to see he
was extremely tall, and his sparse frame was almost skele-
tal. He had a long cadaverous face, with deeply-recessed
eyes beneath eyebrow strips of startling whiteness. His hair
was the same, a great shock of white, clearly impervious to
the assaults of brush or comb, and surmounting him like

some kind of halo. A devil's halo, was Baxter's private assessment. The man was seated on an armchair, with a small table beside him. On the table stood a frosted glass containing some orange-coloured liquid, and beside that rested two books and some papers.

It was noteworthy that when Halloran next spoke, there was just that altered degree of inflection in his tone, which indicated clearly to the listening Baxter that George Halloran was no longer the senior officer present. And quite right, too.

Baxter knew a boss-man when he saw one.

'May I present Philip Baxter,' announced Halloran.

The white-haired man made no move. He was still studying the new arrival, who was returning the compliment. It was hard to be sure, with these bushy-haired types, but Baxter assessed his age at a possible fifty-five, perhaps sixty. His host was one of that rare breed who needed to issue no orders or outward signs of authority. It was quite obvious that wherever he went, and no matter what the circumstances, he was in complete command. Power seemed to radiate from him, settling around him like an aura, and Baxter knew intuitively that whatever this enterprise might be, he was looking at the man who would run it.

'Good day to you, Mr. Baxter. My name is Gregory Ryder. Please take a chair. Oh,' he waved a dismissive hand, and the sun's rays flashed from an enormous diamond on one finger, 'and this is Estelle.'

Baxter had noted the woman fleetingly on his way from the house, but was now able to give her his proper attention. She lay on a wickerwork chaise-longue, raised at one end to support her head. An enormous straw hat covered most of her hair, but it was a lustrous black, tucked away behind her ears. Even the dark glasses could not conceal the sensuous beauty of her tanned face, and she regarded him with frank interest. He tried very hard not to stare at her, but it was no easy task. Estelle had a long lean body which was a rich golden colour, and the slender proportions of a fashion model. Aside from the hat and the glasses, she was completely naked.

Turning resolutely away, Baxter found a chair, and

28

placed it so that he could see only Gregory Ryder, who watched the performance with no sign of interest. Halloran and Williams drew up chairs of their own, so that they formed a small semi-circle facing the white-haired man, with Baxter in the middle.

'I wanted to see you personally, Mr. Baxter, because in enterprises of this nature, I consider an absentee employer to be a fool.' Ryder spoke without emphasis, but each word shimmered like a bubble in the air before dispersing. 'As to whether we shall meet again, I cannot forecast at this stage. It may not prove to be necessary.'

He paused, as though giving Baxter an opportunity to come in, which was accepted quickly.

'If we don't meet again, how do I get paid?'

The white slits which were his eyebrows moved slightly up Ryder's high forehead.

'Excellent,' he breathed. 'The words of the true mercenary, straight to the heart of the matter. Have no concern, Halloran here will be the paymaster, not only for you, but also for the group in your charge.'

This was the first mention that had been made of anyone else's involvement. Baxter had never thought there was anything he could achieve alone which could possibly merit the level of payment offered. It seemed that this was his opportunity to learn a little more.

'Fair enough,' he nodded, 'but I'd like to go into more detail about this group you mentioned—'

He stopped talking as the diamond flashed again from the raised hand, and a brilliant spectrum of white, green, gold and blue caused him to blink quickly.

'I have already dealt with every detail to my satisfaction,' Ryder informed him. 'My interest in that side of things is now at an end. Halloran will brief you as to precisely what is involved and what is expected. One final point. Should you fail, and I consider that a very remote possibility, I am already satisfied that it will be from no lack of effort on your part. Therefore, you have my assurance now that no blame will be attached. However, there is one other possible outcome, which it would be unrealistic to ignore. It might occur to you, at some point in the proceedings, that your reward is

29

disproportionate to the total involved. You might go further, and decide to change the proportions. If you should reach that regrettable conclusion, Basil, or one of his merry band, will execute you. A drab note to end on, but I always make things absolutely clear from the outset.'

Basil? Who the devil was Basil? Unless—Baxter turned towards Williams, who was sitting on his right. Williams smiled happily, and nodded his head in a conspiratorial fashion. It was more effective than if he'd worn a black skullcap and pronounced sentence from the dock of the Old Bailey. It seemed to Baxter that the heat of the sun evaporated momentarily, and the air became chill. Nonsense, of course, he reminded himself sharply.

'Well, I mustn't detain you,' dismissed Ryder. 'I know you all have a great deal to discuss. I wish you good hunting.'

The others rose to their feet, and Baxter followed suit. They all returned the chairs to their original positions, and Halloran began to lead them away.

'Goodbye, Mr. Baxter.'

The woman Estelle spoke at last, a deep musical sound that brought Baxter's head round for a final look, and he was glad of the excuse. He would gladly have spent any length of time drinking in that body, as it glistened in the sun. She tipped one side of her hat in an informal salute, and he knew the eyes behind the dark glasses were mocking him.

'Goodbye, Estelle.'

He managed to say it without weighting any of the syllables. Estelle's place in the scheme of things needed no underlining, and Baxter was too long in the tooth to make any false moves in the direction of a woman so clearly the property of a man like Gregory Ryder.

When the three men had disappeared inside the house, Ryder turned his impassive glance towards the reclining woman.

'What did you think of him?'

She shrugged slightly, causing the small hard breasts to lift up and down.

'He seems all right. Very cold eyes.'

Ryder smiled thinly, and was not deceived. His knowl-

30

edge of women was almost as deep and far-reaching as his knowledge of men, which was considerable.

'We must see how this comes out. If everything goes according to plan, I expect to be spending a few days away. If you behave yourself, I might let you have him while I'm gone. You'd like a little something to play with, I expect?'

She pouted, but not sufficiently to provoke him, in case he changed his mind.

'When you're away, Gregory dear, it can get awfully lonely in this great big place.'

Ryder inclined his head, as though accepting the compliment. Estelle had annoyed him by her obvious interest in this fellow Baxter, and the offer to allow them to further the relationship was far from the bonus he had made it seem. Ryder knew all about the way in which Baxter treated his women, while Estelle did not. That was something she could learn, to her cost, while he was not there to protect her.

Meanwhile, the men had gone into an upstairs room, which was laid out as an office. There was a large central table with several chairs around it, a desk in one corner, a smaller desk with a typewriter, two filing cabinets and three telephones.

'This is where we work,' explained Halloran, pulling out a chair at the centre table, and sitting down at the head.

Baxter sat in a chair where he could command a view of both the doors leading out of the room. He chose the spot instinctively, and without any thought that he might be in danger. Baxter would never sit with his back to a door, not even in a restaurant. Basil Williams took a seat, facing him across the table, and Baxter looked at him speculatively, trying to fit the man to the new role into which Gregory Ryder had cast him. Anyone less like a killer would be hard to visualise, and yet the fact had to be faced. These people were in deadly earnest, there was no question about that, and if Ryder said the little roly-poly figure opposite represented his execution squad, then it was a fact.

Williams showed no consciousness of being scrutinised, but simply rested his elbows on the table and waited for the proceedings to commence. George Halloran took a packet of cigarettes from his pocket, and a silver lighter. He lit up, pulled a glass ashtray towards him, and left cigarettes and lighter handy for the next time. It was not to be a five minute meeting, noted Baxter.

'Right,' began Halloran, 'let's get on with it. Mr. Ryder has laid down the ground rules, so I think we are in no doubt about where we all stand. You, Baxter, will take sole responsibility for one part of this operation. That includes recruitment of the necessary personnel and obtaining certain equipment. To all those people, you will be the boss, and they will have no inkling that anyone else is involved. O.K.?'

Baxter looked doubtful.

'I'm a little bit chary about agreeing to anything before I know what this is all about,' he demurred.

It was a fair point, and Halloran wagged his head in agreement.

'Right,' he said briskly. 'Have you heard of Merridew and Carr?'

The names meant nothing to the listening man.

'No,' he admitted, 'I can't say they're familiar. Who are they?'

The merest hint of a smile flitted across Halloran's face and was gone.

'Not so much a question of who are they, as what are they,' he corrected primly. 'You obviously do not read the City pages in your *Telegraph*.'

There it was again, reflected Baxter. Anyone might have said 'in your daily paper', but not Halloran. He actually knew which paper to quote. These people could probably tell him which of his socks needed repair.

'Not often,' he agreed. 'Not my line of country.'

'Quite,' purred Halloran. 'Merridew and Carr is one of the oldest bullion companies in the City, which is to say the world. The ins and outs of the bullion trade are fascinating, totally fascinating, but they don't need to concern us here today. We are concerned only with the existence of the gold itself, which, as I need hardly remind you, is acceptable currency anywhere in the world, at any time. The pound, the dollar, the mark, these things rise and fall, at the whim of the investors and the politicians, but gold is a constant. Basil, I wonder if you'd be good enough to pass me that map.'

Baxter had noted the cardboard tube which lay on the table, and wondered whether it might have a part to play in the proceedings. Williams now handed it up to Halloran, who slipped off the metal cap and drew out a roll of paper which he proceeded to flatten on the table-top. It was a section of the Ordnance Survey Map on which someone had been drawing in red ink.

'This is the City of London, four inches to the mile,' Halloran explained. 'We are especially interested in the river, around Limehouse Reach. This building here is a simple storehouse. Well,' and he gave a small disclaiming grin, 'perhaps simple is an exaggeration. It is in fact as secure a building as man's ingenuity can make it. The walls are eighteen inches thick of solid concrete. There are no windows lower than thirty feet from the ground. There is only one entrance, and that is protected by sliding steel doors, which are six inches thick, of the highest quality reinforced steel. These are the crude, but nevertheless effective, physical barriers. In addition, there are more scientific security aids. The doors are controlled electronically, and in two stages. Stage One is operated by the chief security guard on the premises, and is a signal that the doors require opening, either for access or egress. Stage Two is operated by the headquarters of the security company, in their City offices, once they have checked the authenticity of the request. So you see, it is quite impossible to get the doors open. There are also photo-electric cells protecting not only the doors, but also the outside walls. Anything breaking one of the beams sets off alarms, not only inside the warehouse, but also, again, in the City headquarters. Behind the steel doors is one further safeguard. If anyone were so ingenious as to get through the doors without going through the electronic sequences of the proper system they would set off another circuit, which automatically fills the entire storage area with tear gas. It's all been quite remarkably well thought out, and there can be no doubt the place is impregnable. It is full of gold bullion, and we intend to remove it, impregnable or not. You're looking thoughtful, Baxter.'

Baxter had been staring intently at the map. The casual mention of the gold had brought him up sharply, but that would have to wait. For the moment, he was concentrating on the objective. He pointed to the red hand-made markings.

'I don't know to what extent this drawing is schematic,' he began, 'but am I right in assuming all this open space around the warehouse is as deserted as it seems?'

Halloran obviously understood what the question was leading up to, and now he nodded his confirmation.

'Absolutely,' he replied. 'There is a clear space at the front and both sides which is at no point less than fifty yards. As far as the rear is concerned, there is nothing between the building and the Thames. You were presumably wondering about the possibility of throwing across some kind of bridge from the nearest building?'

'Just a thought,' muttered Baxter.

'And a good one,' approved his instructor, 'but untenable, I fear. There's nothing these people haven't thought of. Now then, you have considerable experience of attacking strongly fortified positions. Could you offer any suggestions as to how this place might be breached?'

It was like sitting an examination, reflected Baxter. Answer only one question; time allowed, forty minutes.

'Breached, yes,' he said. 'That can be done. A straightforward assault with a heavy enough tank, and the doors would go down. As to the tear gas, I'd simply issue the men with masks. But, having done that, we've really done nothing at all, have we?'

Williams, who had been silent up until that point, now spoke.

'I don't follow what you mean.'

'Just this. Getting inside the place is only the beginning. The main purpose of the exercise is to remove the bullion. I don't know the details, but I know enough to be certain there's a lot of work involved. The stuff has to be carried out, loaded, driven away in several vehicles. It would take hours, without interruption. The way this place is wired up,

I doubt whether we'd have ten clear minutes before every policeman in London was on the scene.'

'Ah,' sighed Williams. 'Yes, I see what you mean.'

'Can't be done then, physically, in your opinion?' queried the listening Halloran. 'Anything else come to mind?'

'Only people. How many guards are there?'

'At any one time, six. They work an odd system of ten-hour shifts. This means that the time of day for relief is forever changing. There are eighteen men required for the shifts, plus two others on permanent standby to cover sickness and holidays. Twenty, all told.'

'Twenty,' repeated Baxter. 'Then we have others. People at the controls of the security headquarters, drivers of the bullion vans, not to mention the staff of Merridew and Carr. Obviously, I don't know all the ramifications, but there must be upwards of thirty people altogether.'

'It's nearer forty,' corrected Halloran, 'but what's your point?'

'Just this. I'd be very surprised if it wasn't possible to bribe a few of them. Out of forty bodies, I'd be prepared to bet that half-a-dozen have money troubles.'

'Very likely,' returned Halloran smoothly, 'but coincidence would be against us. What we should need would be to have our chief security man and our headquarters man both on duty at the same time in order to get the doors open. Plus, we should also have to have in our pockets the visiting guards who make an hourly routine check. No, the coincidence factor would rule out bribery.'

Baxter was not surprised by this reasoning, but it was the first he'd heard about the checking procedure.

'You didn't mention the hourly visits before,' he accused.

'So I didn't. Sorry.'

But, if the expression on his face was anything to judge by, Halloran was not in the least contrite. They were interrupted by the mellow tones of a gong sounding inside the house. Williams stretched his shoulders and looked at the chairman.

'Yes, we'll have to go. Isabella gets furious if we don't pay proper attention to her food. Come along Baxter, you'll enjoy this. We'll get back to the job in, say, a couple of hours.'

Baxter was not pleased. He'd come here to be briefed, not to eat two-hour lunches. His expression was not lost on Williams.

'Look at it this way,' urged the tubby man, 'this is a big operation, not a five-minute attack on the local newsagent. There's a lot to do. A lot of preparation, a lot of discussion, plenty of detail to be ironed out. When this thing lifts off, we've all got to be absolutely confident that it'll go like clockwork. We have to be secure in our minds, because we shan't get two goes at it. Take it easy, old son. A rushed job is a messy job. We don't want that, eh?'

His tone was placatory, and the reasoning was sound.

'All right,' agreed Baxter, 'that's fair enough. One last question, though, before we go. I'm to be paid a quarter of a million as my fee in all this. What sort of money are we talking about, in all? What's the total tally?'

Halloran had got up from the table, and stood listening patiently.

'Oh, didn't I mention that? One can't be absolutely accurate in these matters, of course, what with shipments in and out. It could vary a little either way.'

'Allowing for that,' persisted Baxter, 'what's our root figure?'

'As near as we can judge? Ten million pounds sterling. Shall we go in?'

CHAPTER FIVE

Baxter helped himself to a second cup of the thick black coffee, and passed the elegant pot along to Williams. He wasn't in the habit of eating very much at lunchtime. A pork pie and a pint of bitter were quite sufficient for his needs as a rule. But, if a man had to eat lunch, this was unquestionably the way to do it. The table alone was a feast for the eyes, with its dazzling white linen, glittering silver, and crystal which radiated a hundred sun-shafts. As for the food, Baxter had on occasion dined with heads of state, but had never known anything which could better the deceptive simplicity of the fare provided by the Ryder cook, Isabella. In the ordinary way, he was no great lover of fish, but in the hands of that amazing woman it became transformed to an entirely new plane of experience.

The table-talk was trivial, with no mention of their common enterprise. Both his companions were seasoned travellers, and they found much common ground about countries they had visited in the past. None of them was forthcoming about the reasons for their presence in the various countries discussed, but Baxter doubted whether his fellow guests had been indulging themselves in holiday-making. One thing he did learn was that the two did not invariably accompany each other. It was possible they were not the inseparable companions he had been allowed to assume, and he was in a frame of mind where no scrap of information was to be rejected.

Neither Ryder nor Estelle was present at the meal, and Halloran explained that Ryder ate only once a day, and that was in the evening. He made no mention of the woman, and Baxter felt it would not be prudent to ask. He must not be seen to show any interest in that direction, and as it turned out, the question would have been superfluous. When coffee was served, Estelle appeared, and joined them at the table. She had dispensed with hat and glasses, and her hair was a glorious cloud around the slender knowing face. She wore a dress now, a sleeveless, ankle-length slash of red, which in Baxter's opinion was more provocative than the sight of her unclothed body had been.

All the men stood while she seated herself, and she thanked them each in turn with a sweeping glance from the dark eyes.

'I trust you have enjoyed the meal?'

She seemed to be addressing everyone at once, but Baxter felt that she was really talking to him. That could be her secret, of course, as he well knew. There was a certain exceptional type of woman who had the trick of making every man in a crowd think he was the object of her special attention. Baxter waited, assuming that Halloran would probably be the one to reply, but to his surprise it was Williams who spoke, quickly, almost anxiously.

'Excellent,' he assured her. 'Do you know, I've never been a great one for eating fish, but that lady does things to it which I've never experienced before.'

She nodded, almost graciously, like the lady of the house accepting a compliment. Some lady, reflected Baxter.

'Isabella is an islander. You normally find that island people develop a special affinity with fish, which is, after all, their traditional diet. Think of some of those Polynesian dishes, or the fish restaurants in the Caribbean.'

'Know what you mean,' agreed Williams. 'On the other hand, England is part of an island, and what's our supreme achievement? The fish-and-chip shop.'

Estelle smiled politely, and gave her attention to Baxter.

'Since I speak so highly of Isabella's skills, you must be wondering why I abstain from them, Mr. Baxter. The answer is quite simple. Every third day, I eat nothing at all, and survive on liquids only. It was advice I received from a leading blood specialist in Zurich many years ago. Given regular rest periods, the blood purifies itself. Would someone please pour me some coffee?'

The last remark relieved him of much of the need to reply, and he simply smiled his acknowledgement. Estelle fascinated him, despite his essential caution. Her voice was cultured, which, by itself, did not impress. There were plenty of people, men and women alike, who affected what they considered to be upper-class accents, but they frequently betrayed themselves by their narrow vocabulary, and their mundane use of safe conversational subjects. This woman was quite clearly completely at ease, and had evidently seen a little of the world, to judge by her verbal restaurant tour.

Halloran then produced cigarettes, and the others joined him in lighting them up. The absence of wine at the meal had interested Baxter. Each course had clearly called for the accompaniment of a selected vintage, but the only drink offered had been iced natural mineral water, with chunks of lemon floating in it. Not that his thoughts were critical. They were engaged on very serious business, and it wouldn't do for anyone to be sitting at that table with his judgement impaired.

An hour had passed since the meeting broke up, and Baxter was now anxious to get back to work. There were several hundred unanswered questions jostling for priority in his mind, and it seemed an unnecessary waste of time to delay resumption. He sat there, not joining in the conversation, and trying not to spend too much time in staring at the woman. Finally, it was she who broke up the party.

'This has been very pleasant, but now I must ask you to excuse me. I have a little shopping to do.'

She stood up, and the men followed suit, none of them taking his eyes off her until she had left the room.

'Remarkable woman,' observed Halloran, and Williams nodded his head appreciatively.

Baxter made no reply, and kept his features carefully impassive, wondering what the next move would be. Surely they couldn't be intending to sit here drinking coffee for the best part of an hour?

As though reading his thoughts, Halloran spoke again.

'Right. It's time you had a look at your quarters, Baxter. I'll get someone to show you the way. If there is anything you lack, you have only to ask. We reconvene upstairs at two-thirty.'

One of the male servants, who had so deftly assisted at the lunch, now materialised and waited for Baxter to follow him.

'Two-thirty then,' he said, and went out.

39

His room was at the rear of the house and upstairs, facing out against the side of the hill. The furnishings were sparse, but adequate for his needs. There was a hand-basin in one corner, and he stripped off his shirt, enjoying the application of soap and water to the upper half of his body. There were thick rough towels to hand, and soon he was dry and refreshed. Although the outside sun was now at its full strength, the interior of the house remained cool, and he lay on the top of the bed, wondering about Estelle. What had she meant when she said she had some shopping to do? There wasn't a shop, nor a building of any kind, within miles. Perhaps it was some local joke, particular to this household.

Putting her resolutely from his mind, he wondered what was to happen after the meeting. It was clearly the intention that he should remain overnight, but he couldn't see the point of it. The meeting he was about to resume was of vital importance, and he was under no illusions about that, but he couldn't see why it should take more than a couple of hours. Give it three, to be on the generous side, which would take them to five-thirty. It ought then to be possible to have him back at the airport by half past six at the latest. Traffic between Palma and Heathrow was fairly busy, and even if one or two flights were fully booked, there seemed to be no good reason why he couldn't be back in London by midnight. Still, he reminded himself, at these prices one did not question the arrangements. These people seemed to know exactly what they were doing, so far, and the thing which impressed him most was their seemingly relaxed attitude. There was none of the high-pressure salesmanship approach, which was so often the way of things on some of his earlier experiences.

There was usually someone laying continual emphasis on the urgency of the situation, an excitable general or colonel, waving his arms about in an attempt to imbue the listener with his own enthusiasm. These people could almost be considering him as a candidate for some vacant management post, watching the way in which he held his knife and fork, and so on. Oddly enough, he found himself deeply impressed with the set-up. He liked the calm unruffled approach, bred of supreme confidence, and which could only signify past success. Even when Gregory Ryder informed him that he would be murdered if he attempted any kind of double-cross, there was no malice in the words, no raising of the voice. It was simply an explanation of company policy, almost standing orders, as Baxter's military mind would have classified it.

A sudden loud noise disrupted his thinking, and he got to his feet, crossing quickly to the window. From the other side of the hill, a silver and white helicopter rose slowly into view, dipping slightly as the pilot adjusted his course, then wheeling away into the cloudless sky to the north. The reflected dazzle of the sun made it impossible to see the passengers, but Baxter had no doubt as to the identity of one, at least. His question was answered.

Estelle had indeed gone shopping.

*　　*　　*

Back in the meeting-room, Halloran once again placed his cigarettes and lighter within easy reach.

'Right,' he began in a business-like tone. 'It's time we got down to the crunch. I think it will be best, Baxter, if you let me talk. You will have a mass of questions, naturally, but they must wait until the end. So, the outline first, and then the nuts and bolts. Agreed?'

'Agreed.'

Williams said nothing at all, and again Baxter wondered what his contribution was to be. However, he had been told not to interrupt, and he held his tongue.

In order to keep the plan from its natural tendency to roll up, Halloran placed a book on either side of the warehouse area, thus serving the additional purpose of bringing it into sharp relief.

'There she is. Now, we've already agreed that there is no way in which the place can be breached without bringing every policeman and security guard in London down on our necks. We also know that it will take hours to clear out the bullion. What we need, therefore, is a scheme which will keep the relief forces away for a period of several hours.

41

This is how we shall do it.' He took a pencil and pointed to the river. 'A ship will arrive at this point here. This part of the scheme is not your department, Baxter, and you need not concern yourself with it. Your only interest is in its existence.'

He looked across for confirmation that he was understood, and Baxter inclined his head. He was content, for the present, to leave it at that. Later, he would want to know a great deal more. He was no believer in the system of people working in watertight compartments. If his part of the operation depended on the activities of other people, then he required to be satisfied that they knew what they were doing.

'In addition to whatever cargo she carries, the ship will also be loaded with excess oil. Now here,' and the pencil moved to the right, indicating a small inlet on the river bank, 'as you see, is a natural inlet. A century ago, it was the old St. Augustus Dock, but it was unsuitable for the heavier traffic which began to arrive, and it fell into disuse. At the same time as our ship arrives, there will be two barges, loaded with scrap car tyres, and they will be moored in the shelter of the inlet. The ship will discharge its oil into the Thames, and it will be set on fire. At the same time, we shall put a match to the car tyres. The result will be the most awful cloud of smoke since the Great Fire of London. I don't know whether you've ever seen the kind of smoke which comes from a mass of burning tyres, but believe me it's awe-inspiring. Naturally, all hell will break loose, and this is precisely what we want. There are three main access points to the scene of the fire. These two roads,' indicated with quick jabs of the pencil, 'and the river itself. We may be quite certain that the fire brigade will arrive in no time, and they are far too efficient for us to take any risks. They will be unable to gain access by Rope Street because a petrol tanker will have crashed into a heavy low-loader vehicle at the intersection, effectively blocking the way in. Not only that, but there will be petrol everywhere, and the risk of a secondary fire. Again, Baxter, this—um—accident is not something you will have to deal with. So, we are now left with only Chandlers Way, and that gives us an extra few vital minutes for the conflagration to get a good hold. On the day of the operation, a group of council workmen will dig a hole at one side of the remaining road, and leave it overnight. This will restrict traffic to single-lane, and cause more delay. I ask you to try to visualise the scene. Here is the ship with all the blazing oil on the water, there are your barges setting up all this devilish smoke. As you can see, the area to the right of the warehouse, which is fairly flat ground, will be the operations area for the fire-fighters. All the emergency services will be out in force, fire-tenders, police, ambulances, and they will be working in the most difficult conditions. It will be night, there will be no moonlight worth a damn, and with the seat of the fire so close, visibility will be no better than three or four feet. That is the point, Baxter, at which you move into action. Another fire-tender will arrive, with your own crew. You will proceed to the clear side of the warehouse, the left. You will run your ladders up to the roof of the building, and that is how you get in. You deal with the guards, and now you are ready to begin shifting the goods. Your men will arrive in ambulances, four is the estimated need. As we all know, the front doors are inoperable, and in any case they are too open to view. Therefore, the stuff must come out through the side windows which, as we have already said, are thirty feet from the ground. It will be loaded onto the ambulances and driven away.'

Halloran laid the pencil on the table, and leaned back, looking at Baxter and awaiting his reaction. Baxter rubbed thoughtfully at his cheek. He had a whole barrage of questions to ask, and was mentally putting them in order. Now, he leaned forward and pointed to the road intersection where the accident with the petrol bowser was scheduled to take place.

'I'm not too clear about this crash,' he began. 'I've seen how fast the police can clear a road accident, when they have to. I doubt whether we could rely on that for much more than an hour.'

'You are absolutely right, and I agree.' Halloran accepted his point without question. 'We should be most unwise at any stage to underestimate the resources either of the police or the fire brigade. They are quite remarkably efficient in

43

these emergency situations, and we must never lose sight of the fact. However, we have a back-up emergency scheme of our own in that situation. One of our people will be observing progress at the crash. If he feels they are getting on too well for our convenience, then he will set fire to the petrol. We hope very much that this will not become necessary, because someone is certain to get hurt if it does. On the other hand, we cannot take the slightest chance of putting the operation in peril.'

Baxter nodded. He didn't like it, but he could respect the forward thinking. His next objection was unlikely to be overcome so quickly.

'All right, so we can disregard that road. Let's concentrate on the other one, the one with the hole in it, and the single-lane traffic. There's going to be delay down there, no doubt about it. I can see my fire-tender and my ambulances getting stuck in a jam.'

'Ah,' Halloran picked up his pencil, and shifted one of the books which were serving as paperweights. Then he indicated a built-up area to the left of the warehouse. 'This other warehouse over here is empty at present, but on lease to a certain company which belongs to us. As you say, it's no use us putting on this big bonfire party if the main guests can't get through the traffic. You will already be inside the area, and waiting. Your vehicles and your men will be in position hours before the fire commences, and all you have to do is drive over there when ready.'

Baxter grinned, despite himself. The thing was beginning to sound more and more viable, but he was by no means finished yet.

'You talked about taking out the guards inside the place. I ought to tell you right now that I won't kill Englishmen. That might come as a bit of a surprise, considering some of the things I've been mixed up in before. All the same, I won't do it, and you'll find most of my men won't either.'

Williams stirred then, looking at Baxter with his wide-open eyes, and an expression of near-incredulity.

'But they are the enemy, surely, exactly like the opposition forces in other circumstances? Nothing personal, old man, but one or two of your exploits have not exactly been

Children's Hour material.'

It was fair comment and Baxter took no offence.

'That's true, but I wasn't dealing with my own kind. These are not opposition forces, as you put it. They're just ordinary Englishmen, doing a job of work, and I stand by what I said. I'll club them, tie them up, any of that stuff, but murder is out.'

'What about gas?' interposed Halloran smoothly. 'A nice sleeping gas would do very well. That ought to salvage your conscience, which, I must say, is as much a surprise to me as it is to Basil.'

Not caring to develop any arguments about this inexplicable quirk of his nature, Baxter contented himself with a grunt.

'Gas, then. You can leave that to me. Now,' and he moved quickly to his next subject, 'gold is damned heavy. As you say, it will take a lot of shifting, but it will also take a lot of transporting. I can't see the average ambulance standing too much of that dead weight.'

'True, but that is your problem,' Halloran told him. 'You must see to it that the vehicles are properly reinforced for the job, with heavy duty tyres and whatever else is necessary.'

That was fair enough, and Baxter acknowledged his role.

'All right then. I'm sure once I get the feel of this, I shall have a few more questions, but right now let me tell you what I think is required by way of personnel. I need at least six men on the fire-tender, plus four ambulance drivers, that's ten altogether. Ten men at ten thousand apiece, that's one hundred thousand pounds. Plus an extra ten.'

Halloran and Williams exchanged glances.

'I think ten thousand is about right for this exercise,' agreed Halloran. 'Might I ask what the extra ten thousand is for?'

'My Number Two,' explained Baxter. 'There's too much detail on a job this size for me to deal with everything personally. I need a deputy. Apart from which, you can call him a contingency reserve. I intend to be very careful that nothing happens to me, but, if it does, you'll know who to deal with. A precaution.'

That seemed to satisfy Wiliams, and, sensing the atmosphere between the two men, Baxter knew that in matters of that kind it was Williams' view that carried the day.

'Then there's the equipment,' he continued. 'I'm going to need uniforms, and I imagine that's my department?'—a quick nod from Halloran encouraged him to proceed—'Then there's the transport. Do I find my own vehicles, or will you do that?'

'That will be taken care of,' he was assured, 'but you will be provided with authentic vehicles. Any modifications necessary to meet the requirements of the job will be for you to arrange.'

'Fair enough. Two things remain, for the moment. Timetable, and up-front cash.'

Halloran sat back in his chair, resting his arms flat on the table in front of him.

'Timetable, then. If we allow two weeks for recruitment, then one week for training, and yet another for unforeseen difficulties, it would seem reasonable to expect you to be ready in one month from today. Do you agree?'

'Yes,' replied Baxter without hesitation.

'Splendid. After that, it will be a question only of waiting for the right evening. Thanks to the splendid improvement in weather forecasting over recent years, we shall be able to plan with tolerable certainty two days ahead. Can't risk any heavy rain damping down all our lovely smoke. Also, there is the question of the moon being in the right quarter. However, these details are not your concern. You also mentioned money. When you return home tomorrow, you will find money waiting. Fifty thousand pounds, to be precise. We estimate this should cover retainers for your men, plus a number of expenses which will undoubtedly occur.'

Fifty thousand. Baxter was impressed. He had not expected quite such generous treatment, despite the scope of the operation. It should be ample to get everything rolling.

'Good. How do I let you know when I'm ready?'

'We shall be in touch from time to time,' hedged Williams.

Baxter was now itching to go home and get down to the job, but Halloran seemed to be insisting that he should remain overnight. There seemed to be no point.

'If this is as far as we can get at the moment,' he said, 'and I think it is, shouldn't I be getting off back to the U.K.?'

Williams spread out the fingers of both hands, almost in a gesture of apology.

'Can't be done, old son,' he regretted. 'Mr. Ryder has arranged a special little entertainment for you this evening. He would be frightfully disappointed if you should miss it, and I'm sure you wouldn't want to be churlish.'

For the second time that day Baxter felt there was a sudden drop in the temperature. This fellow Williams was going to need special watching before the operation was ended.

'Naturally not,' he confirmed.

'Well, that's about as much as we can do, I think, for the present. We'll see you later. Shall we say six-thirty?'

Baxter went back to his own room, his mind a turmoil of activity. It had been some time since he was actively engaged, and he welcomed the familiar tingle which always heralded the approach of total involvement. And fifty thousand quid to play with, by way of opening expenses. He was going to enjoy this, all of it, and the thought of the actual operation brought a sudden smile to his lips. He, and the rest of them, were about to bring into reality the ambition of many a hopeful newcomer to London.

They were going to set the Thames on fire.

CHAPTER SIX

Jennifer Fiske tapped quickly at the door of the inner sanctum then went through, approaching the desk with long, easy strides.

'Got him at last,' she announced, quietly triumphant.

'Thank the Lord for that,' breathed Jameson, 'I was beginning to think we might have a sleeper on our hands. May I see?'

He held out his hand, and she placed a sheet of paper in it. The image of the face in front of him, as reproduced by the computer printer, was somewhat below studio standards. It was, nevertheless, a perfectly acceptable likeness for purposes of identification.

'Not one of mine,' he stated definitely. 'I don't claim that my memory is infallible, but I'm pretty sure I'd remember this chap. Who is he?'

'His name is Basil Williams,' she informed him. 'There seems to be no reason why you should know him. He's not in our line of work at all, or, I should say, he hasn't been up to now. Appears to be some sort of gangster. A hit-man, as the expression goes.'

'Does he, by George.'

Jameson looked again at the picture.

'Perhaps that explains why it took so long to track him down,' he mused. 'Where'd you get this, Miss Fiske?'

'From the F.B.I.,' she replied, confident of the reaction the information would produce.

Her boss squinted narrowly, to see whether she was indulging herself in the dangerous pastime of pulling his leg.

'F.B.I.,' he repeated slowly. Then he leaned back. Sometimes this young woman, brilliant as she was, was a little too cool even by his refrigerated standards. 'Since I take it we've not yet found it necessary to confer with the Federation of British Industries, I assume you refer to the Federal Bureau of Investigation.'

'Washington D.C.,' she confirmed, po-faced.

'Our information was wrong, then? Chap isn't English at all?'

'Oh yes he is, but none of our usual people know anything about him. Not at the level at which I've been working, at least.'

Her features remained entirely devoid of expression, as she stared blandly at the departmental head. There was a whole wealth of meaning behind her words, which required no elucidation between them.

Hector Jameson had been entrusted with a unique role in the country's intelligence services. His tiny organisation, known only as Department G, had no loyalty to any other agency. Jameson was directly answerable to a minister of cabinet rank. His access to funds and resources was virtually limitless, and he was accountable to no-one but the minister, either for expenditure or methods. At the same time, he was able to utilise the resources of all the major agencies, with recourse to records and manpower, indeed all but the topmost echelons, and even these could be penetrated if the cabinet minister felt it justified.

The net result was that Jameson and his entourage—more often referred to as his 'gang'—became overnight the most cordially detested group of people in the entire intelligence system of the country. The initial reaction to the department, when it was created, was an attempt to freeze it out. No-one saw the need for its existence, since it was held that Department G's terms of reference were more than adequately covered by one or more of the old-established agencies. 'Senseless duplication' was the most favourable of the expressed views, which tended to run more to such phrases as 'monstrous meddling'. Faced with entrenchment politics on all sides, Hector Jameson had quickly shown his mettle. A lesser man would have run howling to his minister, setting off a memo-swapping war between the various factions, a ploy which would have driven everyone even further into their emplacements, with no benefit or credit accruing in any quarter.

Jameson had quietly gone looking for an executioner.

All the leaders in the field of computer advancement recruit people of outstanding ability, and set them to work on improvements in technique, innovations which will push back the frontiers of possibility. Not for them the crude mechanisms of accountancy and memory retrieval. They are dreamers, visionaries of a new order, because they accept no limitation of the possible. They envisage boundaries beyond boundaries, and have the sound technical background to make today's dreams tomorrow's realities. For them the microchip, so beloved as the new toy of the commercial world, is as outmoded as the hammer and the water-wheel. They speak in other terms, and even their language is incomprehensible to all but themselves.

One of them was called Jennifer Fiske.

She was twenty-eight years old, an outstanding physicist who had early recognised that the practical future of the subject lay in computers, which she promptly set out to master. When Jameson found her, she was head of the new techniques branch of an international space research combine, a position she had achieved by a combination of outstanding achievement and ruthless determination. She used her striking physical attractions as one more weapon in her formidable armoury of intellect and imagination, and, at first sight, there was little Jameson could offer which would tempt her away from her satisfying existence.

He had to look for her Achilles heel, and when he located it, was surprised at its dramatic simplicity.

Jennifer Fiske was a patriot.

Her grandfather had died in a blazing tank at El Alamein. Her father would never walk again, having stepped on a booby trap during an army exercise in Belfast. There was an elder brother, currently second in command of a fighter aircraft station. The earlier history of the family revealed other military involvements, and Jennifer herself had at one stage entertained serious thoughts of enlisting. Only the dissuasion of a much-loved university don had changed her mind, and Jameson would be forever in his debt.

Even so, it had not been a simple matter to recruit her, but he had finally achieved it.

Her first job was to find the key to the computerised systems of the major agencies. With the privileged clues Jameson was able to supply, the task presented little by way of technical difficulty. The main obstacle lay in the girl's own moral objections, but these he was eventually able to satisfy. Once that bar had been overcome, his progress was swift. By availing himself of existing records, he quickly built up a dossier of incompetence, unwarranted delays, and, in a few instances, downright bungling. Again, he showed some of the quality which had prompted his original selection.

Many another man, armed with the evidence which would discomfit his opponents, might have been tempted to bring it to light. Had that been done, a few heads might have rolled, and certainly there would have been a torrent of unfavourable criticism. That was not Jameson's way. Instead, he hosted a series of informal lunches, at which he would mention casually the information he held. The last thing he wanted, as he was at pains to point out, was to cause any embarrassment to his fellow professionals. No doubt they would be glad to know what he had learned, and what they would now be in a position to rectify, and would they please accept that he was passing it on as a matter of professional courtesy.

The various key men with whom he had such talks were not fools. They had been given a chance to get themselves off the hook, and they knew it. From that time on, there was a new atmosphere in the world of intelligence. Jameson and Department G were not after all the insufferable intruders they had at first seemed. Not bad chaps at all, in fact, and after all they had their job to do, the same as everyone else.

All this was known and understood between Jameson and the girl as they faced each other across the desk. When she spoke of 'the level at which she had been working' he knew at once that she had been unofficially tapping other people's systems, in the hunt for the man Williams. But, even so, the F.B.I.?

'What on earth prompted you to try Washington?'

'Simple. None of our people knew him, unless he was on one of the restricted codes. If he was, or is, you'd have to get at that by going upstairs. You've made it quite clear that this is a private fight up to now. I had two alternatives. Either I could come to you and report no result, which I don't care

51

for any more than you do, or I could take a flier on the F.B.I.'

'But the C.I.A. haven't got him?'

'Nope. Not at my level.'

Not, in short, at the level of unlawful entry, he reflected.

'Go on, then, I must hear this. Don't get too many English gangsters.'

Jennifer nodded, a small gleam of malice now in her eye.

'It appears that Mr. Williams was positively identified as having some involvement with a spot of gun-running into Cuba. There was some disagreement about payment. The guns were transferred from a cabin cruiser off the Florida coast. When the argument began, people started using the guns. Five people were killed, apparently, and one of them, up until today, was friend Williams.'

'Ah.'

Jameson inclined his head in satisfaction, and relaxed back.

'That explains it then. Williams somehow got away, and planted a few pieces of evidence to indicate that he was one of the dead. That being so, there was no need for the F.B.I. to tell our people he was on the wanted list, which is why there's nothing at Scotland Yard or Interpol. Very nice. Very nice indeed, Miss Fiske.'

'What do we do?' she asked.

'Do?'

'Well, yes. Am I to tell Washington their man is very much alive, or not? I'll bet they'd love to have a chat with him.'

'No doubt,' asserted Jameson drily, 'but the answer is no. We've bigger fish to fry at the moment. When this is all over, whatever it is, we can think about turning Mr. Williams in. Where is our tame desperado at the moment?'

The girl knew from his change of tone that he was now enquiring about Ben Hardcastle.

'He's been in the cypher room for the past seven hours,' she reported. 'I think he's gone to sleep on the cot.'

Jameson's mouth twitched irritably.

'Sleep?' he queried. 'You and I have contrived to keep awake. We've both been on duty for almost thirteen hours.'

'Yes, we've had work to do,' pointed out Jennifer. 'All

you gave the redbrick hero was half a dozen cards to memorise. If that's supposed to occupy him for seven hours, he's in the wrong job. Besides, isn't it taken as the sign of a good operator, the ability to go to sleep at odd times? The basis is that they never know when they'll get another opportunity. That's what you teach them at your murder academy.'

The man behind the desk stiffened.

'I take it that is a reference to our survival training establishment, and I don't care for your tone. Anyway, go and wake him up. It's time to bring him up to date.'

She went out without a word, returning quickly with the refreshed Hardcastle in tow.

'Pity to disturb you,' greeted Jameson acidly. 'Miss Fiske was quite motherly about you.'

'Really?'

The newcomer turned his head to grin at his companion. She, in turn, pursed her lips and glared at their superior, who twinkled with malicious glee.

'Clucking like a hen,' he confirmed. 'And now, unless you want to go back to bed, perhaps you could spare the time to come up to date.'

'Ready when you are, boss.'

Hardcastle sat down and looked attentive. Jennifer turned, as if to leave the room.

'No, I'd like you to hang on, Miss Fiske. We're coming to a stage where it's important for all three of us to know exactly what's going on. Other people will be involved from time to time, but we are the only ones who will ever be in possession of the whole picture. Please have a chair.'

She dragged one of the cheap plastic seats across the room, and placed it so that the three of them formed a triangle.

'There's no doubt in my mind that Baxter is preparing to go to war,' began Jameson. 'I've had a report from Majorca, and Miss Fiske has also been busy. Take a look at this chap. Ever seen him before?'

Hardcastle stared at the multi-dotted picture of Basil Williams for long seconds, then shook his head.

'New to me,' he decided.

'To me also,' contributed Jameson. 'Interesting chap. Got a bit of a record in the States, where they believe him to be dead. Your friend Baxter met him at Palma Airport, and went off in a car with him. His name is Williams, Basil Williams. We believe him to be a dangerous man. They went for a ride out in the country, and the destination was most interesting. Our chap couldn't get too close, but I think we have enough to maintain our interest. Well?'

He stopped speaking, because it was evident that a question was to be asked.

'You speak of "our chap",' Hardcastle observed. 'You make it sound as if the department has somebody like me hanging around every airport in the world, just on the off-chance that he might come in handy one day. Thought we were supposed to be a small group?'

'Oh we are, we are. We've no-one in the islands at all. Nor on the mainland for that matter. No, this man has been kindly made available to us by some of our friends in other places. He has marvellous cover, assistant attaché or something of that kind. Spends most of his time running around after stranded tourists, looking for missing girls, that kind of thing. Doesn't get much in our line at all, so he's really enjoying this. It appears that Baxter and Williams went out to a rather swanky villa in the hills. The place is on the side of a hill, and the only access is by a long private road through open country. There's no way of getting in closer than half a mile without being spotted. Obviously, they went there to meet other people but there's been no visual confirmation as to who they are. Still, we know a bit about the house itself. It has been rented for six months by a shipping line, so-called. The very company of which George Halloran is a director, under his Charles Cartwright pseudonym. The tenants own a helicopter, the same machine which we know from our records to have been used in the past by Gregory Ryder. It seems reasonable to assume that one or both of those gentlemen is currently in residence at the house. There is also reputed by the locals to be a beautiful woman on the premises. That may or may not be true. Very romantic-minded, the Spanish. They'd find it difficult to accept a wealthy establishment of that kind without some mysterious femme fatale coming into the picture. So, she may exist and she may not.'

'Then there's the pilot. The man who flies the chopper,' suggested Hardcastle.

'There has to be someone, certainly,' agreed Jameson. 'We have no evidence that Ryder or Halloran possesses that particular skill. The last time we had any news of the machine, it was in the hands of one Max Bauer. Bauer has a bit of a history in the smuggling world, both of contraband and illegal aliens. He might be the pilot, and then again, he might not.'

Jennifer Fiske had listened in silence up to this point, but now she made a contribution.

'Don't forget the mysterious beauty,' she interjected. 'No reason why she shouldn't fly the thing. It isn't very difficult, you know.'

Jameson had no intention of letting the discussion become side-tracked into some feminist argument.

'Absolutely,' he cooed. 'That could well prove to be the case. For the present, let us be satisfied with the facts we have. It is quite evident to me that something is on, and our business is to find out what it is, and where it is due to happen. I have one other piece of information, which may or may not be relevant. This will be news to you as well, Miss Fiske, since I first heard it myself only a few minutes ago. It seems that Mr. Halloran turned up recently in Macao. There is no evidence that he behaved in any way differently from any other visitor. However, Macao, as you undoubtedly know, is little more than a stone's throw from Hong Kong. The steamship company, which we believe to be owned by Ryder, has only one tangible asset, in the shape of an aged cargo vessel named s.s. *Sunderland Lady*. The *Lady* plies in and out of Hong Kong, and she recently had some kind of re-fit. Having stayed in those waters for many years, she is now bound for Marseilles, which is odd. The captain is an old pirate by the name of Marco Leonides, a Greek originally, and a man who knows the Mediterranean better than I know the London theatres. Which, in case you miss the point, is praise of a high order. It may be something, it may be nothing, but it is worthy of note. In any case, I shall make arrangements for the *Sunderland Lady* to receive close scrutiny when she docks at Marseilles. At present, there is no need for you to do anything other than to be aware of the situation.'

He paused for a moment, and Hardcastle spoke.

'Bit odd, isn't it? I don't see where there's much to be gained by stirring up something in the Mediterranean. I mean, there's so much strife already that one more disturbance wouldn't make much difference. I would have thought there'd be plenty of places in the Third World which would be easier to exploit.'

'Apart from which,' added Jennifer, 'the major powers already have such a large presence everywhere, it's difficult to see how a private war could have much impact. I'm with Hardcastle on this. Assuming that the trip to Marseilles is for the purpose of loading up with munitions, isn't it far more likely that she's going to offload them somewhere on the route back to Hong Kong? I can think of half-a-dozen places on the way which are ripe for that kind of intervention.'

She was conscious, as she finished speaking, of Hardcastle's grateful glance, but ignored it.

'I agree,' stated Jameson, to their joint surprise. 'However, despite the temptation, we can't afford to extrapolate too much, not with the scanty information we have. One piece at a time, that's our game. Professor Hardcastle, your particular responsibility is to be Baxter. These other people tend to remain in the background, but he's the man in plain view, the one with the gun. He's all yours. I'll lay on a bit of help for the job of surveillance, but the responsibility will not be shared. You have it all.'

'If the bird hasn't flown. Literally,' observed the girl. 'Don't forget the helicopter. He could already have left in that, for all we know.'

Jameson's eyes were like polished steel as he looked at her.

'Naturally, the possibility has been taken into account. Any movement of the helicopter will be reported, and monitored. I think you'd better go to the airport flat from here, Hardcastle. If I have to move you at short notice, you'll be right on the spot. Conversely, if Baxter should come back to London, using, of course, the return ticket which has been causing you such concern, you'll be on hand to meet him.'

Ben Hardcastle got to his feet, looking down at the girl.

'Buy you a drink?'

But it was Jameson who replied.

'I'm afraid Miss Fiske has no time for socialising. I'm going to have to ask her to remain on call here.'

Jennifer shrugged and sighed.

'Perhaps another time.'

Alone in the fourth storey apartment at Heathrow, Hardcastle lay on the bed, thinking about Baxter, and wondering what his next move would be. He had learned so much about the man during the past weeks, that it was almost as though they were old friends. There was a viciousness in Baxter's make-up which would always preclude that. But, nonetheless, he felt he knew the man intimately, could make a reasoned prediction as to how he would act under a given set of circumstances. It was odd to know so much about someone who was, in fact, a perfect stranger, who would walk past him on the street without a glimmer of recognition.

That set off a new train of thought. Would they ever meet at all? And, if they did, in what circumstances? Was it possible that somewhere along the line he might have a face-to-face encounter with Bad Major Baxter, and, if he did, would it culminate in the death of one of them?

He was uneasy at the prospect, and for a variety of reasons. Although he had acquitted himself well at what the Fiske referred to as the murder academy, he had only once found himself in a life and death situation so far. On that occasion, the ultimate decision had been taken from him by a burly S.A.S. sergeant, who had dispatched his opponent without a visible qualm. Hardcastle had never quite convinced himself that he would have been able to kill the other man, unaided. It wasn't that he lacked the necessary skill, nor was he physically afraid. But there was that inside him which revolted at the final act of killing. He might have overcome it, in the course of those next few crucial seconds,

57

but the opportunity had gone, and he'd never been quite certain. It could come to the fore again now, and with an opponent with whom hesitation would be fatal. Baxter had killed times out of number, and not always men. He would have no compunction in adding to the list one well-trained fully grown agent, if his plans were threatened.

As always, with this particular piece of self-examination, Hardcastle recognised the futility of agonising. Pulling his mind resolutely away from the purely hypothetical, he concentrated instead on the hard information already known.

Despite himself, and although it had been made clear that others would be dealing with it, he couldn't help but fantasise about what he privately designated the Hong Kong connection.

There had always been a streak of the romantic in his make-up and he rather liked the concept of some rusty old tramp-steamer, paddling in and out of those mysterious Far Eastern waters. He liked the image of the piratical Greek skipper, Leonides, slipping from one shady transaction to another on ill-lit quaysides. The whole picture was far more exciting than tailing a man through the streets of London. Of course, as Jameson had been quite right to point out, it might not be any of their concern at all. Still, he hoped it was.

After all, George Halloran had not travelled all that way for no good reason.

CHAPTER SEVEN

One month earlier, another strange meeting had taken place off Hong Kong. Captain Marco Leonides was lying on his bunk when the watch-officer's voice came over the blower, announcing that a fast launch was approaching the ship. The unshaven skipper cursed and swung his feet to the deck. Fast launch? They were two hours out from Hong Kong, and it couldn't be the coastguards. Not that it mattered if it was, not this time. Many a time in the past the old s.s. *Sunderland Lady* had carried cargo which would not have passed the most superficial scrutiny, but this time she was clean. Rubber was what it said on the manifest, and rubber was all anyone would find in the hold. It could be someone on the crew, of course, trying to slip through a bit of contraband. That would be no surprise, not with this lot. His crew were as fine an assortment of waterfront sweepings as could be found anywhere in the world, even here on the China Seas.

He peered at himself in the tiny wall-mirror, and frowned. It was just as well the interruption had come when it did. He ought to be getting about the business of smartening himself up in readiness for docking. Now there was this interference, this launch that had to be dealt with. Jamming a greasy old cap on his head, he went topside to see what was going on. The sea was placid, and the immaculate-looking, powerful launch was almost alongside when he reached the bridge. Could have been sent to shame him, he reflected, comparing the glitter of her metalwork with the poor old *Lady*'s rusting iron and dingy paintwork.

A voice came clearly through the light breeze.

'Ahoy there, aboard the *Lady*. Is Captain Leonides there?'

The second mate looked at the skipper for instructions. Instead, Leonides took the loud-hailer from the waiting man, and gave his own reply.

'This is the Captain. What is it you want?'

At least they weren't pirates. There'd have been no time wasted on chit chat with those gentlemen. They were more likely to cut your throat first and get down to conversation later. Besides, not many pirates spoke English.

'The name is Cartwright,' came the reply. 'I'm from the owners. Like your permission to come aboard.'

Owners? Captains like Leonides didn't have much traffic with those people. The s.s. *Sunderland Lady* had had a long and chequered career, which had dipped sadly downhill of recent years. The present owners were some fourth rate company with a registered office somewhere in South America, which probably meant some shady individual had a desk and a telephone on a Panama quayside. Well, if the man had taken the trouble to come so far off-shore he might have something to impart which would be worth listening to.

'Aye aye,' he shouted. 'Come aboard.'

The second mate accepted the return of the loud-hailer.

'Am I to stop the ship, captain?' he asked.

'What for?' snapped Leonides. 'They have the legs of us, and a bit more besides. Let's see what kind of seamen they are.' Then he thought better of it. The man Cartwright might not be a seaman at all. Probably wasn't, if he represented some money-grubbing owner, and it wouldn't look too good if they lost him. 'Well, order half-speed. And tell the men on the ladder to take extra care. I'll be below.'

He'd be damned if he was going to be dancing attendance on some lackey of the owners. Back in his cabin, he surveyed the squalor in which he lived, and wondered whether he ought to tidy up a little. Certainly some of these empty bottles could be dispensed with, and he stood by the open porthole tossing them out.

Marco Leonides was sixty-one years old, and a man with almost half a century of sea-faring behind him. As a boy, he had early become a regular member of the little fishing fleet which was the economic backbone of his native village in Greece. At fourteen he had taken to the sea proper, as cabin boy and later deckhand in the thriving Mediterranean traffic. The outbreak of the Second World War had caught him far from his native land, and he spent anxious months in deciding where his duty lay. The obvious thing was to make his way home, and join in the resistance to the hated invaders, but he doubted the wisdom of such a move. He lacked the mountaineering skills of the inlanders, the inborn ability to merge with the countryside. Whatever talents he had, whatever skills he had acquired, were of the sea. He put the problem to the bosun's mate, a grizzled Armenian veteran of an earlier war.

'You'd be no use to those people,' was the verdict. 'You'd most likely be in the way. What do you know about crops or goats? Not much, I'll be bound. So you couldn't even pass yourself off as a local, except along the shore. No, you're a seafarer, and you'd do better to stick to what you know.'

The young Leonides listened to this wisdom with alarm.

'But I have to do something,' he protested. 'I don't call this doing much, humping stores around from one port to another.'

'There'll be plenty to do, always is in a war. Always people to get out of one country and in to another. Good people, escaping from bad people. They'll need seamen, never you fear. They'll need you, my boy.'

And so it proved. There was plenty of work to be done, and all under the noses of the Germans, whose domination of the Mediterranean in the early years was indisputable. The young seaman became adept at the business of getting into rocky coastlines under cover of darkness, and many a family was ferried to safety in this way. Sometimes their future plans were vague, since they were without papers, but here the position would be reversed, and they would be rowed in to some other, more friendly place, albeit without the benefit of official clearance. The traffic did not end with people. There were army and military supplies to be made available to underground movements in occupied territories, and Leonides was always in the forefront. The war finally ended but the traffic continued, with slight changes of emphasis. What had hitherto been a praiseworthy effort, became suddenly illegal activity. Instead of guns for partisans, the ships were transporting cigarettes, alcohol and other rare stores. The enemy changed his face too. Instead of the detested Germans, the seamen found themselves counter to the very people they had spent long years in helping. It was all very confusing, and, after one particu-

61

larly hair-raising experience, Leonides left the traffic and applied himself seriously to the business of the higher forms of seamanship.

It took him a further ten years to achieve the coveted master's ticket, and even then command evaded him. The bigger lines had their own training and promotion schemes, and even the secondary companies were looking for people with rather more authentic histories. He was finally given his own ship by a company which made it clear that they would require the exercise of his earlier talents. Well, if that was the price demanded for the mastery of the bridge, he was willing to meet it. For many years he plied his old trade, his intuitive knowledge of every Mediterranean port coming to the fore again and again. His brushes with the authorities became legendary, until eventually the company decided with reluctance that he was too great a risk. They had an associated company which specialised in the Far Eastern trade, and Leonides accepted the new position philosophically. Professionally, it was the end of the line, but at least he would still be a skipper, and he was prepared to settle for that. During the next few years, he moved from one rusty old tub to another. Then, three years ago, he had been given the s.s. *Sunderland Lady*. He was fifty-eight years old at the time, and increasingly aware of the passing years. Somehow, he had felt in his bones that this was to be his last command, and the evidence suggested that he and the *Lady* would probably make their exit from the shipping lanes of the world at about the same time.

The *Sunderland Lady* had been launched from Tyneside in nineteen fifty six. She was a cargo vessel of six thousand five hundred gross tons, traditionally constructed, with well-decks fore and aft, and rather optimistic accommodation for twelve passengers. There were four twin-berth cabins and four singles, situated amidships, comfortable enough in their way, but scarcely of a standard likely to cause concern to Cunard or the other great companies. Owing to the vicissitudes of the ebb and flow of international commerce in the few years following her launching, the *Lady* enjoyed a somewhat chequered career, passing through the hands of one owner after another. Some of her most glorious moments had come during the several wars which raged in the Far East, where she had smuggled out large numbers of refugees from under the noses of advancing armies. Thanks to the skill of a certain master carpenter, an ingenious inner shell had been constructed below decks amidship. This gave the appearance of being the interior of the hull, but was in fact concealing a space, three feet in width and running half the length of the ship, a kind of elongated cupboard, in which dozens of people could be secreted. The device had escaped detection time and again, when suspicious hostile navies had halted the merchantman, whose exploits became subsequently something of a legend in those far waters.

Those days were well behind her when Captain Marco Leonides took her in charge. He knew the *Lady*, as he knew every ship within a thousand miles, in common with the rest of the sea-going fraternity. They were like a giant squabbling family, those mariners, an unlikely pot-pourri of all nationalities and backgrounds, competing, frequently fighting, and yet bonded together by their common exile in alien longitudes. Oh yes, he knew the *Lady*, and felt an immediate affinity with her ageing appearance. They were of a kind, these two, coming jointly to the end of their long careers at the seamy end of the trade.

The man called Cartwright tensed himself to grasp at the rope-ladder as it bobbed and danced a few feet away from his reaching hands. In another part of the world, a number of people, had they been party to the scene, might have been forgiven for thinking he was watching George Halloran about to make the transfer. The man on the launch was indeed known by that name in Majorca, but here, in the heated waters off Hong Kong, he was Cartwright. It was a matter of no consequence, since he held no proper entitlement to either name.

The s.s. *Sunderland Lady* rolled slightly, bringing the ladder those crucial inches closer, and Cartwright made his move, grabbing firmly, and swinging clear with his feet. Then he was making his way upward, hand over hand, to where sunburnt arms were waiting to haul him over the side. Once aboard, he stood for a moment, smoothing at his white linen jacket and frowning at the second mate, who stood with folded arms, inspecting him with evident amusement. Cartwright had never met Leonides, but he knew the watching mate was too young.

'Where's the skipper?' he demanded.

'He's waiting below,' was the reply. 'I'll show you the way. That was a nice jump you made just now. You been at sea before, then?'

Cartwright shook his head in denial.

'No,' he rejected stiffly, 'but there are such things as gyms on shore. One attempts to keep fit.'

As he followed the mate he was taking in the close-up picture of the *Lady*. The years of high winds and salt sea spray had taken their toll, along with the lack of adequate maintenance by a series of penny-pinching owners. There was heavy pockmarking on the funnel, and rust had eaten its inexorable way into winches, ventilators and other iron-work. He had already seen from the land the tell-tale red streaks on the hull. The woodwork was no better, dingy and peeling, and the whole effect was one of advanced dilapidation. Yes, he confirmed mentally, the *Lady* would do very nicely. Very nicely indeed.

Now he followed his guide down an uncertain metal companion and was shown to the captain's quarters. An untidy figure of a man stood in the middle of the cabin watching his entrance with little sign of welcome.

'Captain Leonides? I am Charles Cartwright.'

Leonides nodded.

'You want a drink?'

Cartwright had spotted the half-empty bottle on his way in, together with the greasy-looking glasses. He really didn't feel that he could bring himself to put one of them near his mouth.

'Thank you, no. Do you mind if I sit down?'

Leonides removed a pile of magazines from his one stained armchair, and waved him to it, at the same time seating himself on the bunk. A lifetime of appraising men had told him at once that his visitor was no clerk. There was a hardness to his body and a confidence in his bearing which had not been acquired behind a desk.

Cartwright, too, had been sizing up his man. He knew a great deal about the captain's history, and the physical appearance of Leonides confirmed everything he had come to expect. Tough, shrewd as ever, but now beginning to lose that extra edge which had been the hallmark of his spotted career. The man was on his way out, just like his ship. They made an ideal combination for Cartwright's purpose.

'You will soon be unloading in Hong Kong, Captain. What are your plans, after that?'

Leonides added a few more wrinkles to his lined brow.

'Plans? I don't understand the question. There'll be another cargo, I fancy, and I'll go wherever it's bound for. I would have thought you'd know more about that than me.'

His tone was off-hand, but not yet belligerent.

'Possibly,' concurred Cartwright. 'Much depends on our conversation in the next few minutes. I have a proposal to put to you.'

Of course he had, Leonides had known that from the beginning. The owner didn't go to all the trouble of intercepting him on the high seas in order to tell him he would be shipping toys down to Australia. His face was a mask when he put the question.

'Oh yes? What might that be?'

Cartwright was not deceived by his seeming indifference. The old captain had spent a lifetime listening to propositions, and he was agog to know what this one might entail.

'It is entirely possible that I might be able to arrange a cargo destined for Marseilles,' he announced quietly.

Marseilles. France. The Mediterranean, and home. Marco Leonides always tried resolutely to avoid memories of his Greek homeland, which he had not visited for years, but Cartwright's unexpected announcement brought the mental images flooding into his mind.

'Marseilles, eh?' he commented, struggling to keep excitement from his tone. 'Few years since I was over that way, but I dare say I could find it.'

'I'm quite certain that you could,' returned his visitor smoothly. 'None better, in fact. There are still a few quaysides along the Med where the name Leonides is not

65

forgotten.'

The captain's eyes narrowed slightly. This man evidently knew something of his earlier history.

'Really? I wouldn't have thought I was that important. Anyway, this job, what is it? It can't be a straightforward cargo, or you needn't have come out here. Contraband, is it?'

Cartwright was not accustomed to reaching the point in quite such a direct fashion, but he was an adaptable man.

'No,' he rejected, 'not contraband. Indeed, we shall go out of our way to make the cargo as harmless as possible. Heavy, but harmless. You will have nothing whatever to fear from the authorities. However, the matter is not quite that straightforward.'

And here comes the catch, thought the listening skipper. Political refugees, or the like. And why emphasise the heavy cargo?

'Mr. Cartwright, you do surprise me,' he said, with heavy sarcasm.

The seated Cartwright's smile was very thin.

'I doubt that,' he countered. 'However, to continue. Let us proceed on the assumption that such a cargo materialises. It would take you very close to home, after all these years. Just a few hundred miles in fact. It is some time since your last visit, I think?'

Leonides scratched at the grey stubble on his chin.

'Five or six years, yes,' he agreed.

'Seven years and five months,' corrected Cartwright. 'You see, we have taken a great interest in you, Captain.'

Too great for comfort, was the sailor's private reaction. Smooth operator, this Cartwright, a man to be watched.

'Well, go on,' he invited gruffly.

'I intend to. Over the years you have earned huge sums of money, at one time or another, but you have not been a careful man. At this moment, you stand in credit at the Hong Kong Merchants Bank to the tune of eighteen hundred American dollars—'

'Zut!' exclaimed the listener.

'—while, in Shanghai, you have twelve hundred English pounds on credit—'

'Just a minute!'

'—and in Perth, Australia, there is another amount of—'

'Where did you get all this?' shouted Leonides, unable to contain himself any longer.

Cartwright was mildly annoyed at not being allowed to complete his little summary, particularly as he was on the last entry, but he permitted nothing of his irritation to show.

'As to how we came by our knowledge,' he continued imperturbably, 'that is of no importance. The point is, do you agree with the information?'

Leonides was visibly rattled, and justifiably so, as he saw it. A man's business was his own, and these people had no right to come poking around in his private life. Still, he reasoned, they were close enough to the truth, and there must be something behind it all for them to have taken so much trouble.

'It sounds all right,' he admitted cagily.

'Oh it is,' he was assured. 'A life on the bounding main, eh? Not much to show for it after fifty years, have you? You're close to retirement, you know. Couple of years, at most. No matter how carefully you save from now on, you're not going to be able to put much away. Not enough to live the way a retired ship's captain should.'

The old seaman was well aware of all this, and it did little for his morale to have this self-satisfied landlubber remind him of it.

'That's my concern, not yours,' he replied, shortly.

'True, but I think I may be in a position to offer you a proposition which will change all that. Which will make it possible for you to buy a little place near the seashore, and have a small income into the bargain. You wouldn't be a rich man, but you'd have enough to spend your days in the waterfront cafés, with your coffee and ouzo, and the respect of your fellow-countrymen. Shall I continue?'

Leonides' mind was already far away, on a sunlit quayside. He knew the very place, and had dreamed of it often in the past. Of late years he had known the futility of the dream, and rejected it. But now, listening to Cartwright, it all came back with a rush.

'No harm in listening,' he conceded.

'Good. We want you to take the s.s. *Sunderland Lady* to Marseilles. There, you will retire from the company's service. A little ceremony will be arranged, a small entry in the newspapers and so forth. Nothing too fancy, but enough to establish that Marco Leonides has finally left the sea. You will then disappear from the public eye. The crew will be paid off, and new men recruited. The *Lady* will have a little renaissance while she's in port. A good spring-clean of the ironwork, a repaint and so on. She will already have had a certain amount of re-fitting. When she is ready to leave, a new skipper will appear, a man of long experience as his papers will show. He will not be unlike the previous captain in his height and build, but his appearance will be different. A heavily-bearded man, with a most fastidious taste in clothes. Not that anyone will be all that interested in him, except the owners, and they won't need to ask any embarrassing questions, because they will already know that the new man is you.'

He paused, to allow the point to go home. Leonides looked bewildered.

'Let me get this straight,' he urged. 'You want me to retire, then to put on some funny whiskers, pretend to be someone else, and come back to my own ship. Why?'

'It will get clearer,' Cartwright promised. 'The new captain, whose name incidentally is Kokis, Michael Kokis, will take the *Lady* to London. Once there he will leave the ship, and his part in things will be ended. As will yours, my dear Captain. Michael Kokis will travel openly to France where he will somehow get lost. Marco Leonides will appear in Greece, and settle down to a long life of doing nothing. Very simple, isn't it?'

'Too damned simple, altogether,' rejoined Leonides. 'You're going to scuttle the *Lady*, I imagine, but you're going to a hell of a lot of trouble doing it. Much simpler to just let me do it right now.'

'If that were the intention, I would have to agree,' nodded Cartwright, 'but our plans are rather more complicated.'

'I'll bet they are,' grumbled the skipper. 'All this play-acting and nonsense. Of course, you've left out the most important part.'

The owners' representative was well aware of the fact, but he wanted the question to come from the new recruit.

'Really? And what might that be?'

'You haven't said what's in it for me,' pointed out Leonides, heavily.

'Ah yes,' Cartwright crossed his legs, smoothing out his trousers with maddening slowness. 'I was coming to that, of course. Your part in things is really quite small, and I think you will find our proposal more than generous. At the satisfactory conclusion of our business, you will receive fifty thousand English pounds.'

He enunciated each of the last four words slowly and carefully, while watching the expression on the face of the listening man.

'Fifty thousand pounds.'

'English,' reminded Cartwright.

'Yes, I heard you.'

Leonides got up from his bunk and went over to his collection of bottles, splashing out a heavy measure of brandy into one of the stained glasses. He stood there, sipping at it, and thinking. There was silence in the little cabin while his mind raced around this new development. Then he seemed suddenly to remember that he had a visitor. Turning towards him he waved a hand towards the bottles.

'Sure you don't want one?'

'Quite sure.'

Fifty thousand pounds. There was a snag in it somewhere, naturally, a big snag. People didn't just go around handing out huge sums to redundant sea-dogs without an ulterior motive.

'Is this all you intend to tell me?' he demanded.

The seated man shrugged.

'If you have questions, I might possibly be able to answer them, but I reserve the right to refuse.'

'Fair enough. You said that the *Lady* would be having some kind of re-fit. What kind?'

There was no harm in telling him that, reflected Cartwright, because he would have to come to know anyway.

'Certainly, I can answer that. The *Lady* will be taking

aboard one thousand tonnes of oil. That inner shell, which used to be so indispensable for hiding refugees, will be ideal for storage, once it has been suitably reinforced.'

'Oil? Why oil, and why hide it? Nothing illegal about oil.'

The visitor held up a hand in deprecation.

'I am not in a position to enlarge on the answer, I'm afraid. Anything else?'

'This thing, whatever it is that you're going to do, will it cost the lives of any of my crew? Or anyone else, for that matter?'

Cartwright could tell from his tone that the slightest hesitancy here could put the scheme in jeopardy. He kept his voice confident and sincere when he replied.

'Absolutely no risk, and you have my assurance on that. No, Captain, our interests are entirely financial, and the last thing we want is for anyone to be hurt.'

He sounded genuine enough, admitted Leonides. The business about hiding the oil still struck him as crazy, but for fifty thousand pounds he could afford to leave a few questions unasked.

'It all seems so casual,' he said cautiously. 'You climb up onto my ship in the middle of the great blue, offer me fifty grand, and then push off again. Isn't there any more to it?'

'Naturally, yes.'

Cartwright reached inside his jacket and pulled out an oilskin package which he proceeded to unwrap.

'If you accept the offer, we shall need to spend some time in going over the whole thing in detail. I have come prepared for that. Do I take it that we are agreed?'

Leonides' hesitation was no more than momentary.

'Provided that what you tell me now doesn't change the basics, yes, we are agreed.'

'Splendid.' The owners' representative began to look at the papers he had removed from the waterproof package. 'Ah yes, I'd almost forgotten that. There is just one thing you should know, now that we are on the same team, as it were. My principals are extremely concerned about security, not only during this project, but subsequently.'

'Subsequently?'

The man talked in riddles.

'Subsequently,' repeated Cartwright. 'You see, it is quite possible that, long after your part in this is finished and paid for, you might begin to think you were shabbily treated. You might feel that you ought to have had more money.'

He looked at the puzzled skipper blandly.

'I don't follow that,' objected Leonides. 'I'm a man of my word, and I've given it. I don't know what you're up to, and I don't much care. That fifty thousand will satisfy me.'

The other man nodded encouragingly.

'I'm sure of it, and personally I am quite satisfied. However, you must understand that I am only a spokesman, a messenger, if you will. I must pass on our employers' message in full. They are people of extraordinary caution. According to what they tell me, you still have a few enemies left in the world?'

'Who hasn't?' shrugged Leonides, wondering at the apparent change of subject.

'Who indeed,' agreed Cartwright. 'But not everyone, I think, can claim the enmity of an entire government. The Israelis have a very long memory, as we all know. Think of Eichmann, and the others. They never close their files.'

The Israelis? Leonides did not care for the direction in which the conversation was now heading.

'You'll have to explain that.'

'I intend to. In 1973, an American freighter developed some mysterious engine trouble, en route to Haifa. She had to call in at Naples for some repair work, and it was all quite unforeseen. At least, it seemed so at the time. The ship was carrying agricultural machinery, as part of the Israeli development programme. That night, a flotilla of small launches appeared, and took the ship by surprise. The visitors were Arabs, who had apparently got wind of the fact that the packing cases of machinery were in fact full of weapons, including two of the latest rocket-launchers. The ship's crew had no chance against the raiders, who gunned them down without mercy. The engines had been tampered with by a member of the crew, who was an Arab agent, and the raiders had brought with them the vital new parts, which were quickly installed. They then hijacked the entire ship, and sailed away. She was found later, riding at anchor off the coast of North Africa, deserted, and with the precious cargo vanished. At the time, it was the greatest seafaring *cause célèbre* since the *Marie Celeste*.'

He had no need to be concerned about holding his listener's interest. Leonides stood, quite immobile, with his head to one side, in an attitude of frozen attention.

'The armaments, on which the Israelis had been relying, turned up in due course in the hands of unfriendly powers. They went to work at once, hunting down the various traitors and informers who had made this episode possible. But there was one man who managed to elude them, and, indeed, they never even learned his identity. It isn't possible to steal an ocean-going ship by filling it with gunmen and sailors, no matter how enthusiastic they are. The ship must have a master, an experienced mariner, who knows exactly what he's about. No one ever found out that the ghost captain was a certain Marco Leonides.'

Behind the stubble of his beard, the blood had drained away from the captain's face, leaving the weather-beaten features sallow.

'I deny it,' he contrived to say, his voice hoarse.

'I'm sure you do,' purred Cartwright, 'but unfortunately I cannot see the Israeli agents being content with a simple denial. In these circumstances, I fancy their questioning might be quite forceful, and it must be faced, we are none of us as young as we were. Personally, I think the matter is best left as it is. After all, who wants to go raking up all this old history? It isn't going to benefit anyone. Indeed, in your own case, the result could be quite to the contrary.'

Leonides had just finished one large drink, in celebration of his impending and comfortable retirement. He poured himself another now, and for very different reasons, shuddering as the raw spirit hit the back of his throat.

'What do you intend to do with these lies?' he asked finally.

'Do? Why, nothing. Nothing at all,' he assured him. 'My dear Captain, it is the dearest wish of us all that our business should proceed smoothly, and with complete trust on both sides.'

'Trust? Huh,' snorted the alarmed man. 'You speak to me

of trust, when you bastards can pull the plug on me at any time?'

Cartwright, having made his point, now proceeded to calm down the agitated man opposite.

'Could, yes,' he agreed, his tone conciliatory, 'but why should we? We are not political people, but businessmen. All we seek is a nice, smooth operation, with everything clicking into place at the right time. Profit, Captain, that is our motive, our sole motive, and we have no interest in side issues. This little matter is no more than an insurance of your continued good will.'

They'd really got him sewn up, thought Leonides. He knew all about the relentless activities of the Mossad, and only in the last few years had he begun to feel safe from them.

'What about the money?' he asked abruptly. 'Do I still get it?'

'But of course.' Cartwright looked him directly in the eye. 'With us, a deal is a deal. So far as we are concerned, this other matter need never be referred to again. Why don't you sit down, Captain, and put it from your mind?'

Leonides plumped heavily down on to his bunk. All very well for this character to say 'put it from your mind'. It was quite another matter to be able to do it. What was he saying now?

'Let us turn our attention to the exact timetable over the next few weeks. On this operation, timing is of the essence. You are scheduled to arrive in Marseilles on May the second. You will then—'

Gradually, Marco Leonides brought his attention to focus on the present, and soon he was immersed in a mass of detail.

Cartwright's pleasant voice droned on.

CHAPTER EIGHT

The taxi crawled another few yards along Upper Regent Street, and from his seat in the rear, Baxter could see the locked mass of traffic at Piccadilly Circus. Leaning forward, he tapped on the glass and pointed to the kerb. The driver nodded, pulled over and stopped.

'Must be an accident in Coventry Street, by the look of it,' he said dolefully, as Baxter stood on the pavement. 'It was clear half an hour ago. That's one-sixty, guv.'

Baxter handed him two pounds, saying, 'Just give me two ten pees.'

He put the coins into an outer pocket, against some future telephone call, and began to make his way through the late-morning crowds. There was a light drizzle of rain, not enough to justify a raincoat, but sufficient for all the females to arm themselves with their deadly array of umbrellas. Because of his height advantage, the umbrella spikes were mostly on a level with his eyes, and he kept a careful watch as each new circle of coloured nylon came towards him. He turned up Glasshouse Street, past the Regent Palace Hotel, and then threaded his way through side-streets until he reached the public house he wanted.

It was as busy as ever, dark and smoky, with no concession to daylight or the approaching summer. There were no tourists here, no suburban shoppers up for the day. This was a London pub, for Londoners who either lived or worked in the area, and the clientèle remained substantially the same the whole year round. Baxter adjusted his eyes to the gloom, then went over to the bar and ordered a pint of bitter. It was two minutes before noon, when Joe Mallory was due, and Baxter stood by the counter waiting. He was anxious to enlist Mallory for this new undertaking, and his earlier telephone conversation with him had been a promising beginning.

He had put in a call to the travel agency, where Mallory was a partner and liked to work when he wasn't busy on other matters.

Baxter announced himself, and wasted no time on pleasantries.

'If you're free,' he said carefully, 'I'll be in the Feathers at twelve noon.'

Mallory's reply was terse, and typical.

'See you.'

It was the first time they had spoken in months, and any other two men would at least have made a polite enquiry after each other's health. These two, with their history of shared experiences, had no need of such niceties. The conversation, harmless even to the most suspicious listener, had been very complete. When Baxter had asked if Mallory was free, he had not meant free to meet him for lunch. It was an enquiry as to whether his man was available, and interested in listening to a proposition. Mallory had fully understood, and his two-word reply was confirmation on both points.

A voice said, over Baxter's shoulder, 'You could always buy a man a drink.'

He turned, and there was Mallory, his long, sardonic face creased in a grin. Despite himself, Baxter found that he was grinning in reply. Mallory always had that effect on people, with his infectious good humour and ready laugh. He was tall and dark and, if not exactly handsome, good-looking enough to cause a stir among the opposite sex. His restless, mobile face seemed to be continually on the lookout for some new experience, while the eyes were ever-watchful. This ceaseless scrutiny of the world around him had stood him in good stead in many a tight corner. He had been instrumental in saving Baxter's life on two occasions, and Baxter, for his part, had been able to return the compliment once only, which left the score-sheet in Mallory's favour. Of all the people with whom Baxter had served, he had never encountered another man with whom he had such a complete rapport, and whose judgement and personal bravery were so much to be relied on.

'You're pretty lavish with the hospitality,' grumbled Mallory. 'Dirty carpets, warm beer. A regular tourist trap.'

'You're losing your tan,' observed Baxter. 'Looks as if you could use a holiday. Think the company could spare you?'

Mallory grinned.

'The company would be delighted,' he assured him. 'They seem to think I concentrate too much on the lady customers. Where are we going, somewhere pleasant?'

'How do you fancy St. James's Park? We could feed the ducks, have a chat.'

'We could get wet too,' objected the American.

'This won't last. Spring shower, that's all.'

A few minutes later they climbed out of a taxi and walked into the park. The rain had kept away most of the usual lunchtime crowds, but, as Baxter had predicted, the drizzle was falling off by this time, and they had the place much to themselves. Without going into any detail, Baxter quickly outlined the non-military nature of the project.

'A robbery?' exclaimed Mallory. 'Us? Not quite our style, would you say?'

'It's unusual, I agree, but it would be conducted very much in our way. Think of it in terms of taking an enemy strongpoint.'

Mallory wrinkled his face in doubt.

'Oh sure. We go in with armoured cars and flame-throwers, right? And who's the enemy, one old watchman aged ninety?'

His reaction was what Baxter had expected it to be, and he was ready for objections.

'It isn't that kind of operation,' he explained, 'more of a commando raid. And no guns. Don't worry, it's not a run-of-the-mill job. We're not stealing furs, or grabbing a payroll. And we shall need eight good men, plus a week's rehearsal, before we pull it off.'

For the first time the listener looked less sceptical.

'Eight men? Must be a big one. I thought those Crown Jewels were supposed to be hard to lift.'

'I expect they are,' grinned Baxter, 'and I've no ambition to find out. Your end would be twenty thousand.'

'Pounds or dollars?' was the quick response.

'Pounds.'

'H'm.'

They walked along in silence, while Mallory absorbed this new and attractive thought. He'd risked his life many times over for far less money, as had Baxter himself, and, as an American, he'd be bound to think of it as an offer he couldn't refuse.

'It sounds too good,' said Mallory finally. 'All that dough for one week's work, and no armed opposition. Why are you so good to me, Baxter?'

'Because I need a deputy. Somebody I know I can trust, and who won't accidentally leave me behind if things get rough. On top of that, if anything should happen to me in the meantime, he has to be someone who could run the thing. You could do it, Joe.'

Mallory shooed an over-confident duck away from his feet as they moved along. The idea was beginning to appeal to him, and he knew that Baxter would not sell him short. They were not exactly friends, as the term is interpreted in the more conventional world, but they had been comrades more than once, with all the deeper implications the term implied.

'How would I get paid?'

'Five thousand when you agree to take the job on. Another five when we go to work. The remaining ten thousand on satisfactory completion.'

Again, they walked in silence.

'Before I commit myself, do you intend to go into more detail? I mean, I'd like to hear more about it, you know?'

'I'm sure you would, but the answer is "no",' rejected Baxter firmly. 'The security on this is one hundred per cent plus, and I can't give out information to anyone who isn't committed.'

'So I just have to take your word?'

The two men paused, and looked each other in the eye.

'It's been good enough before,' Baxter reminded him calmly.

One final pause, and Mallory nodded his head.

'O.K. Put me down. When do I get the five Gs?'

'Right now.'

Baxter pulled a bulky white envelope from his pocket, and handed it over. Mallory held it for a moment, grinning.

'Just like that?'

'Count it,' invited Baxter.

77

'What for?' shrugged the other man. 'You wouldn't gyp a simple soldier.'

He stuck the envelope carefully into an inside pocket, tapped at his chest as though in confirmation, then said, 'Who else did you have in mind? Is there any room for Jimmy Sparkes on this?'

'I thought about Sparkes, yes. And that chum of his, the tall one, Porter. They work well together.'

'Right. And what about that guy who sings all the time? You remember, he damned nearly drove us crazy that night over in Macao. What's his name again?'

'Judd. Yorkshireman. Eric Judd. Yes, he'll do.'

'Then there's little what's it, the electronics man—er—'

The rain was beginning again, light spots which carried the threat of heavier showers to follow. A young couple, who'd been spending their lunch-break in tossing scraps to the ever-greedy birds, gathered up their belongings, ready to sprint for shelter.

'Look at those two silly buggers,' observed the girl. 'You'd think they were waterproof or something.'

The young man with her followed her gaze to where two men strolled along, deep in conversation, and seemingly oblivious to the increasing rain.

'Tell you what they're talking about, if you want to know.'

'Go on then,' invited the girl, busily tucking a headscarf inside her coat.

'Horse-racing,' pronounced her companion confidently. 'Horse-racing or women. There's nothing else takes your mind off the weather like that.'

'Ooh Fred,' and the girl nudged him. 'Do I take your mind off the weather?'

'Come here, and I'll show you.'

They lost interest in the men, who were now almost out of sight.

They didn't even notice the small City-clerk type, wrapped carefully against the elements, who was following about a hundred yards behind the two men.

CHAPTER NINE

In Hong Kong it was hot.

Most great cities have their fashionable residential areas, their not-so fashionable, and their slums. There are business sections, amusement districts and self-styled artistic quarters. Often too, there is a waterfront, either from sea or river-mouth, with docks a hive of activity by day, and half-lit desertion by night.

Hong Kong contains all these segments a-plenty, but nowhere else in the world are they flung together with such haphazard disregard for symmetry. Nowhere else is the fashionable to be found cheek by jowl with the demi-monde, the city type with the pedlar, the great artist with the honky-tonk dancer. Hong Kong has been likened to a great simmering stew of humanity, and the comparison is not inept. It is almost as though some giant hand had taken Jack the Ripper's East End, the early San Francisco China-town, the Parisian Left Bank, and added to these the solemn enclaves of the City of London, the heady artistry of Florence and Milan and the feverish excitement of the Klondyke gold-mines, in a great distillation of eras and social groups, and dumped it unceremoniously on the coastline of China. Here it has thrived and prospered. The confines are stark and immutable, so there can be no question of pushing out boundaries to form acceptable lines of demarcation. People have had to adapt to the environment, and the environment, in its turn, to the people. There has had to be compromise and adjustment between social groups and conflicting interests, of a kind and on a scale which is without parallel elsewhere. The basic rule has been simple. Adapt or perish. Faced with this unalterable edict, oriental and occidental alike shrugged shoulders and pocketed their differences. Never the twain shall meet? Anyone repeating that old saying would do well to add in parentheses 'always excluding Hong Kong'.

And in Hong Kong it was hot.

Captain Marco Leonides, of the s.s. *Sunderland Lady*,

rolled reluctantly off his bunk and retrieved his soiled old cap from the floor. That Frenchman would be coming aboard at any minute, and the only feature to distinguish the captain from most of the crew was the misshapen peaked headpiece which he now jammed down over his ears. The ship was almost motionless at her berth, with only the gentlest rocking to remind those aboard of where they were, and now and then the rusty groan of a straining hawser.

The heat over the island was unseasonal. At this time of year it was often cloudy, although that damned humidity was always present, and even fog was not at all uncommon. Well, the rain would start at any time now, and that would cool things down at first, but the *Sunderland Lady* would probably miss its cooling benefits. What mattered at the moment was that it was hot, making a man's skin clammy, and doing nothing to improve the temper.

The huge docks were as busy as ever, but the unusual temperature had reduced the normal bustle to a more mannered pace. By contrast with the leisurely movements of the dock-workers, the young European seemed to be hurrying along, but this produced no particular surprise. All foreign devils were considered to be partly mad, and the ones with fair skins seemed to be the worst of the lot.

Marcel La Roche was in a good mood. An incurable optimist, he had managed to convince himself that somehow or other he would be able to raise the money he owed to that smiling villain, Li Chang. He was, after all, a Frenchman, of good birth and education. It was not in the nature of things that he should find himself threatened by people of that class, and certainly not for such a trivial sum as fifteen hundred HK dollars. This unexpected commission from the captain of the s.s. *Sunderland Lady* had arrived in the nick of time, there was no doubt about that, but La Roche had already adjusted it in his mind to the natural workings of fate. He'd been unlucky this time, that was all, and he would learn from it. In future, his gambling would be more subdued, no more than a little flutter from time to time. It was unthinkable that he had actually stood in that little gangster's office, pleading with him for more time. People like that were damned lucky to have Europeans frequenting their grubby premises, and should make allowances accordingly.

Li Chang had been excessively polite, almost fawning, during the interview. If it were left to him, he explained, he would be only too pleased to extend the young monsieur unlimited credit. Alas, he was not the master of his own fate, but merely a servant of harsh businessmen. Just that very day, he assured La Roche, he had personally approached those shadowy figures, suggesting that matters could be left for at least another month, but they had been inflexible. It was not, he hastened to add, that they did not trust Monsieur La Roche. That had never been a factor in their reasoning, and he hoped it never would. Their concern was that so many things could happen to prevent the gentleman from keeping his word, things quite outside his control. They quoted figures in support of their argument. The Crown Colony of Hong Kong was a violent place, with an appalling record of murder, stabbings, street assault, and abduction. He, Li Chang, was a simple man, and quite unable to comprehend anything as complicated as statistics. He must, however, accept the thinking of his masters, and they had assured him that the likelihood of one of the catastrophes overtaking Monsieur La Roche during the next month was of the order of fifty-fifty, and they felt the odds were against them. They were putting themselves at risk, even by granting him one week, and this was solely because he was known to be a gentleman, and a good customer.

La Roche smiled grimly at the recollection as he strode along. That little matter would be settled before the day was out, and he would see to it that the experience was not repeated.

A fleet of heavy vehicles trundled slowly past the walking man, on their way to the great container terminal of Kwai Chung. In the ordinary way, La Roche was not interested in commerce, except to the extent that the nature of the cargo affected the design of the carrying ships, but he could not resist reading the markings on the giant wooden cases. In a matter of minutes, a representative sample of the colony's diverse activities rolled past his gaze. Soft loads, like cotton yarn, man-made fibre garments, toys, foodstuffs, cigarettes. Heavier items too, such as air conditioners, television sets, steel pipes, heavy duty PVC. It was a source of continual astonishment to the Frenchman that such an enormous range of products could pour without any seeming end from the disorderly hubbub of the colony.

With so much legitimate trade to be had, it struck him as incongruous that he should be involved, however obliquely, in something which was outside the law. The matter was never mentioned, and indeed Captain Leonides had given him quite a different explanation, but La Roche had not been deceived.

The Frenchman was a designer draughtsman with one of the larger shipping companies, and was paid a handsome salary for his work. But, having brought with him the same expensive tastes which had hastened his departure from France, he quickly found it necessary to seek private commissions in order to supplement his income. As a rule these consisted of minor alterations to the great fleet of privately owned yachts and launches, which were the recreational pride and joy of the well-to-do, but this particular job was unusual.

'Tanks, Captain? I am to design tanks for you?'

'That's the idea,' confirmed Leonides. 'It's a little private invention of my own, so I shall be paying you direct. When I go to the owners, I want to be able to show them proper drawings, to prove it can be done. Originally, I thought we could adapt an existing inner shell, but it won't do, for many reasons. So we must start from scratch.'

La Roche nodded. It could be done all right, he had no doubts about that. The point was, why?

'And what will they carry, these tanks?'

Leonides looked cunning, and placed one finger along the side of his nose before replying.

'You must appreciate that I am placing enormous trust in you, Monsieur La Roche. If my idea is accepted, it could bring about a small revolution in the coastal trade. Not just here, but all over the world. I must rely on your discretion.'

The designer nodded impatiently.

'Quite so, monsieur, but you appreciate I cannot give you

a proper design unless I can calculate my stresses. For this, I must know the contents.'

That seemed to make up the captain's mind.

'Oil,' he said briefly.

La Roche looked politely puzzled.

'Oil,' he repeated, his facial expression making it a question. Leonides snapped his fingers. 'Absolutely. The world has gone container mad. These bloody great floating oil wells, fouling up every ocean, and what's the result? They can't get into half the ports in the world. Special plants have to be built, miles from anywhere, to take in the oil, tens of thousands of tonnes at a time. Everyone is dancing to the tanker's tune, but I'm going to change all that. Plenty of people, small people, don't want the extra charges involved. If I can supply a few hundred tonnes, right at their own back door, I can do it cheaper and quicker.'

'I see. So you are not proposing to turn the *Sunderland Lady* into a small tanker?'

'No, no. You miss my point. The oil will be a little extra. The *Lady*, and ships like her, will carry on with the normal trade. At the same time, there will be this extra bonus for the shippers, and believe me, there will be no shortage of customers. I shall be a rich man, you'll see.'

Again, the designer nodded politely. It was clearly time that Captain Leonides retired. There was no future in this hare-brained scheme. The oil companies would block it from the outset. Still, that wasn't his concern. He had not kept this appointment in order to talk the customer out of the job. This excitable man was offering two thousand HK dollars for prompt action. If he wanted a drawing and specification for tanks, tanks he should have.

'It is certainly an original idea, Captain,' he said tactfully. 'Now, as to practicalities, how much oil do you wish to carry?'

'About a thousand tonnes. It needn't take up too much room. I was thinking about positioning them on the upper deck. If we start behind the back of the fo'c'sle, and end well short of the engine-room, we shall have about a hundred and fifty feet to play with.'

La Roche was already sketching a rough side elevation of a typical three-islander.

'Starting about here, you mean?' he pointed with his pencil.

'Right. Now if we take the tanks as three feet wide, and break them up at twelve-foot lengths, we ought to finish about there.' It was the captain's turn to point. 'Discharge plates at the forward end on each one.'

The Frenchman looked at him.

'Aren't you proposing to use pumps?'

'No, I've thought about this quite a lot. Pumps are a damned nuisance, and they're always letting you down at the wrong time. These are only tiddly little tanks, after all. We're just as well off with a valve at the rear, and a goose neck air pump forward.'

La Roche considered what the captain was proposing. It would mean that the plate in the side was little more than a bung. With the plate out, and the air pressure coming in from above, the tank would simply empty, in much the same way as a barrel of wine. The lack of technical refinement was distasteful to his engineering-trained mind, but its expediency was undeniable. It was cheap and it would work.

'Forgive me, Captain, for speaking the obvious, but remember this is all new to me. You have the advantage of having been planning for some time. These new tanks are going to have an influence on what cargoes you carry. No more soft goods, you realise, or your stability will go to hell.'

Leonides shrugged irritably, and the gesture was misinterpreted by the watching man, who assumed that the captain had no wish to be reminded of difficulties. The assumption was wrong. The old seaman's annoyance was at the suggestion that he might have overlooked such a basic point.

'I've been riding these old fruit-boats since before you were born, monsieur,' he rejoined heavily. 'The *Lady* will stabilise if the double-bottom tanks are filled with sea water.'

God in Heaven, this landlubber would be warning him about free-surfacing next.

Sensing that he might antagonise the skipper, thus putting his fee in jeopardy, La Roche dropped the subject, and spoke instead of the time available for the job. He was dismayed to learn that the completed drawings were required within thirty-six hours. It would mean he would have to work deep into the night, and the arrangements he had made with a certain speciality dancer would have to be postponed. But the thought of the smiling Li Chang stifled his objections, and he went away to apply himself to the task.

It was in the middle of the second night that he realised suddenly the true purpose behind what had seemed such a crazy scheme. That old fox, Leonides, had really fooled him for a while, with that nonsense about carrying oil. What he, La Roche, was designing, was a near foolproof smuggling space, but not for oil. Wine, perhaps, or spirits. Contraband of some kind. He chuckled, in the darkness of his room, where the only light came from the suspended neon tube above the drawing-board. Cunning old devil, to have taken him in like that. No wonder he wanted the drawings done privately. He'd no intention of letting the owners know what was going on, now or at any other time. What he'd said was probably true after all. If he was going to smuggle a thousand tonnes of liquor each time he made port, he really was going to be a rich man.

La Roche spent some time cogitating as to how he could profit by this new knowledge, but abandoned the thought eventually.

Now, as he climbed aboard the soot-grimed *Sunderland Lady*, he felt almost light-hearted. A small breeze was coming from across the Pearl River, and brought a welcome coolness to his damp brow.

Captain Leonides was waiting for him below, with a carefully-composed look of gravity on his face.

'Ah, there you are, monsieur,' he greeted, 'and right on time.'

'You were most pressing on that point, captain,' reminded the Frenchman. 'And here are your drawings, together with full specifications.'

His smile faded as he noted the shrug with which

Leonides accepted the proffered papers.

'I trust there is nothing amiss, Captain?'

'Nothing that needs to concern you.' The captain unfolded the sheets and looked at them perfunctorily. 'Yes, a very nice job, monsieur. You are to be congratulated on the quality of your work. What a pity it is all to be for nothing.'

Nothing? The young visitor thought of Li Chang, and his face dropped.

'I don't understand,' he said urgently. 'My fee—'

'Will be paid,' he was assured. 'And out of my own pocket, just as I promised. But your work will remain on the drawing, I fear. The owners got wind of my idea, and have cracked down hard. They want no part of it. They are not men of vision, like me, but grubby little clerks, who cannot see a golden opportunity when it is dangled in front of their noses. However, a bargain is a bargain, and Marco Leonides is a man of his word. Your fee, monsieur.'

There was no finesse about the captain. No cheque inside an envelope, not even an envelope. Just four large five hundred dollar notes, and none too clean, but they looked good to the eager La Roche. It was a pity about the old man's idea, of course, but you couldn't blame the owners. They'd spotted right away what he had in mind, and quashed it at once, as any self-respecting firm would. He took the money gratefully, refused the offer of a drink, and left. La Roche was not a man who enjoyed wakes.

Captain Leonides watched the youthful figure striding away through the dock-side confusion, smiling at his recent visitor's jaunty step. The young designer had believed him all right, he had little doubt about that. He could put M. La Roche from his mind. There were a number of matters now requiring his attention.

*   *   *

The portly figure of Li Chang attracted little interest as he made his way down the crowded side street. He was a familiar figure, as were the two young men who strolled along a few feet behind him, their loud Western clothes standing out among the more traditionally garbed vendors and pedestrians. Li Chang looked neither to left nor right, but the eyes of his companions were never still, roving and probing at passers-by, buildings and shop-fronts. The jostling crowds, busy about their own affairs, seemed to melt mysteriously as the little procession advanced, allowing sufficient room for their progress, then closing as by some hidden chemistry after they had passed. Although they were only a few hundred yards from the great open harbour itself, there was no trace here of the shipping and docks activity which flourished so close by. The streets and the crowds could just as easily have been duplicated in any of the great cities of the mainland, for this was Kowloon, facing across the harbour to the island of Hong Kong itself. Geographically, it was situated on the mainland, but politically it had been ceded to the British under the Peking Convention of 1860. To the teeming masses of the interior, Kowloon represented the gateway to freedom, and scarcely a day passed without the appearance of fresh faces in the crowded tenements and byways. No one really knew the exact size of the population, but it certainly exceeded two million and could quite possibly be as high as three.

Li Chang knew little of such matters, and cared even less. His sole interest lay in the inherent Chinese addiction to gambling, a trait which knows no political frontiers, but whose roots are deeper and more elemental. To him, the ever-swelling tide of immigrants represented nothing more complicated than an increased number of potential losers. Adherence to this simplified approach had made him a wealthy man, and wealth, regrettably, creates its own problems, in the shape of enemies. It was because of such people that he was compelled to employ the services of such as the two young thugs who now accompanied him, and whose relentless vigil would preserve his person and his property. Reaching a certain doorway, he paused. From inside there arose the smell of rich foods and spices, to mingle with the thousand and one street aromas which hung in the still air.

One of the young men went past his patron and inside the crowded café. After a moment or two he emerged again, nodding to the waiting men, and bowing his head. Li Chang went in then, and threaded his way between the tightly-packed tables. The proprietor, alerted by the bodyguard's inspection, walked in front of him, bobbing and smiling, and ensuring the uncluttered progress of his distinguished visitor. At the end there was a curtained narrow doorway. On either side there was just room for one small table, and seated behind each was the watchful figure of a man. The proprietor made himself scarce, while one of the men rose, inclined his head to the impassive Li Chang, and pulled the curtain aside for him to enter. Before going through, the gambler raised one hand in signal to his escorts, who fell out on either side, each leaning against the wall adjacent to the tiny tables. It would have been improper, and indeed a gross breach of etiquette, for them to follow him further. Their master was now under other protection, and would remain so until he re-emerged.

Li Chang mounted slowly up the steep wooden stairs which confronted him until he reached a narrow landing. Here stood a massive Shanghainese whose wary and scarred face betokened a life other than that of the doorkeeper he now seemed to be. This man made his best attempt at a courtly bow as Li Chang passed him, to knock twice at a panelled door before entering.

The room was almost spartan in its simplicity, and was dominated by a single desk, of which the lacquered surface was a glowing tribute to the bygone craftsman who had created it. Behind the desk sat a small man, whose lined and wise face was so frail as to be almost ethereal. Li Chang bowed deeply from the waist and waited.

Han Lee studied his visitor impassively, and wondered what it was that had prompted the gambler to seek this interview. It would have to be something of importance, to excuse the unmannerly way in which the approach had been made. There were rules to be observed in these matters, procedures to be followed. The normal waiting time for a personal confrontation was at least twenty-four hours, but this man had claimed that his business was too urgent for delay. It was possible that his growing strength and personal wealth was bringing with it a concomitant inflation in the newcomer's assessment of his own importance. If such was the case, then he must, of course, be disillusioned.

The old man spoke, and the words were like the rustle of autumn leaves in a dark forest.

'You honour my poor house with this sudden visit.'

Li Chang was staring at the rich textures of the rug on which he was standing. He swallowed nervously at the sound of the rebuke, and wondered fleetingly whether he had been too importunate in asking for this audience. Slowly he raised his head, his mind fumbling for the correct words.

'Excellency, I crave pardon a thousand times for this intrusion. When an ignorant villager finds something of value, it is his duty to seek the guidance of a man of letters.'

Straight to the point, noted Han Lee. A crude fellow this, but, at the same time, no fool. Li Chang was not the man to risk giving offence without a good reason, and he was certainly doing his best to achieve the right note. He smiled slightly, and some of the tension went from the face of the standing man.

'In what way may a poor scholar be of service to a man of such eminence?'

In halting phrases, interspersed with such flowery verbal tributes as he could recall, Li Chang explained about the sudden payment of a gambling debt by the foreign devil called La Roche. The young Frenchman had celebrated his economic release by spending the night in carousing with a certain young woman named Silver Lily, who had promptly reported back to Li Chang. He, in turn, felt that the information, although of no value to him, ought to be passed to those who might make use of it.

Han Lee listened politely. There was little that passed in Hong Kong that escaped his notice. Information flowed in ceaselessly from all sides, much of it useless, but none ignored. Only that day it had been brought to his attention that a certain ship's captain had recruited six skilled workers in steel, to join his ship for the next sailing. It had been an odd thing for a merchant captain to do, and anything odd usually repaid a little scrutiny. Now, here was this fellow, Li Chang, supplying another scrap of information which might assist in solving the puzzle. When the story was told, he nodded.

'You must forgive the mind of an old man, Li Chang, but I know little of ships. You tell me of this great puzzle, but I cannot decipher it.'

Li Chang was uncertain whether the words were serious. Surely it must be obvious what was going on? Aware that he must at all costs show no sign of impatience, he cleared his throat.

'It would seem, Excellency, that the man Leonides has a plan to smuggle fire-wines from one country to another. I have heard it said that there is much profit in this. It seemed to me that information of such value should be in the proper hands.'

It was out now, an overt attempt to court the favour of Han Lee, and everyone he represented. If only the old devil would twitch an eyelid, or a facial muscle, anything that might give his audience an inkling of what was going on behind those faded eyes. But his listener was too practised a hand for any such self-betrayal, and continued to stare at him steadily.

'The ship of which you speak, where is it bound?'

'To Marseilles, in the land of France, Excellency. As your worship knows, this is the homeland of cognac, a spirit which has found much favour, even among our people. The duty on this wine is heavy everywhere, and it would be a load worthy of bearing.'

Cognac? Yes, indeed it would, admitted Han Lee privately. Perhaps this pirate of the fan-tan tables had brought him information which could be turned to profit after all.

Li Chang watched him carefully, anxious for his verdict, and his face fell when it came.

'There is nothing here for us, Li Chang. Such matters are not our concern. I shall inform the Council that your visit here was well-intentioned, but no more. And now, I find my heart and my head are in conflict. It is the price of advancing years. My heart tells me to press tea on an old friend, but my head tells me the friend is anxious to be about his affairs.'

Li Chang was keenly disappointed that his news had fallen so flat, but, at the same time, he was relieved not to be chastised for wasting the great man's time. With much bowing and showering of compliments, he made himself scarce. Outside, he even bowed to the enormous Shanghainese, who could scarcely conceal his disappointment at not being called up to demonstrate his muscular prowess.

Inside the room all was still for several minutes. Then Han Lee picked up a small silver bell which rang a high sweet note as he shook it. The door opened at once and a second burly figure, the twin of the one at the head of the stairs, bowed low and waited.

'There are enquiries I wish to make.'

CHAPTER TEN

Ben Hardcastle was disappointed to find that Jennifer Fiske was not in her customary seat at the controls of the mighty Wurlitzer, as he privately designated the computer. Despite her absence, the equipment continued with some mysterious function of its own, the only sound in the room being a gentle whirring, plus an occasional staccato chatter from the printer. He knew from experience that there would be no point in reading the print-out, which seldom made use of any plain language. He would be faced, he knew, with a complex array of meaningless symbols, the key to which was only in Jennifer's mind. Where was she, anyway? Perhaps she had at last succeeded in programming herself out of the necessity for her presence. Or, more chillingly, the reverse. It was an increasingly popular theme with the more advanced science-fiction writers that the ultimate programme would be for the controller to integrate himself/herself fully within the heart of the machine, bone, sinew et al. A thoroughly nasty concept, and, in the case of the delectable Fiske, a monstrous misapplication of the said bone and sinew, which had clearly been designed for more earthly purposes.

'Ah, here you are,' greeted Jameson, not quite smiling as Ben entered his room. 'Sit down, my dear fellow. A certain amount of progress, I think.'

'You have the reports,' replied the other. 'Our friend Baxter certainly had a talk with the American, Mallory. We've no idea what they said to each other. Could have been just chatting over old times, for all I know. Even a loner like Baxter must feel the need for human contact sometimes.'

'True,' conceded Jameson, 'but if that's all it was, he went a strange way about it. They could have stayed in that pub, had a few drinks, gone to lunch, picked up a couple of women, anything. Instead of which they elected to go walking in the park, and in the rain, to boot. Not the most usual kind of get-together for a couple of active chaps. No, I think we may take it, as Holmes would have said, that the game is afoot. Our man got thoroughly wet.'

Hardcastle nodded assent.

'You could be right. I certainly hope you are. To tell you the truth, boss, I'm getting a little bit disenchanted with all this. I have devoted eight valuable weeks to Mr. Bloody Baxter. So far I've done nothing which could not have been done just as well by some flatfoot. Makes a bit of a mockery of all my training, not to mention whatever qualifications I am presumed to have which got me into this racket in the first place.'

Jameson sighed inwardly. The complaint was familiar, and justified. It was inseparable from the very nature of any kind of intelligence work, irrespective of the field, that ninety per cent of the time was occupied in carrying out tasks which could have been performed quite adequately by a lively-minded errand boy. It could not even be claimed that the work was essential to form a solid platform from which to launch some vital assault. Most of it proved to be unnecessary duplication, wrongly-based, or, worst of all, totally pointless. All this was drummed home during survival training, as were the brighter spots. If an assignment proved to have a five per cent interest content, that was to be considered as above average. A job which ultimately contained even two per cent of excitement or danger was rare indeed. These hard facts were instilled into people time out of number, but rarely did they register in the early stages. Being human, the people on the courses applied an inborn technique of selective listening. They abstracted and retained the words they had come to hear. Excitement and danger had far more appeal than boredom and routine, and were in any case more acceptable components of their own visualisation of the kind of existence for which they were destined. It was only field experience which brought home the realities, and which was now causing the man opposite to fret.

'Life isn't all K.G.B. defectors and hand-made Berettas,' he pointed out venomously. 'In this job, one spends more time at the shoe-repairer's than the gunsmith's. Anyway, as I just said, there is no doubt that we are making progress.

I've had a little more information from our people in the Far East since you were last in. I thought it would interest you.'

Far East? Oh yes, the ship—what was it—the *Sunderland Lady*. On its way to Marseilles, when last reported. Well, anything would be more interesting than the hourly reports on Baxter. Hardcastle put on a look of polite attention.

'Yes, I'd like to hear that.'

'Good. My initial report simply said that there had been some activity aboard the *Lady*, while she was berthed in Hong Kong. I now learn that she has been fitted with additional storage space of some kind. According to the specifications, this takes the form of extra oil tanks, which of course is nonsense.'

'Oh? Forgive me, but I know nothing about ships. To me, it would seem quite logical for a ship to build extra tanks. Maybe she is due to make longer voyages or something.'

There was a decisive shake of the head behind the desk.

'Out of the question. She isn't a paddle steamer or what they call a coast-hugger. She is a fully equipped ocean-going vessel, designed to travel for weeks, if she has to, without refuelling. No, professor, those tanks will carry something else, and my guess is armaments.'

'From Hong Kong? Sounds a bit far-fetched, doesn't it?'

Jameson was unable to decide whether his agent was being deliberately obtuse, or whether he was genuinely missing the point. On balance he decided to give him the benefit of the doubt, but his tone had dropped a degree or two when he replied.

'I do not mean to imply that the arms would come from that direction. The big manufacturers are mostly on this side of the world, if one excludes the United States. Marseilles has a history of smuggling which extends back for a thousand years. It is practically a clearing-house for every form of illegal traffic. It would be my guess that the guns or whatever will be taken aboard while the *Sunderland Lady* is there.'

Despite himself, Hardcastle was aware of disappointment. If Jameson's theory was right, then the whole business would fizzle out.

'So it's really that simple, is it? All you have to do is to arrange for extra-tight surveillance of the ship. Once she's loaded up, the French authorities can move in, and there's one war down the drain. Pity, really, just when things are warming up.'

The look of horror on his superior's face was not assumed.

'My dear fellow, what are you thinking of? I wouldn't dream of anything of the kind. Wouldn't suit our book at all. I'm not interested in arresting a few miserable gun-smugglers.'

'No, of course not, but it would go beyond that. A little pressure, a little negotiation, a promise or two of light sentences, and you'd soon find out who was behind them.'

'Really, Hardcastle, your naïvety continues to astound me. Do you really imagine we'd ever get close to the people who mattered? We should find ourselves up against layer after layer of protection. Believe me, in an operation of this kind, throwing a few front-line personnel in jail solves nothing.'

Which left only one alternative, in the listener's mind, and one which was clearly unacceptable.

'What's your option? You can hardly let them start their war, wherever it happens to be.'

Jameson pressed his finger-tips together, very much in the manner of a clergyman about to deliver a sermon.

'Wrong,' he corrected. 'That is precisely what we shall do.'

'Oh come now,' protested Hardcastle, 'you can't be serious. We're talking about war. People will get killed, innocent people mostly. I don't believe I'm hearing this.'

'Just wait a moment, and think further. Wherever this—um—disturbance is scheduled to take place, you can be quite certain it's about ready to blow. All the preliminary work will have been done. It is not in the nature of things that someone appears with a load of munitions and then suggests that a war would be a good idea. No, no, the actual supplies are the very last step in a carefully planned operation. If we should interfere with this particular shipment, it would serve only as a delay. Other arrangements would have to be made, and we might not be so lucky next time.

We might not be in on the ground floor at all.'

'We'd still have Baxter,' objected the other.

'True, but it might be decided that he's become a risk, and they could opt to go ahead without him. No, no, there'll be no interference at this stage. Let them load the guns, let us monitor the movements of all concerned, and then we go in fast and hard. I wonder where it will be?'

Hardcastle didn't care to dwell on the thought. Although he could follow the cold logic of the argument, he found it impossible to free his mind of the terrible implications. Jameson's thinking might be the only practical way to deal with the wider issue, but that would be of little comfort to him when the television pictures began to arrive, showing defenceless women and children facing bayonets.

'I'm beginning to think I have no place here,' he said softly. 'I haven't your breadth of vision. I know a general has to sacrifice twenty men in order to save a thousand, but I lack the tactical mind. My sympathies are with the twenty, every time.'

Jameson regarded him levelly for some seconds. He could appreciate the struggle going on in the other man's mind, which was perfectly understandable. At the same time, it was unacceptable. With the scale of operation with which the department had to deal, there was no room for mealy-mouthed sentimentality. To use the man's own argument, if twenty had to die to save a thousand, then die they must. Fortunately for all concerned, the decision did not rest with Hardcastle.

Lightening his tone, he said:

'Well, we mustn't get ahead of ourselves. Early days yet. Any number of things can go wrong, as we all know from experience. Meantime, you've got a job to do, and so have I. When is the next report due on Baxter?'

'Fifteen minutes. I ought to get back to the flat.'

'Do that. And Hardcastle, don't go dwelling on all these dark possibilities. Doesn't pay in our job. One step at a time, that's the ticket. Keep after Baxter. I think you'll find the next few days will produce something to keep us all occupied. Shan't have any time to waste on speculation then. I think it's time you brought your tool kit up to date, incidentally. Fiske will see to it for you.'

The reminder that he might shortly need a weapon brought the younger man back to earth sharply.

'She wasn't there when I came in,' he announced, getting to his feet.

'I'll see she gets in touch,' came the promise.

An hour later, he was sitting in the Baker Street flat, trying to become absorbed in the trials and tribulations of an Australian sheep-raiser on television, when the door chimes sounded. Thankfully, he switched off the set and went to the door, staring through the tiny spyhole. Jennifer Fiske winked at him, and he opened the door.

'Well, well,' he greeted, 'come in.'

She stepped inside, and walked past him, peering around. Closing the door, he stood watching her. She was wearing a safari suit in blue denim, which had been tailored to show off the rangy body to maximum advantage. A large pouch-bag dangled from her shoulder, and she stood with a thumb hooked in the strap while she inspected his quarters.

'Tidy devil, aren't you?' she observed. 'Thought you might be. My place is a slum.'

'The bathroom is through there,' he pointed, 'you can check my toothbrush if you like. I also change the sheets regularly.'

'I can see you would. Is there a drink?'

'You offend me, madam. What would happen to my macho image if I didn't have a well-stocked bar? Whiskey all right?'

'If it's malt,' she replied negligently. 'Straight please.'

He carefully selected a chunky tumbler, and poured out a generous measure. The pale amber liquid picked up the dying rays of the sun as they slanted through the window. She took it, nodding her thanks.

'Where's yours?'

'Coming up. I'll stick to beer, I think. Could be a long night if Master Baxter decides to take off somewhere. Cheers.'

He held up his glass in salute, and they drank. Jennifer parked herself on an upright chair, shifting her bag over the back. He sat opposite, very conscious of her presence, and

97

at the same time aware that he must not too quickly place his own interpretation on her motives.

'Brought you a present,' she announced, 'from the Lord High Executioner. One Webley .38 automatic, plus two clips. Why two clips? Does he think you might want to start your own war?'

He shrugged.

'Who knows what he thinks? He has some very outlandish notions of the value of human life, judging by our last conversation.'

She cocked her head on one side, inspecting him.

'Yes, he told me about that. Worried you a bit, did he?'

He thought carefully before replying. This girl might be in his flat, drinking his whiskey, but for all that she was very much Jameson's confidante, not his. The seeming informality of the occasion must not deceive him into forgetting whom he was addressing. Now he shrugged.

'I can understand his position, naturally. He has to take a global view, and there isn't always room for the niceties of life. That's one of the reasons he's the boss, and I'm just a humble employee.'

'Oh pshaw,' she scoffed. 'You're about as humble as a secondhand car salesman. But there is a difference between you. I think you would probably kill if there was no alternative, and on a one to one basis. Our revered master would think more in terms of minimal strikes and the like. Personally, I don't care for any of it, but if I had to make a choice, I'd elect for your philosophy.'

Hardcastle began to feel uncomfortable, not liking the direction in which the conversation was heading. What was the girl aiming at, some kind of alliance between them? An anti-Jameson front? Because if she was—

'Anyway, this is all too gloomy for words,' she went on. 'We ought to find something more agreeable to talk about, on a sunny evening. I have a subject, if you want to hear it.'

He grinned then, aware that she was playing with words.

'Me too,' he confessed, 'but I was intending to wait until the drink thawed you out.'

She responded with one of her lazy smiles.

'Steady Bonzo, I think we're on different tracks. I have a

theory about the operation which might surprise you a little. Unless I'm mistaken, our revered leader is misreading the signs.'

'The signs? How do you mean?'

Instead of replying, she held out her glass.

'Get me some more of this, and I shall expound.'

He poured her another drink, but made no effort to match her by swallowing his own beer. The glass was still half-full.

'Expound away,' he invited.

'Very well.' She rested her glass on the table beside her, and relaxed into the chair, her arms resting on either side. 'Let's consider what we have. One undoubted mercenary, in the shape of Philip Baxter. One con-man, large scale, George Halloran. One dangerous criminal, Williams. In the background, quite possibly the mysterious Ryder. Remember that the only one of those with a known history of involvement in civil wars is Baxter.'

'The others seem like pretty good candidates,' interjected the listening man.

'Candidates yes, but no more at present. Next, the ship. She has been equipped with some new superstructure in Hong Kong, of all places. Why? If all she has to do is carry a few guns, they could easily go in the existing hold, with some crates of farm machinery to make it look good. Apart from which, there's plenty of shipping available a lot nearer home, which would probably require no adaptation at all, assuming adaptation to be necessary.'

Hardcastle made a wry face.

'Good questions, but I haven't any answers.'

'Here's one possibility,' she suggested. 'These new additions attract a lot less attention in a place like Hong Kong. The Far East trade consists largely of ancient vessels on their last legs. They're always being patched up, one way and another, to keep them afloat for a few more trips. If the same kind of work were done on the Clyde, for instance, it would be well reported. People might even ask questions, and whatever it is these people are up to, the last thing they want is to answer questions.'

'O.K. so far as it goes,' he pointed out, 'but it still doesn't answer your other point, which is why they didn't find a

99

ship a bit nearer home, which could do the job as it stood.'

She nodded, evidently pleased to have aroused his interest.

'Right on, as the Australians say. So perhaps it isn't the ship at all. Perhaps it's the skipper they really want. I've run a probe on Captain Leonides, and he's as colourful an old rascal as you could find in a month of Sundays. His career in World War Two would make a dozen movies, and there isn't a bay or an inlet on either side of the Mediterranean that he doesn't know like the back of his hand.'

It was clear from the warmth of her tone that Miss Fiske had developed a regard for the aged Leonides. Her information about him was very much in line with what Jameson had already indicated.

'Go on,' he invited.

'Let's go back to Hong Kong,' she said, apparently changing direction. 'If I asked you to make a guess as to who showed interest in the *Sunderland Lady*, we'd be here for hours. Not the Americans, not the Japanese, not even mainland China has shown the slightest flicker. The people who have are the Triads. What do you know about them, Ben?'

It was the first time she'd ever called him by name, and his initial reaction was one of such gratification that he almost forgot the question.

'The Triads?' he repeated, composing himself. 'Well, let's see. They are a very old secret society, quite possibly the oldest in the world. They prey on Chinese nationals in every sphere of life, but I wasn't aware they ever interfered with other races. Evidently my information is incomplete.'

'No,' she denied, 'I don't think it is. I think your information is sound. They don't interest themselves with non-Chinese matters, except for the occasional co-operation for the common good.'

'Well, they are now, aren't they?' he protested. 'I mean if they're starting to meddle in this war—'

'Which I begin to doubt exists,' she interrupted.

'Eh?'

For once he was at a loss for words. Staring at her face, he tried to discern whether this might be one of her put-downs, but she returned his gaze quite calmly.

100

'Jameson is looking for a war, we all are. One of our very best leads is Baxter, and he's become a kind of symbol. Baxter equals war equals Baxter. He's far and away our best bet, and, as a result, Jameson refuses to think of him in any other context. The very mention of Baxter's name, and our leader hears the rattle of distant gunfire.'

'After all, that is what this is all about, isn't it?' remonstrated Ben.

'Is it? I'm beginning to wonder. Baxter is the only name we have to date in this caper who has known mercenary connections. We know Ryder and Halloran are shifty money-men. We know Williams is little more than a gunman. Now, stir in the other ingredients. A ship's captain who can sail the Mediterranean blindfold, plus the Triads. I think we're onto something big, but it's not a war. It's some kind of crime. What we've been watching is the putting together of the components for some large-scale criminal undertaking.'

Hardcastle shook his head, not so much in denial as in an attempt to clear it in readiness for this new thinking.

'But Baxter's not a crook, he's a soldier.'

Jennifer pointed a finger, in admonition.

'He's a man who will hire out his considerable skills for money. If I were planning a crime on some scale, and I didn't want to risk the usual run of conceited bully boys, I can think of no one I'd sooner recruit. He has no criminal record, the police are not at all interested in him. Not only would he not be spotted beforehand, but he'd also have a good chance of getting away with it afterwards. Think about it for a moment, while I inspect your bathroom.'

She went away, and Hardcastle lit a cigarette. Whether she was aware of it or not, Jennifer's absence was exactly what he needed at that moment. Her powerful physical presence was a severe handicap to clear thinking on his part. His every instinct wanted to agree with her, rather than to do anything which might disturb the welcome and increasing intimacy of their present situation. With her out of the room, he forced himself to examine closely the new line of thinking she had imported into the conversation.

All in all, he conceded, it could make sense. If it did, the sooner they confirmed her theory, the better. They could then hand over what they had to the proper police authorities, and get back to their own line of work.

'Have you thought about it?'

Jennifer was back, and he looked up, nodding. Then he looked again. She had undone the bun behind her head, and her face was now framed by gleaming blonde hair.

'Wow,' he said. 'I've never seen your hair down before. It's beautiful.'

'Thank you, sir.' She poked him lightly in the shoulder, and went over to resume her seat. 'Well?'

'I think it's possible you're right. We'd need more information before we can be sure. Meantime, don't you think we ought to tip off the boss?'

'Hector?' she scoffed. 'Oh, I've tried, believe me, but he won't have it. The man has a fixation about Baxter, and I can't shift him.'

Hardcastle was disappointed, and showed it.

'That's too bad. Well, I suppose that's it. We just carry on as before. After all, it's only a theory, and we ought to know, one way or the other, before too long. Agreed?'

He got up to pour himself another glass of beer, and was standing by the drinks cupboard as he put the question.

'Almost.'

She came and stood beside him, delicate perfume wafting around his head. He remained quite still, conscious that a wrong move might spoil everything.

'What does that mean, almost?' he breathed.

'Just this,' she said softly, 'until now, I've been able to live with the idea that you might get yourself killed, preventing a war. That's why we do what we do, and it's all in the game. But I am not prepared to see you throwing your life away because of some purely criminal case. That would be wasteful, and I won't have you wasted, Ben Hardcastle.'

He put down the glass then, and turned to her.

'What's this I hear? I thought you were a real tough lady.'

'I am,' she confirmed, looking up at him, 'but I have my limits. I want you to promise me that you'll be extra careful from here on. Crime is not our business, and I don't want any heroics. If we're to have something going, I don't expect to have it ended by a third party.'

He took her gently in his arms, and she moulded into him. After a while, she murmured into his chest, 'I still haven't checked those sheets.'

CHAPTER ELEVEN

Basil Williams lay contentedly on the bed, his head propped up by pillows, and watched. The tall, willowy girl had skin with the texture of silk and the colour of mahogany. Some of them marred what had gone before by an indecent hurry to be off, but this one contrived to make something of an art of putting her clothes back on. Conscious of his scrutiny, she smiled at him reminiscently as she slipped the cream silk dress over her head, and shrugged it into place. Then she stood in front of the mirror, adding a final smoothing with long, slender fingers. A quick pat at her hair, and she turned, walking over to him with easy flowing steps.

A mischievous grin played around the red lips as she looked down.

'And what is this, *chéri?* Can it be that I am perhaps leaving you too soon?'

She was quite right, of course. He didn't want her to go at all, as she could clearly see. At any other time, he would have pulled her down beside him, and rectified things, but the time was getting on. He smacked her playfully on the rump.

'There will be another time, my little one. Here.'

He took his wallet from the bedside table, and began to extract some large banknotes. She shook her head.

'It is not necessary, monsieur,' she said quickly. 'Monsieur Girard has said—'

He silenced her with a forefinger.

'Monsieur Girard is most generous, but this is a little gift between friends. He need not know of it. I would like to do this for you. Please.'

She hesitated. Her instructions had been quite clear, and Girard was not a man to be trifled with in such matters. But he was not infallible, as this morning had clearly shown. She had been concerned that this M. Williams was a highly dangerous man, and that she might be hurt. If so, she would of course be compensated. She had approached the assignment with some trepidation, and had been more than agreeably surprised. The customer might be a dangerous man outside, but in the bedroom he was a cuddly lamb. With his little round body, and his smiling face, he reminded her irresistibly of the happy plaster figures in St. Catherine's. All he lacked were the spreading wings at the shoulders.

'Monsieur is very kind,' she said gravely, taking the money. 'Are you sure you would not wish me to deal with your small problem before I leave? It would be a pleasure.'

He shook his head regretfully.

'Unfortunately, little one, I have business. You understand.'

She nodded, patting him on the cheek.

'A bientôt,' she murmured.

'I hope so, pretty one.'

The door closed behind her with the gentlest of clicks. Williams got up from the bed and went to the window. What a glorious day it was, he reflected.

Any coolie, transported from the teeming harbour of Hong Kong, could have been forgiven for imagining he had died in his sleep, and woken up in some heavenly paradise. For this was Nice, where immaculate white sand lined the sparkling blue of the Mediterranean. No sea-going tramps here, no cranes or warehouses. Only the sleek and well-cared-for luxury yachts, and the gleaming white sails of the fast racers. No shuffling work force, merely the leisured parade of golden men and women, all busily engaged in proving that their existence was entirely without point. That, at least, was the estimate of the watching man.

Turning, he climbed under the shower, and switched it to full cold, yelling as the icy needles drove at him, then enjoying the refreshment of his skin. Mustn't be too long, he reflected, since he had agreed to meet Girard at noon.

Marcel Girard was sitting on the stone terrace, talking to his companion, when he saw a portly figure emerge from the cream Cadillac which had pulled up below. It was two minutes before twelve.

'The Englishman keeps good time,' he observed.

The other man grunted with satisfaction. They made an odd contrast, these two. Girard was suave and elegant, every inch the urbane cosmopolitan. The other one was shorter and thickset, with an air of sinister purpose about him, which the expensive suiting could not disguise.

'Remember what I told you,' warned Girard softly. 'This man might look like a Montmartre pastry-cook, but he is not one to be trifled with.'

'You're repeating yourself, Girard,' replied the other man rudely, 'I heard you the first time.'

Girard flushed slightly, but left it at that. Necessity, as they say, makes strange bedfellows, and certainly this brute Pagnol was not the kind of associate he would have chosen.

Jean Pagnol looked out of place among the polished and sophisticated surroundings along this section of the coast, but not far to the west lay the great port of Marseilles, and there he was in his element. Now in his early forties, he had spent twenty years in advancing to his present eminence. Twenty hard years, in which dexterity and skill with fist, knife and gun had marked his progress from the sewage in which he was spawned to the affluence he now enjoyed. Versatile though he was in all forms of violence, it had been his special aptitude with another weapon which had earned him his soubriquet. A short truncheon of steel-encased teak was never far from his reach. With this he could break an arm or a leg, or a skull if the offence warranted, and he was a fearsome sight with this instrument in his hands. He was known far and wide as The Club, and rejoiced in the recognition. There were few activities on the Marseilles docks from which The Club did not exact his toll, and he had a small army of retainers to assist him with any difficulties.

When Marcel Girard had first been approached about the matter of the s.s. *Sunderland Lady*, he had realised at once that Pagnol would have to be involved, sooner or later. The sensible thing would be to bring him in at the outset. Apart from other considerations, such a move would appeal to the man's enormous vanity.

Basil Williams was now advancing towards them. Girard stood up to greet him. Pagnol remained where he was, almost as if to indicate that he stood for no man. When they were settled, Girard spoke first.

'I invited M. Pagnol because he is a man of enormous

influence in such matters, M. Williams. I am sure our little conversation today will advance matters with smoothness.'

Williams looked curiously at the man of enormous influence, and summed him up at once. His influence undoubtedly came from the wrong end of a machine-gun, but that was probably all to the good. This was hardly work for a senior officer of the Salvation Army. He got straight down to business.

'Our needs are very simple,' he explained. 'A ship will arrive in Marseilles from Hong Kong. There, she will pay off six members of the crew. When her cargo has been discharged and fresh cargo taken aboard, she will sail for London. We need six good reliable men to replace the discharged seamen. They will accompany the ship to London, where they will be required to perform certain duties. After that, they will have to make their own way home. We shall pay these men well, and, of course, we shall also pay an administration charge to you gentlemen.'

He smiled from one to the other, well aware that he had really told them nothing of value, but enough to arouse their interest. Girard waited a few moments to see whether Pagnol wished to take the lead, then spoke.

'I do not quite see why you need us at all, monsieur. Anyone can hire sailors.'

'True,' agreed the Englishman, 'but these men must be willing to turn their hands to any task, even things of which ordinary seamen know little. I was hoping that M. Pagnol might know of such men. One of them, incidentally, will replace the first mate.'

The Club stirred restlessly. He was not adept at all this verbal pussy-footing around. He liked a man to come out and say what he meant.

'You need crooks, right?'

Girard winced, but Williams only smiled the wider.

'Let me say this. We should not hold such a background against a man. Even if they had a record of violence, we should not consider that a disqualification.'

Pagnol grinned then. He had a feeling that if they could only dispense with this pouf Girard, he and the Englishman could talk turkey.

'Let's talk about money,' he suggested.

Williams made no demur. He had made a special visit to the Crédit Lyonnais on his way to this meeting, and his wallet was bulging.

'These matters can be expensive to arrange,' he said smoothly. 'Just as a token of our good faith, I am authorised to make you gentlemen an advance of one hundred thousand francs.'

'Not here.' Girard's tone was sharp. 'You say this is a token only. If we should be able to help you in this matter, what sort of sum would be in your mind?'

Williams left the question unanswered for several seconds, leaving them both to wait.

'One million francs,' he announced.

'Additional?' queried Pagnol, close-eyed.

'Of course. The money today, as I have said, is merely to cover your initial expenses.'

'We're interested,' declared Pagnol, and it was significant that he made no attempt to consult Girard.

'Splendid,' smiled Williams. 'Well, gentlemen, I really think that is as far as we can go today. If you would like to give the matter some thought, and particularly to consider those men you would put on to the work, may I suggest we have a further talk in a week's time?'

He was evidently about to take his leave, having thoroughly whetted the appetites of his listeners, but The Club was not so lightly to be dismissed.

'Stay a moment,' he urged. 'You ask us to take a lot on trust, monsieur. The kind of men you speak of, they are expensive. They are also men who do not care to have their time wasted. Girard here speaks well of you, but to me you are a stranger. I like to know who I'm dealing with. How can I guarantee these people that you are in a position to deliver on these promises?'

Basil Williams opened his eyes wide. Had his early-morning companion been able to see him at this moment, she would probably have imagined she could actually hear the bells of St. Catherine's.

'Tell me, M. Pagnol,' he whispered. 'What news is there of Papa Louie?'

The silence now was deep. The disappearance some weeks earlier of Louis Legrand, one of the most prominent and influential racketeers of the entire Mediterranean coast, was still shrouded in mystery. He had left his casino in Cannes late one afternoon, claiming that he had an important business appointment. No-one queried this, even mentally, because of the hour. Legrand's *cinq à sept* activities were an open secret in the circles in which he moved, and his discretion was legendary. The identities of the ladies concerned were jealously guarded, and it would have been an unwise enquirer indeed who dared to probe. That was the last time anyone had seen him, and the resultant suspicion and unease among the criminal fraternity had created tension along the entire coastline.

Now came this foreigner, this Englishman, casually mentioning the missing man's name in open conversation. More than that, he actually used the nickname which was employed only by a few of the hierarchy. Girard and Pagnol looked at each other significantly.

'I have not seen M. Legrand for some time now.' Although the question had been addressed to the squat Pagnol, it was Marcel Girard who replied. 'I think he may have decided to take a vacation.'

'Possibly,' returned Williams smoothly. 'I must say, the last time I saw him, he was looking far from well.'

Again there was that weighty silence at the table. Nothing open had been said, but the two Frenchmen understood fully what they were being told. Papa Louie was no more, and this smiling roly-poly man knew all about it. The Club made a guttural noise in his throat.

'I have heard enough,' he decided. 'I will make a few enquiries, M. Williams. I leave it for you and Girard to arrange a further meeting.'

So saying, he levered himself up from his chair, nodded briefly and was gone.

'You must forgive Pagnol,' excused Girard. 'He is a man of considerable talent and resource, but he is not a diplomat.'

Williams scarcely heard him. He was still thinking of the last time he had seen Papa Louie Legrand.

Estelle stood sideways, admiring the flat line of her stomach. It was at moments like this that she reaped the benefits of her strict regimen of low-calorie, no-fat diet and rigorous daily exercise. The cream satin nightdress clung to her like a skin. Her deeply tanned back was entirely bare, and two thin shoulder straps led down to the deep scoop line of her breasts. She would do, she decided.

She would definitely do.

What time was it? Still twenty minutes before he was due. It all seemed rather pointless really, all this dressing-up, but nonetheless she had her instructions. The instructions had come from Ryder himself, and she knew better than to deviate from them.

'Very nice, madame, if I may be permitted to say so.'

Max the chauffeur, who also flew the helicopter when necessary, spoke from behind her, where he was busy with an ice-bucket.

'You may not,' she advised him peremptorily.

She was never quite sure about Max, despite Ryder's assurances that his only interest lay in the direction of young men. Estelle had caught him looking at her on more than one occasion, and what she had seen had made her shiver.

He had a long, thin needle in his hand, which he now inserted with great care into the cork of a bottle of champagne, pressing gently at it to prevent snapping, until it reached the required depth. Then he deftly screwed a small syringe to the top, and squeezed a few drops of a colourless liquid down the inside of the cork.

'There we are,' he announced triumphantly, 'he will sleep like a baby.'

'That stuff is all right, I suppose?' she asked anxiously. 'We won't kill him by accident?'

The man's face contorted with a sardonic grin.

'Not by accident, madame, no,' he assured her. 'He will merely sleep for two hours, perhaps three. Long enough.'

She nodded, wanting to be convinced. That side of things

110

was out of her hands anyway. Estelle had asked no questions for a long time now. A girl could not expect to live a life of luxury, and in palatial surroundings, without being called upon to make some return from time to time. On the whole, she had no complaints. What had Max meant when he said they wouldn't kill him by accident? Did it mean that later—no. There was no point in her thinking about what might happen later. Any more than there was any point in dwelling on the past. She had learned long ago that if she was ever to have any peace of mind, there could be no loitering over memories. That way lay nightmares at best, even perhaps insanity.

'Is there a proper drink in this place?' she demanded.

Max nodded. Mr. Ryder had given very explicit orders about the alcohol rations, but a couple wouldn't hurt her.

'Certainly, madame. I took the precaution of bringing along a little cognac, just in case.'

Estelle accepted the glass from him gratefully, noticing the smallness of the measure. They were certainly taking no chances on her not giving a good performance, she thought wryly.

'Is that all the time is?' she grumbled.

'Patience, madame. It will take the gentleman a good hour to drive here from Cannes.'

Louis Legrand was cheerful as he drove along the sweeping cliff road. He had no eyes for the glorious Mediterranean panorama at that moment. After all, this was his territory, and he could see the view at any time. Right now, his thoughts were busy with quite a different kind of beauty. The striking wife of the English colonel had seemed quite impervious to his gallantries on their first visit to his casino, but Legrand had not been dismayed. There were rules in these matters, an elaborate ritual not unlike the formal set dances of an earlier century, and he was an expert player. On her second visit she had been unaccompanied, showing that she, too, understood the pattern of movements. On that occasion she had confided to him that her husband was a poor hand at bridge, and despised the game anyway. Many of her friends were experts, and she yearned for a proficient partner. Legrand, an expert at any game involving cards, had gladly offered his services. It had been a disappointment that two weeks had passed since that conversation, with no further word nor appearance from the lady. Then, yesterday, had come the telephone invitation. A small, private party, he must understand, with very low stakes. Such a prospect might, perhaps, not interest him? But of course it did, greatly. He did not know whether there might really be any bridge to be played, and did not much care. The game was on, in the wider sense, and that was what drew him.

The address he had led him to a small village up a private road, three miles inland. This was wealthy terrain, and Legrand felt more relaxed than ever as he climbed out of the Ferrari, and approached the front door. A maidservant opened it, and inspected him.

'Your name, monsieur?'

'Legrand. Louis Legrand.'

'Ah yes. Madame is expecting you. If you will please enter, monsieur, you will find madame in the first room at the top of the stairs.'

The door closed behind him, and that was the last the outside world saw of Papa Louie Legrand. Fifteen minutes after his arrival, Max the chauffeur put his head round the kitchen door.

'You may go now, Michelle. You are satisfied with the arrangements?'

Michelle was already dressed in her outdoor clothes, and had been waiting for him.

'Oh yes monsieur,' she assured him. 'I am more than satisfied.'

'Good. The car is yours, as promised. Dispose of it quickly.'

He took her by the arm, and stared down into her face. His expression brought her quick alarm.

'You will now forget all this,' he instructed, his voice flat and filled with threat. 'If you ever see me again, you will know I have come to kill you. Also your mother, and the sister with the little baby. Now go.'

He handed her some keys. Two minutes later a red Ferrari, with a pretty girl at the wheel, was heading east along the coast. The girl's face was frightened.

At the same time, a burly man was walking through a field at the back of the house, with the limp figure of a man slung across his shoulder. He was walking towards a silver and white helicopter. Behind him, and carrying a small bag, strode a tall dark-haired woman.

*   *   *

Philip Baxter reported at six-thirty as instructed. Halloran and Williams were already in the room, and there was a third man, a newcomer. He had heard the noise of the returning helicopter, and deduced that the languorous Estelle had returned from her shopping foray. This chap had presumably arrived with her.

'Ah, there you are, Baxter,' greeted Halloran. 'What will you have to drink?'

Baxter looked enquiringly towards the newcomer, who sat quite still, in a deep chair by the open window, his face deathly pale.

'Of course,' boomed Halloran cheerfully, 'you two haven't met. This is Louis Legrand, a business associate. Nothing to do with our little scheme. He's popped in to see Mr. Ryder on something quite different.'

Baxter could tell at once that there was something radically wrong. The man Legrand made no attempt to shake hands, or even to look at him. Given other circumstances, Baxter's assessment would have been that he was mortally afraid.

Halloran shrugged, and poured him a drink. Williams clapped him on the shoulder, raising his glass.

'Always enjoy this time of day,' he proclaimed. 'The sun about to set, all those gorgeous perfumes coming in from the garden. Really very pleasant indeed. And good company, eh? Mustn't forget the company.'

Anyone would think Williams was entertaining guests in his own home, he was so thoroughly at ease, and clearly enjoying himself. And why not? The table was immaculate again, and they were obviously in for a feast. The only jarring note was the sight of Legrand. The others chattered

113

away, as though he wasn't there, but Baxter inspected those tight features from time to time, and wondered about the nature of his business with Gregory Ryder. Of whom, incidentally, there was as yet no sign.

The dark little manservant, Pedro, glided in and spoke softly to Halloran who bent his head to listen, then made an announcement.

'Mr. Ryder will not be able to join us for dinner. We are to proceed without him.'

'Oh dear,' exclaimed a dismayed Williams. 'I do hope that doesn't mean he's cross with us.'

It was then that Legrand spoke for the first time, in his good but accented English.

'But what of our meeting, monsieur? How long am I to wait?'

George Halloran shrugged.

'I have no instructions yet on that, M. Legrand. Come, let us have some food. Believe me, you'd be sorry to miss experiencing one of our chef's creations.'

The Frenchman remained where he was, biting rapidly at his upper lip.

'Old English custom, gets drilled into us at school,' stated Williams heartily. 'Bad lads have to wait outside the headmaster's study until he decides to see them. Could be five minutes, could be an hour, who knows? No use in sitting there sulking, Louie. Might as well be with us. Beats the school grub, believe me.'

Legrand looked at them each in turn, then made up his mind. The English were mad of course, as he'd known since childhood. Here he was, a kidnap victim and a prisoner, and they were treating the whole thing as if it were one of their jolly tea-parties on the lawn. They didn't fool him, with their hearty backchat, especially the fat one, Williams. Papa Louie had heard all about him in the past, and would have preferred to be without his company. Well, he might as well eat, as sit here worrying.

'That's the spirit,' said Halloran. 'Come and sit here, on my left, won't you?'

He waved Baxter to the seat at the foot of the table, and Basil Williams took a chair opposite the reluctant

114

Frenchman.

The parade of dishes began again, but this time they were accompanied by a series of excellent wines. Baxter was not an enthusiastic wine-drinker, but he had learned to distinguish the real vintage from the supermarket plonks, and speculated idly as to what the bill for such a gourmet experience would amount to in a London restaurant.

Williams was not to be put down, despite the gloomy countenance of the man opposite him.

'Always maintain, you know, that we'd have got on better with the French if only they played cricket. Germans too, for that matter. Do you play at all, Baxter?'

The game of cricket, in Baxter's estimation, was even more futile than football, since it was hedged around with laws, plus centuries of those unwritten laws known as fair play. His early hopes of becoming a devastating fast bowler had soon been brought to an end after he had injured a large number of young batsmen. He could not see what all the fuss was about. They had a bat with which to defend themselves. It wasn't his fault if their heads and shoulders kept getting in the way of the ball.

'Not since school,' he replied. 'Used to bowl a bit.'

Williams' eyes gleamed.

'Guessed as much,' he rejoined. 'Bit on the quick side, I expect. You're built for it. Not like me,' and he patted ruefully at his middle. 'I was a spinner. Six paces, arm over and let fly. I played up until a few years ago, the club game you know. Meet some wonderful chaps, going round. I remember one match, at Pinner—'

He burbled on. Baxter listened politely, but Halloran actually encouraged the reminiscences, and perhaps it was just as well, reflected Baxter. It would have been a silent meal indeed, if it had been left to himself and the worried Frenchman to keep things going. Legrand ate very sparingly, he noted, but made good inroads on the wines, and never refused when the ever-attentive Pedro hovered at his side.

When the meal was cleared away there was coffee on the table along with brandy, port and cigars. The staff withdrew, leaving the four men alone in the room. Legrand, unable to contain himself any longer, spoke suddenly, interrupting one of Williams' stories in mid-flow.

'I have been here three hours, and it is intolerable. You are all like a bunch of cats, playing with a mouse. Well, I am no mouse, as you will discover. When this business is settled, I will remember you, all of you. Papa Louie is not the man to be treated in this fashion.'

He spat the words out venomously, then emptied his glass, and reached for the brandy. Halloran looked at his watch, then rose and went out of the room. Williams tutted.

'Spoiled my story,' he complained. 'Bad form, that.'

Baxter lit a cigar, thankful for the interruption. He had been unable from the beginning to see why they insisted on his remaining. As for the promised entertainment, whatever it might have been, that had obviously had to take a back seat, owing to this new development, the business with Legrand.

Halloran re-entered, carrying some papers. Legrand watched him intently, but he said nothing until he had resumed his seat.

'I am to tell you, Legrand,' and the absence of the formal 'monsieur' was very noticeable to the attentive Baxter, 'that Mr. Ryder has considered the matter with great care. Your excuses for non-payment are no longer acceptable. Mr. Ryder is prepared to accept your casino in full payment. I have the necessary legal documents here for you to sign.'

'Sit down.'

Williams' words flicked across the table like whiplashes. At the same instant, he had produced a heavy calibre automatic pistol from his jacket, and was pointing it steadily at the Frenchman. Legrand had half-risen from his seat, but he looked at the eyes behind the weapon, and subsided slowly. Halloran reached forward, clearing a space in front of the unhappy visitor, then placing the papers in front of him.

'You will sign there, there and there,' he commanded, setting a pen beside the documents.

'You cannot make me sign,' breathed Legrand, and there was a new determination in his tone. 'It is ridiculous. Two million lousy francs, that is the extent of my debt. My casino

116

is worth five times that. Six. I will not sign. You cannot make me.'

'True.' It was Williams who spoke. 'We cannot make you sign. But we can kill you. Easily. And it will be a pleasure, my old frog, believe me.'

The words were flat and lifeless. Legrand had dealt with violent men all his life, and he knew he was staring at death. The Frenchman was widely known and respected for his courage. Had there been one chance in a hundred of his turning the tables, he would have grabbed for it. But there was to be no escape from this situation.

He picked up the pen, and scribbled quickly, then threw it to the table. Halloran leaned across and gathered up the papers, studying the signatures, and comparing them with a specimen which he had ready.

'Good,' he pronounced. 'You have acted very wisely.'

'Which is more than I can say for you, Englishman. Or these others.' Legrand's voice was strangely controlled, as he stared around at his enemies. 'You think my power is confined to pieces of paper, a few legal documents? You will learn otherwise, my friends. You will learn something of Papa Louie when this business is done.'

Baxter felt there was truth in the words. A man like Legrand would have his own brand of muscle. Strong-arm men, and political pull. He would make a formidable adversary, casino or not.

'And now, Baxter, to make this properly legal, will you just witness these signatures, please?'

He looked up in surprise at Halloran, who waited expectantly.

'Me?' he queried. 'Why me?'

The man at the head of the table spread his arms.

'These documents transfer the ownership of properties to a certain leisure company,' he intoned. 'Basil and I are both directors of that company, and our signatures could easily be challenged later in a court of law. It is essential that we have a completely independent witness. So, if you please.'

He held up the pen. Baxter hesitated, and Williams turned to look at him. Well, he decided, there couldn't be much harm in it. Rising, he walked up to the waiting

Halloran and took the pen.

'Where do I sign?'

The others all watched as he bent over, and none more closely than the sweating Legrand, who would certainly have attacked him had it not been for the unwavering presence of the gun in Williams' hand.

'Thank you. Please sit down again, won't you?'

Baxter went back to his seat, and waited to see what would happen next. He was glad to observe that the gun was now gone from Williams' hand. Halloran pushed his chair back from the table, but remained seated.

'I think that now concludes our business,' he stated in formal tones. 'Basil?'

What happened was so fast, and so unexpected, that it seemed to take place in a blur.

Williams lunged across the table, grasping Legrand by the hair. At the same instant his right hand scooped up a gleaming fruit-knife and he plunged it deep into the Frenchman's throat. The victim had been given no opportunity to move, or even speak, before the blade was deep inside him and his life blood was spurting out on to the snowy tablecloth.

Baxter sat, transfixed by the speed of it all. He watched in fascinated horror as Williams pulled the dying man's head forward, so that it lay on the table in an ever-widening crimson pool. There were strange sounds coming from inside Legrand, gurgles and bubbles of half-words, but nothing intelligible. It took him several seconds to die, seconds during which Williams stared down at the top of his head, with a strange and unholy light in his eyes. Halloran sat watching, his face expressionless. As for Baxter, he had no idea what his own face might be showing. Horror probably. Disbelief certainly. The sheer unbridled savagery of the casual execution had taken him completely unawares.

Slowly, almost reluctantly, Williams released his hold. There was no sound now from the motionless figure. Then he did a strange thing, an act which was somehow even more obscene than what had gone before. He patted the head of the dead man, almost with affection.

'There, there,' he cooed.

Baxter was conscious of the bile churning in his stomach. He had witnessed, and taken part in, countless acts of violence and brutality, but nothing to parallel this. It was not the fact of death. Death had its place in the scheme of things, even murder. Given the setting, and the circumstances, he could have accepted it. But not this setting, nor these circumstances. The whole thing was alien.

Williams had now subsided into his own chair, and was gazing at his handiwork with that detached expression which Baxter found so chilling, a thin film of sweat on his upper lip. Halloran broke the silence.

'I think I'll smoke my cigar outside,' he said stiffly. 'You coming, Baxter?'

No second invitation was needed. Baxter got up and walked past the sprawled corpse of Legrand, not trusting his eyes to meet Williams' unblinking stare. Outside, he was glad of the light, scented breeze which had sprung up, and took several deep breaths before following Halloran along the side of the swimming pool.

'Messy business, that.' Halloran's voice was calm and controlled.

Baxter made no reply. These people had intended that he should witness the execution of the unfortunate Legrand. One reason for their doing so was obvious enough. As a demonstration of what happened to people who ran foul of them, it could not have been more convincing. But there might be more to it than that, he realised, and the way to find out was to keep his own counsel for the present.

Realising that his companion did not intend to reply, Halloran strode on a few more yards, then spoke again.

'Yes, decidedly messy. Still, chap had it coming to him, no argument about that. Puts you in a rather difficult position, I'm afraid.'

In the half-light from the house, he could just make out Baxter's features. If he was watching for any sign of alarm, he was to be disappointed. The only expression visible was one of puzzlement.

'Me? I don't follow you, Halloran. You gave the order, and Williams carried it out. I just happened to be around.

What are you driving at?'

Halloran half-turned towards him with no interruption to his stride.

'Why, the papers of course. Dated and signed. You are the last person known to have seen Papa Louie alive. It could be made to look bad.'

They couldn't really think he was that naïve, wondered Baxter.

'Leave it out,' he scoffed. 'If you try pinning this on me, I'll sing like a canary. You must think the police are pretty stupid. Or me, for that matter.'

'Police?' echoed Halloran. 'We don't need to involve those people, thanks very much. They're too damned fly by half, and nosy, to boot. No, we shan't be troubling them, I think.'

'Well, then—?' said Baxter, and left the question in mid-air.

When Halloran next spoke, it was rather in the manner of a patient professor addressing a group of recalcitrants.

'The late, unlamented Legrand was a powerful man, with many friends in low places. They are not people to bog themselves down with procedures such as trials and cross-examinations, and the like. They work largely on instinct and intuition. They make decisions swiftly, and then act on them. I rather fancy, in your case, that they would act even faster than usual. However,' and his tone became consoling, 'these are theories only, flights of fancy. There is no reason why such information should ever be passed to them. Don't you agree?'

Of course. This was their way of ensuring not only his co-operation but also his continuing loyalty, realised Baxter. He could visualise only too well the kind of people who would be seeking to avenge Legrand, and Halloran was right. There would be no standing on ceremony. These smooth-talking swine had sewn him up more neatly than anyone had ever managed to achieve in the past. One word from them, and he was a gone goose.

'You really are,' he enunciated slowly, 'as ruthless a set of bastards as I've ever mixed with.'

Halloran chuckled, seemingly not remotely offended.

120

'I always think it clears the air, when all the concerned parties understand one another.'

Baxter realised something else, for the first time. He must be careful to stay clear of Estelle's shopping list.

When she went shopping, it was for people.

CHAPTER TWELVE

In the absence of a national body, the police authorities of the United Kingdom achieve a degree of co-operation which is the envy of many another country. But, even with computerisation, there is a limit to the quantity of information which is disseminated on any scale, and for sound reasons. An attack on a newsagent in Aberdeen is hardly likely to arouse any great interest in Devon. A hit-and-run driving case in Liverpool is of no concern in Southampton. These are local matters, and dealt with by those on the spot. By mutual consent, the number of criminal activities deserving of wider attention is restricted to certain major categories.

Even if all crimes were notified to a central clearing house, there would have been nothing to connect a number of bizarre little incidents which took place over a period of weeks, and which bore no signs of a common thread.

Chronologically, the first of these occurred in the town of Salford, Lancashire.

*   *   *

Police Sergeant Eric Dawes eyed the waiting P.C. warily.

'Back already?' he queried. 'Didn't expect you for an hour at least. Too much to check, was there? What time will they be ready for us?'

P.C. Hunter cleared his throat, pulling out his report sheet.

'No, it's all done, Sarge. Bit strange, really. Almost nothing gone at all.'

Dawes put down his pen and waited.

'What do you mean, almost nothing?'

The clothing manufacturers, Rowland and Black, were one of the town's largest employers, and a break-in at their premises was a serious business. There must be miles of expensive suiting material in their storerooms, not to mention the rows of ready-made suits and overcoats which rolled off their assembly lines.

122

'All that's missing is twelve uniforms. Firemen's uniforms.'

'Firemen's—? They can't have checked properly. Nobody's going to waste time clobbering Rowland and Black's just to nick a few uniforms that they can't sell anyway. You should have insisted on their being more thorough. I thought you were a bit sharp back.'

Hunter did not relish having to contradict his superior. Sergeant Dawes was a bit irascible at the best of times.

'They were very thorough, Sergeant. Since that big fire two years ago, they've put in this system of progressive stock control. It's bang up to date every day. They can tell you where every yard of material is, and they showed me how it works. There's no mistake, Sergeant. The only missing items are the uniforms.'

Dawes sighed. Despite his inbred cynicism, he was aware that P.C. Hunter was a thorough and capable man. But the report made no sense, and that was a hard one to swallow. There was plenty of attractive stuff out at that factory, and yet he was being asked to believe that a bunch of villains had made off with some firemen's uniforms. It was daft. They were of no use to anybody, except firemen. The inspector wouldn't like this.

'All right, lad. You've done all you can. Gawd knows what the boss'll say. Leave it on the desk.'

Several weeks would pass before they had occasion to recall the pointless little crime.

*   *   *

Tommy Evans pushed open the door and walked gratefully into the fat-laden atmosphere of the all-night café. At the counter he ordered his usual meal of two eggs, sausages and chips, collected a cup of tea, and sat down at a table, waiting for his number to be called.

'Wotcher Tommy.'

He turned towards the voice, and saw a well-known face grinning at him from another table.

'Hallo Sid. You going or coming?'

To an outsider it might have seemed an odd question, but

not to these habitual travellers of the great commercial highways. The two drivers were both London-based, and Evans was simply enquiring whether his chum was on his way out of London or going home.

'I'm going to Liverpool,' was the shouted reply. 'Machine parts, nothing fancy. Couldn't drop me off a nice Fiesta by mistake, could you? My barrer's getting past it.'

'Fat chance,' returned Evans. 'You'd look a bit silly driving one of my load. I've got ambulances up.'

'Number eighty-three,' shouted a woman's voice.

Evans got up to collect his food, and the next twenty minutes ticked away as he cleared the plate, wiping it carefully clean with the last of his bread and butter. Then he turned his attention to the crumpled newspaper from his pocket, and became absorbed in the comings and goings of his football heroes.

At another table, in the far corner of the café, two men sat over half-empty tea cups. They were not known to the other customers, but there was nothing about them to attract special attention, and they were dismissed as newcomers.

Tommy Evans looked at the scarred clock above the counter, and put his newspaper away. Then he stretched and yawned, got up and prepared to leave. At the far table, one of the strangers tapped his companion on the wrist.

It was dark outside, but at least the rain had stopped. Evans stood for a moment, buttoning up his leather jacket, then walked round to the lavatories at the rear of the premises. It was high time they smartened up these bogs, he grumbled to himself. Most places these days had decent facilities, strip lights and all that. This one was years behind the times. He wasn't the only one who said so, and if it wasn't that this was the best grub on the whole route, he'd seriously think about keeping his foot down, next time.

Another man followed him in, and stood beside him.

'They'll be all right if there's a pile-up tonight then,' said the stranger.

Evans squinted at him.

'How d'you mean?'

A second man had entered and was advancing towards them.

'You'll be right on the spot,' explained the other. 'That is you pulling all them ambulances, isn't it?'

A joke. Evans grinned.

'Oh, see what you mean. Yeah, that's me.'

It was confirmation enough. The second man struck him hard at the back of the head, and, as he crumpled, the man beside him caught him swiftly round the shoulders. They knew what they were doing, these two, and there was no need for conversation. The attacker produced a roll of sticky tape, and sealed the mouth of the unconscious man. They then each took one of his arms, looping it round their shoulders, and dragged him to the door. A quick check outside to ensure there were no new arrivals, and the little procession made its way round to the bushes at the back. Evans was stretched out on the ground, and more tape applied to his hands and feet. They went through his pockets, removing all keys.

'Nice few quid in here,' said the second man, waving a shiny wallet.

'Leave it out, Eddie,' snapped the other. 'We're not bleeding tea-leaves.'

The second man shrugged, and replaced the wallet.

'He'll do,' decided his companion, straightening up. 'Good for a couple of hours, at least. Plenty of time for us.'

'Let's go, then.'

They strolled casually back into the lighted area, and made their way out to the rows of parked vehicles. One minute later the café lights reflected briefly against the white paintwork of a small fleet of ambulances, as a long articulated trailer nosed its careful way out on to the trunk road.

*   *   *

'Hurry up now lads, supper's waiting.'

Prison Officer Francis put no emphasis on his words. There was no need to be rough with this lot. First offenders, mostly, and all with light sentences; they weren't out to give him any trouble. All they wanted was a quiet life, with no disturbances. Nothing which would interfere with their release at the end of the six or twelve months' imprisonment

125

which they were serving. If you could call it imprisonment, that was. Cushy number, really. Working all day out in the fresh air of the farm, then a couple of hours watching the telly, or playing cards, then banging up for the night. They were better off than real farm workers, when you got right down to it. All they worked was an eight-hour day, while the farm people often worked ten or eleven, especially now the light evenings were coming in. You could see them across the highway, still hard at it, while these offenders were packing up for the day, and going back to a waiting meal.

They were nearly all present now, and standing in the rough semblance of a squad. Only two to come, and there was one of them, dawdling across from a barn as though time was of no importance.

'Move yourself, move yourself,' called Francis. 'We haven't got all day.'

The late arrival fell in at the end of the waiting group, and muttered something to the man next to him. Francis looked at his watch. Where the devil was Davis? Not like him to be late. He was one of the most orderly of the whole bunch.

'Where's Davis?' he barked.

The enquiry was a pure formality. He knew perfectly well that no-one would answer, unless spoken to directly.

'You seen Davis?'

He addressed the question to the nearest man, who shook his head.

'Not me, sir. Haven't seen him for hours.'

'You?' to the next man.

'No sir, he wasn't on the weeding party.'

He received the same response, with variations, from every man present. To listen to this lot, you'd begin to wonder whether anyone named Davis really existed. The first small naggings of worry began to form in the officer's mind. He tried his last ploy, one that was certain to produce results.

'You realise that Davis might have been taken ill, do you? He could be having a heart attack or something. All you're doing by covering up is causing a delay before he gets proper treatment. You could be killing him, one of your

126

own. Well?'

The men exchanged low-lidded glances. Mucking the officer about was quite in order, almost mandatory, within their code. This was different. If Davis was ill, they wouldn't be doing him any favours by delaying his discovery. Finally one man spoke.

'I saw him about half an hour ago,' he admitted, with evident reluctance. 'He was over by the hedge, doing repairs, I think.'

'Which hedge? There's miles of bloody hedges.'

'One alongside the road,' completed his informant.

Francis turned his head. From his present vantage point, he could see clearly the line of the hedge, some quarter of a mile distant. There was no sign of anyone, but then, Davis could have fallen over. The unease in his mind grew.

'All right. You and you. Get over there on the double. See if he's lying down somewhere. Smartly, now.'

The two men jogged away.

Twenty minutes later the work-party truck rolled in at the prison gates. The officer on gate duty walked out to make his routine enquiry, to which he was certain he would get the routine answer.

'All correct, sir?'

'No, sir. One short.'

The standing man blinked as he looked at the grim features of his colleague inside the cab.

'One short?' he repeated disbelievingly.

'Davis,' confirmed the other. 'He's done a runner.'

The governor sat in his office, re-reading the file on Ian Charles Davis for the fourth time. There wasn't a single blemish on the man's record, not even a late-on-parade note. Davis had received a three-month sentence on what was originally a drunk and disorderly charge. Since it was his first offence, he would normally have been let off with a ten-pound fine and a warning, but his behaviour in the police station had put paid to that. He had almost wrecked the place, and it had taken five officers to subdue him, all of whom bore the marks of the fracas. As a result, a simple charge of D and D had been supplemented by others, and the magistrates could not tolerate attacks on police officers.

It was quite clear that the alcohol was responsible, but that could not be accepted in justification. Prior to the offence, Davis had spent six years in the army, where his record had been exemplary. Since discharge he had been employed on various overseas assignments, the details of which were somewhat obscure, but which appeared to have brought him no discredit. Altogether, it was rather a sad business, that a chap like that should lose control of himself for a few hours, and finish up in a correction centre as a result.

He'd been with them now for six weeks, and had been in every sense a model prisoner. For such a man to have absented himself, there must have been a reason, and the governor had spent two fruitless hours in trying to learn what it was.

While his recent guardians were puzzling their brains as to what could have prompted such uncharacteristic behaviour, Ian Charles Davis was sprawled in a comfortable chair in a hotel room, enjoying a glass of cold beer and listening to the quiet tones of the man opposite. Ginger Davis was not one to make decisions lightly, and the idea of walking out of his open prison would never have occurred to him, had it not been for Joe Mallory. Davis owed allegiance to no country, no flag, but he would go through fire and water for the Yank, as he called him. This job he was talking about was going to be run by Baxter, the one they knew as Bad Baxter, and Davis had served with him before. Good soldier, good organiser, and a man you could trust, was Baxter. But Davis would not have walked out of prison on his say-so. It hadn't been Baxter who had dragged him out of that blazing storehouse, with three bullets in him. He could remember it now, as though it were yesterday, as he lay helpless on the floor, watching the fiery beams above him, and knowing he was finished.

Then, from nowhere, had come the grinning, smoke-streaked face of the Yank.

'You lazy limey bastard,' he shouted, grabbing him painfully by the shoulder, and inching him gradually away. 'Lying around when there's work to do. You'll be fined two days' pay for this.'

Oh yes, he remembered every detail. Remembered how

the Yank had humped his useless body up on his back, regardless of the whining lead from the advancing rebels, and shoved him into the back of a jeep. The roar of the engine had sounded sweetly in his ears, just before he lost consciousness.

And here they were again. The old firm, looking somewhat more presentable than on some previous occasions, but the same old firm, for all that.

'When do we leave, then?' queried Ginger.

'Some time tomorrow,' replied Mallory, 'there'll be a telephone call. And where we're going, no-one will be looking for you.'

*   *   *

When the Borough Surveyor walked into the yard foreman's office, he wasn't looking very pleased, and small wonder. His equipment schedule was tight enough as it was, without people stealing it.

'What's all this about a vehicle missing?' he demanded.

'Sorry to drag you down here, guvnor, but I thought you might know something about it,' apologised the foreman.

'Well, I don't,' snapped his visitor. 'All I know is I was dragged out of a meeting with the Borough Engineer, so I hope it's justified.'

He looked sternly at the foreman, who remained unperturbed. He'd been with the borough for thirty years, and there wasn't much new under the sun. These top people might come and go, but John Wilkes was part of the scenery.

'It's one of the ten hundredweight diesels,' he explained. 'It was here last night when we locked up. Then this morning, when we came to work, it was gone.'

'Told the police?'

'Well no, not yet. I thought you ought to be consulted first.' Good word that, 'consulted.' Wilkes had used it to soothe many a savage breast in his time. 'For all I knew, there might have been some emergency during the night, and you'd had to call out the standby crew. I'd have looked a proper mug if I'd called in the law, and it turned out the

129

Town Hall knew all about it.'

The Surveyor nodded. You could never tell with Wilkes whether he was being thoroughly co-operative, or gently putting you through the mincer.

'No, it wasn't me,' he denied. 'A ten hundred eh? Anything in it?'

'Not a lot. Compressor, couple of drills, a few sledges and shovels. Oh, and road barriers and lamps. Just the usual kit. Not much use to anybody but us. Unless we've got competition.'

'Eh? Competition? What does that mean?'

'Well, guvnor, I mean if anybody else wants to start his own little firm, digging up the High Street at peak periods, he'll have all the gear, after last night.'

Despite himself, the Surveyor grinned.

'See what you mean. Bigger and better holes, eh? Well, they don't want that stuff, that's for sure. It was the waggon they were after. Plenty of people can use a nice ten hundredweight.'

Wilkes looked doubtful.

'But that's just it, guv. There were four others in the yard, all at the same time, and they were empty. Two of them were brand new.'

'H'm.' The Surveyor looked at his watch. He could still get back to his meeting, if he hurried. 'It does seem a bit odd. Still, it's no use you and me wasting time on theories. Leave that to Inspector Smart of the Yard, that's what the police are there for. You deal with it, John. I want to get off.'

He went back to his car, but Wilkes' words lingered in his mind. It would be a hell of a lark if somebody did start digging their own holes. He was due to make an after-dinner speech at a coming function. There ought to be some little joke he could concoct around this incident. What would they call the company? Holes Limited. No, that was a bit crude. Traffic Disruptions Inc.? No.

He'd think of something.

CHAPTER THIRTEEN

The insistent piercing racket from the alarm on his wrist penetrated the stillness inside the tiny tent, and Ben Hardcastle groaned. Opening one eye, he stared at the offending mechanism to confirm that there was no mistake. The illuminated face stared back, in unrelenting affirmation that it was indeed four-thirty a.m. Unzipping the sleeping-bag, he rolled clear and started his little chemical stove. This would be his fourth wearying day of watching Baxter and his men at their antics. It had all seemed quite straight-forward when Jameson had issued his brief command.

'Nip up there and keep an eye on them,' was what he'd said.

Quick to say, but laborious in execution, was Hardcastle's verdict.

Once Baxter had returned to England from his brief trip to Majorca, things had begun to happen. Agents from 'friendly' departments had been watching certain of the major's former comrades, and the previous weekend had marked their disappearance from familiar haunts. Contact had been lost with all but two of them, but those two had been worth following. They had met at a boarding house in Aberdeen, and within a matter of hours the rest had ma-terialised, including their leader, for which Hardcastle was profoundly grateful. Baxter, although he had no reason to suspect that anyone was monitoring his movements, had nevertheless taken evasive action as a matter of habit. As a result, they had lost him, and it was a vast relief to all concerned when he turned up in Aberdeen. From there the whole party had moved out, evidently bent on a camping holiday, judging by their equipment. They were reported as having set up camp out on the lonely moors, and that was when Hardcastle had been briefed to watch them.

Not that there was much to watch. The university man knew a keep fit course when he saw one, and that was exactly what the quarry were up to. It made boring watch-ing for the most part, except for the unarmed combat and

131

the weapon training. It was clear, even to such a non-military eye, that each man was an expert. The course was less a matter of learning than of brushing up on familiar techniques, and already there was an extra zip to their movements, which had not been evident on the first day. Jameson had reasoned that the party was getting itself in trim for early action. When pressed as to how long the preparation work might take, he had thought for a few moments.

'Chaps like that? Professionals? Give 'em five or six days. One week at the outside. I'll be surprised if they're not on the move by next weekend.'

After that, he had issued his edict, and Hardcastle had commenced his tiresome vigil. He would much have preferred to remain in London, since Halloran and Williams had both returned, travelling quite openly and seemingly without a care in the world. There had still been no news of the top man, Ryder, nor of his beautiful companion, if indeed she existed. Hardcastle rather hoped she did, and conjured up many a daydream about her, as he lay on his stomach, field glasses trained on the distant opposition. Olga Pulloffski, the beautiful spy, he recalled. Perhaps she'd be a little like Jennifer Fiske—no, mustn't start thinking about her. Think about brewing the tea, and getting the circulation going. Then a quick breakfast before Baxter and his crowd started the day's programme.

It was already getting on for five o'clock.

*　　*　　*

'Cuppa tea, Major. You've got five minutes.'

Philip Baxter stirred himself awake, reaching automatically for the enamel mug which Ginger Davis was holding out. The man had no right to look so fit and alert at six o'clock in the morning.

'Thanks, Ginger. I'll be there.'

He sat up in the narrow camp bed, shivering in the morning cold. The poets seemed to find a lot of magic in the early morning mist which blanketed the heart of Scotland. It was all right for them, they didn't have to sleep in it, and worse still, go running about in it. He took a grateful sip of the hot sweet tea, the traditional 'gunfire' of the infantryman, and reviewed the situation rapidly in his mind.

They were now up to full parade strength, and he had personally selected every man in the company, and he had chosen well. They were all hard-bitten professionals, with at least half a dozen campaigns behind them, often more. Another qualification which he had insisted on was that every man had been wounded at least once. In Baxter's reckoning, there were plenty of people who could display the outer signs of bravery at least once, and once was not enough. He preferred a man who knew what it was to feel the obscene intrusion of hot lead inside himself, and still came again. Theoretically, there was no great physical danger to be found in the coming exercise, but Baxter was not putting his faith in that theory. He had seen Basil Williams' work at close hand, and there were to be other men on this job, men outside his control. He, and his force, were needed for the acquisition of the bullion, but after that they were expendable. When that time came, he wanted to be surrounded by armed fighting men, men whose allegiance was solely to him. He was under no illusions about the kind of people he was dealing with.

In addition to the common basic requirements, he had picked out those who had some special skill, which would contribute either to the operation itself, or to the successful social knitting of the group.

Ginger Davis was the keep-fit fanatic, a qualified physical training instructor whose task it was to keep them all on their toes, Baxter included.

Jimmy Sparkes was the comedian of the troupe, with his endless supply of sharp East End gags. Jimmy's inseparable companion was the lugubrious Gloomy Porter, a lanky Brummie who would complain endlessly about everything, from start to finish. There were two Irishmen, the O'Rourke brothers, a devil-may-care twosome whose sweet tenor voices had led many a sing-song in strange circumstances. Their purpose with him was more serious, since they had both spent a period as regular firemen.

Cookie McLeish, a giant Glaswegian, was the camp chef.

A great barrel of a man, equally at home in a bar-room brawl or on a battlefield, Cookie was never happier than when trying to coax the appetites of jaded men with his ingenious culinary preparations. Cookie would have been the one who prepared Baxter's tea that morning, because he would not allow anyone else near his equipment.

All weapons were under the eagle eye of Deadeye Dick Judd, a quietly spoken Yorkshireman who preferred to be stripping down a Bren gun to lying on his bunk, even in his spare time. There would be no unforeseen jamming of weapons while they were in his care.

Finally, there was the Australian, Graham, inevitably known as Oz. Baxter had first encountered Graham during the Vietnam war, when the thick jungle territory had almost been responsible for their respective platoons wiping each other out. The mistake had been recognised in time, and he and Graham had subsequently become monumentally drunk during a rest period. It was some years later when they met again, as mercenaries upholding some corrupt far-off government, and quickly became comrades. Oz Graham was a man who needed excitement, and not of the kind to be found in more peaceful surroundings. He was a natural soldier, and a good mixer, a valuable asset to any enterprise where there was danger and reward.

A good crowd, and Baxter was pleased with his choice. Usually, in the past, he had had to make do with the personnel supplied to him, and there were frequently people with whom he would gladly have dispensed. This time, he had been in on the ground floor, and if any of this lot let him down, he would have only himself to blame.

It was now Wednesday, and if all went well, they would be moving down to London on Friday. The balloon was due to go up either on Saturday or Sunday, and they would be in position well beforehand.

It was time he was getting dressed.

Baxter had not yet told the men very much detail about their objective. The first task had been to weld them together as a unit, and to check on their physical fitness. They had commenced training on the previous Sunday, and it was gratifying to observe how quickly they had all

134

adapted to the régime. There had been a few creaks and groans on the first day, but by and large they had all kept themselves in shape. The mercenary soldier can never be certain when the next possibility will present itself, and he prefers to be ready at all times. He could be putting his life at risk within twenty-four hours of signing up, and he has no intention of losing it through lack of fitness.

'Let's be 'aving yew.'

The familiar barked command sounded, out on the barren hillside, and figures began to emerge from the little scatter of tents, laughing, muttering, or grimly silent, each according to his personal chemistry. Baxter trotted out and fell in beside Joe Mallory. It was his rule that they should both join in with as many activities as possible.

'You nearly didn't make it,' greeted his second-in-command. 'That would have cost you your breakfast bacon.'

'Ridiculous bloody rule,' grunted Baxter, 'must have been some fat officer who made that one up.'

'Guess so,' agreed the unrepentant American, who was responsible for the regulation. 'Are you going to tell us a bit more about this war of ours today, chief?'

Baxter nodded.

'After lunch. The O'Rourkes'll get a shock. They're going to find themselves instructors, all of a sudden.'

'Yeah?'

Mallory cocked an eyebrow, but asked no further question. He knew there would be no answer until the proper time. In any case, Ginger Davis was calling them to order.

'All right, my lovely comrades-in-arms. We're going to take it easy this morning. Just a gentle trot, then back for our nice brekkies.'

This provoked immediate suspicion on all sides.

'How gentle is gentle then?' queried Jimmy Sparkes.

'Five miles. We'll be back in no time.'

Davis waited until the expected boos and catcalls had died down. Then he began running on the spot.

'Settle down, you 'orrible soldiers. With me now. Off we go.'

He set off briskly into the mist, the others close behind

him, two by two. The grey shroud closed behind them as they vanished across the moor.

*   *   *

Captain Marco Leonides shook hands with the owners' Marseilles representative for the third time, while the little photographer did his work. No-one knew better than he how important it was that the historic moment of his retirement from the sea should be properly logged. The owners' man, a little clerk named Dubois, couldn't see what all the fuss was about. They didn't normally bother with all this pomp and ceremony, but still, he was not averse to having his photograph appear in the local paper. It would be one in the eye for Marie, for one thing, who seemed to think his job was of no importance at all.

For Leonides, the ceremony marked the successful conclusion of what he had come to regard as Stage One of the operation. Stage Two would commence when he reappeared at the quayside in his new role as Captain Kokis, but that was not yet. Many things had happened since his dramatic ocean encounter with the man Cartwright, and the last few weeks had been among the most suspenseful in his long career. What with those Chinese steel-workers aboard, and the continued suspicions of the first mate, plus his own self-doubts about his ability to carry off the impersonation when the time came, Leonides had not enjoyed the trip. On top of which there had been a particularly heavy storm in the Indian Ocean which had threatened to tear away the new tanks before the job was half completed.

The Chinese had not been made welcome when they joined the ship's crew. They were not seamen for one thing, and they kept very much to themselves as a group. Their leader was a man known only as Chin, a giant figure from the New Territories, who ruled his team with an iron fist. His English was limited, but adequate, and he quickly made it plain that he knew his job, and would brook no interference. To Chin, this little task was nothing, a simple job of construction involving no personal risk, and not worthy to be recorded among his great achievements. For was he not a

136

Sea Rabbit, with all the honour that proud title conveyed? To be a steel construction worker was in itself a mark of distinction in the well-defined social hierarchy of the colony. Those able to claim, in addition, membership of that honoured fraternity could indeed walk upright among their fellows.

When it was first proposed that a tunnel should be built, to link Hong Kong island with the Kowloon peninsula, many eyebrows were raised. Even the foreign devils, famed for their instability, had surely excelled themselves with this piece of madness. Work began in an atmosphere of scornful derision, even though the project provided work for many hundreds of men. But what kind of work was it? It was not seemly for a man to go burrowing in the ground beneath the sea, as though ashamed to show his face. They were more like rabbits than men, rabbits of the sea. And thus was born the label, Sea Rabbit. And yet, the work went ahead. Foot by foot, the madman's dream began to emerge as a possibility, then a probability, and finally a triumphant reality. In 1972, the tunnel was opened, a testament beyond question to the expertise of the Western invaders, and to the workforce who had achieved this miracle. No longer a shameful breed of men, the Sea Rabbits found themselves transformed into an honoured group, which could hold its place in any assembly.

Chin had been a young man then, and his sweat had formed part of the foundations for every yard gained. Along with all his fellow-workers, he regarded the great tunnel as his personal achievement, and there were few to contest the claim.

It was natural that he should attract attention in higher places, not the least of which was a certain ancient brotherhood, rooted deep in the structure of Chinese society. No change of dynasty, no revolution, no cultural upheaval was permitted to disturb their smooth and time-honoured procedures. The man Chin was absorbed for the customary probationary period of five years, after which he was awarded officer status at Stone Step Six. With continuing good service he had been promoted to Five, which was the highest level available to those without certain qualifications. It was in this capacity that he had been in-structed to take charge of the modifications aboard the s.s. *Sunderland Lady*. The increase in the original number of technicians from four to six had been at his insistence, and the request met without demur.

For a man who could construct such a monument as the undersea tunnel, the task of putting a few steel plates together presented few problems. There was a period of adjustment, as the men accustomed themselves to the roll-ing of the ship, but after that the work proceeded smoothly.

The first mate was a man named Fleischer, a good-looking German in his early thirties. Fleischer had been a brilliant cadet, and destined for early high office in the great pas-senger-carrying line with which he had trained. Unfortu-nately, and like many a man before him, he had been unable to strike the right balance between the social duties expected of him, and the seamanship which was also required. Over-addiction to the lady passengers, and to the ships' bars, had led finally, and after repeated warnings, to his downfall. By this stage, he should have been awaiting the news of his first command, instead of which, he was first mate on a third class ship belonging to a fourth class company, and even that would not last if there was any repetition of his behav-iour on a recent trip to the East Indies. As a man, he neither liked nor trusted the Chinese, and to have half-a-dozen of them as surplus crew was difficult for him to accept.

Captain Leonides knew his man, and had rehearsed, well in advance, his explanation for their presence, and for the work they were doing.

'It's no use for you to complain to me,' he said, during one confrontation in his cabin. 'You won't come up with any argument I haven't already put to the owners. Yes, it is a crackpot scheme, and no, it won't work. I know that, and I've told them so.'

'A thousand tonnes of oil? Who's going to buy it? Nobody, that's who. Bloody civilians, with their half-assed ideas. I would have thought you, as the captain, would have refused to go along with it.'

Leonides eyed him carefully.

'You're right, Karl, and I did. Know what they said? They

said, "Captain, you can do what the hell you like. These tanks are going in, and if you don't want to sail with them, we'll have to find someone who will." That's what they said.'

'You should have told them to take their tanks and ram 'em,' asserted Fleischer vehemently.

The captain nodded sadly.

'Yes,' he agreed, 'I should. And thirty years ago, when I was your age, I probably would. A man sees things differently when he's on his last trip. Particularly one that's practically taking him home.'

Fleischer had accepted the position, albeit reluctantly, and the construction of the tanks forged ahead.

After the bargain with Cartwright had been struck, the captain's role in the final drama had been spelled out in detail. In consequence, Leonides had given a lot of thought to the filling of the tanks when the time came. Those to the aft would be charged with fuel oil, and would be emptied first. The forward tanks would contain diesel which was lighter and more flammable. The diesel would thus float on top of the crude, and when thoroughly alight would be sufficient to set fire to the heavier oil beneath. The surrounding waters would be an inferno, and it would be his task to ensure that he and his skeleton crew were well clear before the conflagration started. Leonides had experienced fire in the past, and knew all about its capricious and unpredictable behaviour. It was easy enough to start a blaze, quite another matter to control it.

During the voyage, he also addressed himself to the task of play-acting his role of the incoming skipper, Captain Michael Kokis. His new identity was unlikely to be challenged, but there was too much at stake for him to treat the impersonation lightly. In any event, it gave him something positive to occupy his time, which was a welcome change from the endless routine of drinking and sleeping, which had been his pattern now for so long past.

And now, here he was, smiling fixedly at the ridiculous Dubois, who had actually combed his moustache for the photograph. Over the heads of the small crowd which had gathered—amazing where people come from when there's free booze, he reflected—he could just see the s.s. *Sunderland Lady*, unloaded now and stripped. There were men busy at all parts of her tired old body, sandpapering, polishing, painting. The old girl wouldn't know herself in a couple of days.

What a pity it was that her brave new costume was destined to have such a short life.

* * *

Sammy Fong eyed his visitor uneasily. He seldom had much direct contact with people from the old lands, but when he did they invariably made him nervous. He had been informed weeks earlier that the man was to be expected, a Stone Step Five like himself, but carrying the words of a Stone Step Two, which was sufficient to strike terror in any quarter of the brotherhood. In all Europe there was only one man of such exalted rank, and he was located in London, England. Thus, in effect, Sammy Fong was to be the link-man between the Two officer in Hong Kong and the Two in England, a responsibility so awesome that it had prevented him from sleeping for much of the previous night. The slightest error of judgement, or even behaviour, on his part, and the outcome would be too awful to contemplate.

Chin sat and looked at his brother officer with interest, mingled with a certain degree of contempt. The man's Cantonese was faulty, and clearly not much used, while his clothes and general appearance were more appropriate to the kind of young men they were now having to recruit in Hong Kong, rather than to a person of his senior status.

Fong's etiquette, too, was clumsy, and falling short of total correctness. It was not that the Marseilles man was not trying his best, indeed his greeting and treatment had been even more flowery than custom demanded. Rather, it was that the small actions and phrases seemed almost alien to the man, things he had had to re-learn especially for this formal occasion, and which played no part in his normal and unquestionably Westernised way of life. His distinguished lord, Han Lee, would not be pleased when he

140

learned of these matters. It was known, in the homeland, that these brethren who dwelt too long among the heathen Westerners tended to be less strict in their application to old traditions and customs. Any such deviations must needs be reported, so that the task of their eradication could be planned.

As for Fong, he was finding it difficult to adapt to the slow formality of the proceedings. A Stone Step Five he might be, with all the dignity and awesome power attaching to that rank, but, on a more practical level, he was a successful gangster and strong-arm man, widely respected among the many criminal groups who dominated the port of Marseilles. Ritual and discussion played little part in the daily life of that community. The quick flash of a knife, or the sudden chatter of a machine-gun, were liable to signal the commencement and termination of negotiations, all inside a few violent seconds.

This job now ahead of them was a straightforward hi-jacking, as Fong saw it. Brandy would be loaded on at Marseilles, in these new tanks, and smuggled into London. Once there, it would be the responsibility of the local boys to get their hands on it. Such a cargo could not be left in the hands of ordinary sea-faring men. It was a fair assumption that a team of local goons would be put aboard the ship, to act as bodyguards to the illicit cargo, until such time as it was handed over at the far end. It would be Fong's job to identify those men, so that he could pinpoint the particular gang who were party to the operation.

'It might perhaps be wise to have the ship watched.'

This suggestion came from Chin, who had spent an hour already in lavish and detailed descriptions of the ship's layout, with accompanying drawings, so that a boarding party would readily be at ease in their new surroundings.

Fong had listened, with all the patience he could muster, to the talk thus far. This was information which must be passed to London, and which showed meticulous attention to detail. But this new proposal, which impinged on his local handling of the matter, was not acceptable at all.

'What for?' he parried.

There were recognised speech patterns for questioning a

proposal, and Fong's curt rejoinder fitted none of them. Chin smiled.

'Would you not feel it advisable to know who carries the fire-spirit to the ship? He who knows his enemies sits quieter by the fountain.'

'I'll know who they are when I get the names of the new crew-members,' Fong promised. 'As for the loading, it could take place anywhere. It doesn't have to be here, you see. It could take place in the middle of the Mediterranean, or off the coast of North Africa. Can't watch the ship all the way to London. Besides, there's another reason.'

He paused for a moment, to let the point sink home, and to whet the visitor's appetite. Chin's face remained calm, with just a hint of polite enquiry.

'We can't afford to have a Chinese face anywhere near that ship, now that your people are off,' continued the local man. 'This isn't Hong Kong, where our men can disappear among the crowd. One sight of a Chinaman in Marseilles, and people think of Fong. It will alert them at once, and I am sure we are agreed that our branch in London must have the advantage of total surprise.'

Chin thought for a moment, then inclined his head.

'I see the force of your argument. Since you mention London, may I perhaps raise one further point? Would you agree that London must be warned that these are dangerous men, with whom they must deal? Although it saddens me to contemplate, I think we must accept the realities. There will be faces to be washed.'

Fong almost smiled at the use of the quaint old expression. It was Chin's way of saying that they would probably have to bump off a few people, before they got their hands on the brandy.

'He who goes prepared among the flowers, will smell them longer,' he quoted.

At least the man hadn't forgotten all his teachings, thought Chin. They had really finished their formal business by this time, but etiquette required that he should linger a further thirty minutes.

When he had left, Sammy Fong stood at his window, watching, as the stately figure made its progress down the

142

narrow street. So much for the old guard, he reflected, with a touch of impatience. All that stuff might go down big with a bunch of peasants in the old homeland, but this was his world, Fong's world, and things were done the modern way.

The man to talk to about the ship's crew was the Corsican, Morella. He was a big wheel in the union, and owed Sammy a couple of favours.

As for that nonsense about finding out who loaded the ship, and where, who cared? The only thing that mattered was that she would be full of brandy when she reached London. Nobody would give a damn how it got there. It would be there, and that was what counted. These old-timers were far too preoccupied with a lot of unnecessary detail.

The decision was made.

The decision that would ultimately put the seal on the death warrant of Sammy Fong, and many other people, who had never even heard his name.

CHAPTER FOURTEEN

Philip Baxter had made the telephone call to a London number at the prescribed time, and George Halloran had answered. He was told to proceed to Aberdeen airport the following day, where a reservation had been made for him on the five-thirty-five p.m. flight to Heathrow. At London Airport there would be a letter waiting, containing certain instructions as to his next move.

Although nothing more was said in explanation, Baxter realised that he would be attending a further briefing session, possibly the last one. It was equally obvious that there would be no possibility of his return the same day, and that he would be required to stay in London overnight. Doubtless the letter would tell him where to report, and also give details of his hotel reservation. They were very thorough, these people, and meticulous as to detail. Baxter approved of that, because it all led to confidence in the enterprise. On the other hand, the arrangements were always weighted heavily in their favour, and Baxter was not a man who relished being led around by the nose.

On returning to the camp, he spent two hours in close discussion with his Number Two, Joe Mallory. The following day he caught the nine-forty-five a.m. plane to Heathrow, thus permitting himself hours in the capital before his due time of arrival. He utilized the time in booking himself a room at a prominent hotel, and in making other precautionary arrangements including the rental of a hire-car. Then, when the early evening flight was due from Aberdeen, he presented himself at the British Airways desk, and collected his instructions.

They were that he should report to the Skyroofs Hotel at the airport immediately on landing, where Halloran would be waiting for him in Suite 1105. Accommodation had been reserved in his name at an adjacent airport hotel, so that he could catch the early morning flight back to Aberdeen, ticket enclosed.

Baxter smiled grimly to himself. If he had followed

blindly the pattern laid out for him by these people, he would have had no chance to leave the airport environs at all. There would not have been sufficient time, which was what they intended. In, work, sleep, out. It was as well for him that he had foreseen the possibility of something of the kind.

It wasn't Halloran who answered his tap at the door of Suite 1105. Basil Williams stood there, with his happy grin, waving him inside, where Halloran sat at a small conference table, waiting.

'Good, good,' greeted Halloran. 'Come and sit down, Baxter. We have rather a lot to get through.'

From force of habit, Baxter made a quick survey of his surroundings. They were in a reception room, capable of housing a small gathering either for social or business purposes. Three doors led off, and it was a fair assumption that there would be two bedrooms and a bathroom.

Again, out of long habit rather than any suspicion of treachery, Baxter occupied a chair commanding a view of all the doors, a move which was not lost on his hosts.

'My word, you are a cautious man,' observed Williams, pulling up a chair.

Halloran nodded approvingly.

'I like to see it. Our friend has no love for being taken by surprise, and that is exactly the attitude we need for our little venture. Now, Baxter, will you please open the proceedings by giving us a report on progress to date?'

Baxter unbuttoned his jacket, and rested his arms on the table.

'Certainly. Oh, by the way, I've had nothing to eat for most of the day, so I ordered some sandwiches and coffee on my way up. Hope you don't mind?'

'It was quite unnecessary,' was the stiff reply. 'A proper meal has been ordered for us all in two hours' time.'

'Well, no matter. I shall be able to eat that, too. Now then, let me tell you what I've been up to.'

He began to outline his activities since their Majorca meeting, and the others listened closely. The recital was interrupted by a discreet tapping at the door, and he broke off.

'That'll be my grub.'

It was Williams once more who went to the door, admitting a white-jacketed waiter who pushed a metal trolley into the room, resting it in the centre. He looked at each of them in turn, trying to decide who was in charge.

'I'm very sorry, gentlemen,' he said finally, staring over their heads, 'I've only brought one cup. The order was for one.'

'That's all right,' Baxter assured him. 'It's for me.'

'Ah.'

The trolley was wheeled across, and behind Baxter's chair. The waiter began placing his cargo on the table, close to Baxter's hand.

'Never mind all that,' snapped Halloran. 'Just leave it.'

'Won't take a minute, sir, no trouble at all,' replied the man, setting out his wares with deft hands.

'Leave it,' repeated Halloran, and now there was no mistaking the instruction in his tone.

The waiter straightened up, clearly offended. He bowed stiffly to Halloran, and walked to the door, where Williams stood waiting. Once there, he turned and bowed again, then was gone.

'He'll probably complain to the union,' grinned Baxter, picking up a sandwich, and biting into it. 'Now then, where was I?'

'You were telling us about your rehearsals with the fire-fighting equipment,' reminded Williams.

'Ah, yes. Well, no problem there. Most of the men have had to use the stuff at one time or another. In any case two of them have been real firemen in their time, so they have been able to give us a professional polish. Let me just give you a brief rundown on our other equipment.'

He carried on with his report, speaking rapidly, and with the confidence of a man who knows what he is about, an attitude which was not lost on his appreciative listeners.

'That about brings you up to date,' he said finally, leaning back, and helping himself to another sandwich. 'Your turn, I think.'

'You seem to have done very well,' complimented Halloran, turning then to Williams. 'Basil?'

'Oh, first class,' agreed the tubby man. 'Most thorough. Give me the military mind every time. I don't like dealing with crooks, they're very sloppy when it comes to administration. Much prefer a chap like yourself, Baxter. Proper approach, and all that.'

'Thank you,' acknowledged Baxter, munching away. 'And now, if you please, I'd like to know more about the rest of it.'

'Of course,' said Halloran.

He opened a slim leather case which had been resting by his elbow, and pulled out the blown-up plan which Baxter had last seen in Majorca. This he spread out on the table, and it was noticeable that there was no tendency now for it to curl. Continual use had eliminated that problem. To begin with, however, Halloran did not refer to the plan. Instead, he sat upright, looking directly at Baxter.

'Let us first deal with the ship,' he began. 'She has already cleared the formalities, and is at this moment on her way up-river.'

'Could you be a bit more explicit?' requested Baxter. 'If she hasn't even arrived yet, how could she have cleared the formalities?'

Williams chuckled.

'That's what I asked,' he interrupted. 'You and I would make a fine pair of sailors. Oh, sorry.'

He broke off under Halloran's waiting stare.

'It is not that simple,' he explained. 'A ship proposing to enter the river must first come under the jurisdiction of a Trinity House pilot, who joined her in this case at Dungeness. From there she proceeded to Gravesend, where the Trinity House man hands over to a river pilot. There are also the Customs and Excise people there, and the Port Health Authority, to check vaccination certificates and that kind of thing. Everything was in order, and she is now on her way to her berth.'

Baxter pointed to the spot originally planned for the fire.

'So she'll be dropping anchor there, some time soon.'

Halloran frowned at his lack of knowledge.

'Certainly not,' he chided. 'People can't just pull up anywhere they choose. They're not parking a car, you know, they will be berthing an ocean-going ship, and they must go where they are directed. In our case, the berth allocated is at this wharf here.'

He pointed to a spot well away from the scene of the planned disaster. Baxter felt uneasy. There could be no guarantee that the smoke would carry that far.

'That must be a quarter of a mile at least,' he objected.

'Rather more,' confirmed Halloran. 'Much too far for our purpose. She will have to sail down to our rendezvous, after her cargo is unloaded, and most of the crew are ashore. The ship, incidentally, is the s.s. *Sunderland Lady*, and she has travelled here from Marseilles. A number of people under our control joined her there.'

Baxter frowned, thinking ahead to the fire, and pointed.

'You say that she will sail to this point here. But that means the crew will have to be aboard. They can't all be in on this business. A lot of them are going to die, surely?'

Williams chuckled happily. At first, Baxter assumed it was an outburst of ghoulish pleasure at the prospect of a lot of harmless men being burnt to death. It was a relief when Halloran's next words proved him wrong.

'Basil's pleased because you have once again raised the same question as he did earlier, although I fancy your motives were rather more charitable. If I read you correctly, your point is that there could be a pointless waste of innocent lives? Yes, I thought so. Basil's objection was rather that it would involve a lot of unnecessary mess, and could hamper the operation.'

The unrepentant Williams met Baxter's stony stare with a bland expression.

'However, and no matter what the motives are, the question stands. Once again, I must apply my nautical expertise. My,' and Halloran almost smiled, 'very newly acquired expertise, let me hasten to add. When a ship is at her moorings, she must, in theory at least, be manned ready for sea at all times. In practice this means that somewhere between one quarter and one third of the ship's complement have to remain aboard. There are twenty-eight crew members on the *Sunderland Lady*. No-one wants to stay aboard while a ship is in port, and there will be no difficulty in sending ashore all the regular crew-members. Seven will remain. The captain, who is our man, and the six new men who joined at Marseilles. They will provide quite sufficient manpower to get the ship down to our rendezvous. There, they will do what is necessary, and make their escape. From that point on, it will be your show.'

It sounded satisfactory, and Baxter was in any case acutely aware of his shortcomings when it came to matters of the sea. Instead of asking further questions, he changed the subject.

'What about this road accident?' he asked. 'Is everything ready to go, there?'

'The accident at Rope Street is all in hand,' was the smooth assurance. 'As also is the hole in the next road, Chandlers Way. No problems are anticipated at either location, and, if anything should occur, it will be dealt with.'

That again was an area over which Baxter had no control, and he was compelled, albeit reluctantly, to accept that the others knew what they were doing. In any case, his mind was busy in quite a different direction. There were seven men coming from the ship. Two more would be driving the crashing vehicles, and probably up to six others posing as workmen for the road-digging. A total of fifteen, not counting the two principals now seated with him. A possible seventeen men in total. His own force amounted only to ten, and Baxter did not care for the odds. If there was any possibility of a double-cross during the final stages, his men could be at a numerical disadvantage. At that moment, he chose to say nothing.

'We've already been through my routine,' he said, 'right up to the time of departure. Obviously you didn't want to discuss the point earlier in the game, but now I think you must tell me where my men will take the bullion. Not much point in pinching the stuff if we don't know where to take it. Another ship, is it?'

Halloran sighed. This was the final piece of the plan which Gregory Ryder and he had thrashed out in such fine detail long months ago. It was a beauty, honed and polished until every eradicable flaw had been expunged, a very personal achievement. Reluctantly, he had been compelled to

149

disclose small sections of it to various people, but up until this point, no-one else had ever seen the thing in its entirety.

'As to its ultimate destination, that need not concern you.' His hand moved downriver, along Limehouse Reach, and passing the vast sprawl of the India/Millwall dock complex. 'For your people, the destination is here. An old cotton warehouse, recently taken over by a firm of car-body renovators. You will drive the ambulances in, and leave them. The rest of your money will be paid to you, and your part in the proceedings is ended.'

'Just a moment,' objected Baxter, 'this will be happening in the middle of the night. It'll probably be two or three in the morning. How are my people supposed to get away? It would look a bit odd, wouldn't it, to have ten firemen and ambulance drivers queuing for the all-night bus? Even if there is one.'

Halloran chuckled with mild annoyance.

'Naturally, this has been thought of. You will leave the uniforms behind. There will be a stack of pullovers and trousers for you to change into. A rough fit, doubtless, but good enough for the time it will take you to get back to your own clothes. Three cars will be made available. They will be reliable, secondhand family saloons, nothing to attract attention. Does that satisfy you?'

'Yes, I think so.' The point was being reached where Baxter was going to have to declare his hand, but there was one other very important matter to be cleared first. 'The arrangement was that I should receive half my fee immediately before the job. Am I to get it now?'

Halloran's eyes moved to Williams, who reached under the table and produced a medium-sized suitcase. This he pushed across to the watching Baxter.

'One hundred and twenty-five thousand pounds,' purred Halloran. 'A great deal of money. A man could be forgiven for thinking he would settle for such a sum. We are putting a great deal of trust in you, Baxter.'

With hands not quite trembling, Baxter snapped the catches and raised the lid of the case. There, set out in rows, were more banknotes than he had ever seen in his life. He

150

lifted out a packet of twenty-pound notes and riffled it. Five hundred pounds. That meant the top layer alone amounted to twelve thousand. There would have to be ten layers, then.

The others watched dispassionately as he removed enough packets to be able to satisfy himself as to the depth. There was no doubt, he decided. It was all there. What was that Halloran had said?

'Did you say something about trust?' he queried. 'I don't think you're running much risk. I'd be a fool to try double-crossing you people. With your organisation you'd suss me out wherever I went, and I know it. The boot is rather on the other foot, as I look at it.'

Williams looked up quickly, but Halloran remained calm.

'I take it that means something?'

'Yes. I've had plenty of time to think about this, and I've tried to cover it from your point of view. When this is all over, my usefulness will be at an end. I could even be considered a liability, knowing what I know, and all around it might be just as well to take me out. Not on any personal grounds, purely a business precaution.'

'My dear chap, I assure you—' began Halloran, but Baxter waved a hand for silence.

'You wouldn't think twice about it,' he stated flatly, 'and your assurances are not enough, I'm afraid. I'd like you both to have a look at this.'

He tossed over a manila envelope, its ungummed flap wide. Halloran stared, but made no move to pick it up. Basil Williams raised a hand, as though to reach out, but changed his mind and clasped his cheek instead, eyes flicking from the envelope to Baxter's face, and back.

'What's inside?' demanded Halloran.

'My confession,' Baxter told him. 'Go ahead and look.'

Halloran pulled the envelope towards him, slipped his fingers in and withdrew a folded sheet of paper, inside which were three photographs. He looked at the shiny pictures first, his face grave, then passed them to Williams, who sucked in his breath.

'I'll be damned,' he said softly, then was quiet as Halloran began to read the document.

151

It took him a full two minutes to read, and the silence in the room was oppressive. Then he passed it to Williams, who snatched at it, reading eagerly.

'It is a very complete statement,' began Halloran, his voice under careful control. 'Very complete indeed. Every detail of your involvement is scrupulously outlined, and no-one could seriously question its authenticity. A few points come to my mind. How did you acquire those pictures of the house in Majorca?'

'I have a chum in the aerial survey business,' explained Baxter. 'There was no difficulty in arranging for a few shots. They're quite good, don't you think?'

Halloran ignored that, anxious to proceed with his questions.

'You name Mr. Ryder, Basil and myself, and describe us very carefully. You also refer to photographs, which are alleged to be enclosed. They are not here.'

Baxter acknowledged this with a bow of the head.

'True,' he agreed, 'but you see, I didn't have them when I wrote that. I was relying on this meeting.'

That brought a look of puzzlement to the questioner's face.

'You mean you have a camera concealed about you?' he asked in some surprise. 'In that case, I can assure you it will be destroyed before you leave this room. Not very clever, if—'

'The waiter,' snorted Basil. 'That bloody waiter.'

'Precisely,' confirmed Baxter. 'A complete professional. I shall have half a dozen shots of each of you from all angles. Those, plus your fingerprints, ought to clinch the question of identity, wouldn't you say?'

'Fingerprints?' snapped Williams, clearly rattled. He was blaming himself for not having suspected the waiter at once.

'Yes. I removed a few small items during my Majorca visit. Nothing valuable, I assure you. Just little things, which one or other of you had handled. I was unable to perform the same service for Ryder, so I'm afraid you two must bear the brunt.'

Williams decided that Halloran had led the exchange long

enough. More action was needed in this unexpected emergency.

'What the hell do you hope to gain by this?' he exploded. 'You're cutting your own throat.'

Baxter's headshake was decisive.

'No,' he refuted. 'Quite the reverse. What I'm doing is to ensure that you don't cut mine. I know it's rather a little habit of yours, Basil. I've watched you do it before, remember?'

George Halloran had understood that from the outset.

'It's a form of insurance, Basil,' he explained. 'Our friend Baxter shows a regrettable lack of trust in his fellow man. This document, you observe, is a photostat. There are other copies. How many, in all?'

Baxter laughed, but there was no mirth behind it.

'Oh come now, Halloran, you don't seriously expect me to tell you that. Let's just say, quite a few, and well scattered. I doubt if they'll ever be posted because you will ensure that nothing happens to me which would make it necessary. And now, if you gentlemen will excuse me, I must be off. My P.T. instructor is an absolute tyrant, and he'll have me parading around tomorrow with the rest, as soon as I arrive back. Sorry about dinner, but I must get my sleep. We shall be in position on Friday, by fifteen hundred hours. Till then.'

The suitcase was heavier than he'd imagined. Neither of the others spoke as he made his way out. It was Williams who broke the silence.

'Bastard,' he breathed. 'He's got us by the short and curlies. You're sure there's no chance of raising the guvnor? He doesn't much care for last-minute changes.'

Halloran shook his head regretfully.

'Out of the question. He's in Washington D.C. and his instructions are explicit. He wants to hear nothing further about this business until he reads it in the newspapers. His parting words to me were that it was now up to the generals in the field. That, my dear Basil, means us.'

Williams grunted. It had been planned from the outset that Baxter would be eliminated, once his part in the work had been brought to a satisfactory conclusion. He was the only link with the top echelon, and, with him out of the way, there would be no possibility of anyone tracing a connection between the thieves and the organisers. The rest of his men were of no importance. The only authority they knew was Baxter, and once he was dead they presented no threat. Williams had been looking forward to carrying out the final piece of treachery in person, and now he was to be cheated of that pleasure.

With one simple stroke, Mr. Bleeding Baxter had turned the tables on them very neatly, and, in the first pangs of frustration, Basil Williams could not see how they were to prevent him from getting away with it. It could even have its effect on another arrangement, a very private matter of which only Williams was cognisant, and which could not be discussed aloud, even with George Halloran. Especially with George Halloran.

'Bloody fine time to tell me I'm a general,' he muttered.

Halloran hesitated. There was one piece of information which Williams did not yet possess, and it had been Ryder's instruction that he should not be told until the following day. Halloran never queried orders from that quarter, and never departed from them. All the same, this new development from Baxter had altered the situation as Ryder understood it, and there seemed to be justification for anticipating tomorrow's explanation.

'Don't look so despairing, Basil,' he soothed. 'There is something you don't yet know, an arrangement which Mr. Ryder made on our behalf, and which I was instructed to pass on to you tomorrow. In the light of this development, I think I must tell you now. As you know, the governor is on his way to Washington.'

Williams put his annoyance aside, and began to listen.

154

CHAPTER FIFTEEN

Hector Jameson was, by his immaculate standards, decidedly edgy.

This is a state of mind which affects people differently. Some will lose control, raising their voices, even fists. Others withdraw into sullen denial of the obvious, or will exact some form of retribution upon an innocent, but convenient, third party. Jameson, naturally, was above pedestrian forms of release. All that happened was that there would be the faintest tightening of the mouth, a barely discernible added inflection to certain words when he spoke. All forms of emotion were, by definition, infra dig, and interfered with the thought processes. For all that, he could not ignore the fact that he was out of sorts, and with reason.

Things were not adding up.

Baxter and his band of cut-throats were in London, and quartered in some disused warehouse. Why? They were men of war, who had spent the past week toning up their fitness, in readiness for their murderous occupation. By rights, they should be aboard an aeroplane, heading for some distant trouble spot, instead of which they had gone to ground.

Then there was the s.s. *Sunderland Lady*. Far from sneaking out of Marseilles on some clandestine errand, she was even now heading for the Thames estuary, with some innocuous cargo. On top of which, one of Jameson's top cards, the Greek Leonides, had formally retired from the sea, taking all his criminal expertise with him. A lesser man would have tailored the facts to fit the theory. It would be a comparatively simple exercise for Baxter's people to sneak aboard the *Lady*, which could then set sail for its unknown war. Fifty years earlier that might have been acceptable, but not nowadays. Trained men did not spend weeks at sea, not when there were fast aircraft which could accomplish the journey in terms of hours. No, unless he was prepared to commit himself to the ridiculous proposition that the war

155

was scheduled for London, England, then he would have to go back to square one.

'Frankly, Miss Fiske, I am disappointed. The various pawns on this board have come together, very much in the manner envisaged at the outset, but in the wrong place. The wrong place altogether. This ship is my last hope. You've alerted the customs people?'

Jennifer Fiske was looking at her most severe. A casual observer could have been forgiven for not recognising her as the same woman who had recently left Ben Hardcastle's bed. In a sense, he would have been right, because they were different Jennifers, and she was resolved to keep them apart. If the dapper Jameson ever caught wind of the situation between them, then one or both would be axed, out of hand. There was no room within the department for anything other than straightforward professional relationships.

'Customs will search the ship, as a matter of routine,' she confirmed. 'They will be looking for munitions. If they have good reason to suspect they have found something, they will report back.'

'But they will do nothing?' he insisted.

She made an expressive gesture.

'They made the point, and it's a fair one, that they can't pretend not to notice if a sub-machine gun falls out of a packing case. But, outside that kind of accident, no, they will take no action.'

Jameson conceded the reasonableness of the qualification.

'Very well. It's the best we can hope for. Personally, I am not very confident of the outcome. I am coming round to the view that the *Sunderland Lady*, whatever else she might be up to, is not connected with our war.'

'And yet all the others are in London,' reminded his assistant. 'Halloran, Williams, and now Baxter's men. The place they are hiding out in is less than a mile from where the ship will berth. I'm sorry to have to remind you of my earlier suggestion, but do you still exclude the possibility that this is not a military operation at all, but straightforward crime of some kind?'

The man opposite clicked his tongue, the nearest he ever

came to a display of outright annoyance.

'One of the basic rules of our curious way of life,' he intoned, in his lecturer's voice, 'is that one excludes nothing. One simply allocates what I like to term credibility ratings. When you first postulated your theory, I did not of course dismiss it out of hand. I have far too much regard for your opinion. However, one did feel that the probability level was low. Low to fair, let's say. In the light of the current information, I'm bound to say that it looks rather more promising. In fact,' and his voice tightened, as the struggle between reason and inclination continued in his mind, 'in fact, I must now rate it as a possible good.'

Jennifer felt no triumph. Her long training as a scientist had eliminated emotional elements from any areas which were work-oriented. The only desirable end-product to an enquiry was that which could best be supported by facts and direct evidence. In the present circumstances, a projected crime would meet those requirements, and Jameson's capitulation did not represent a personal victory on her part. The pleasure that she was experiencing was for quite different reasons. The receding possibility of some foreign war carried with it the increasing likelihood that Ben Hardcastle would come out of this business alive, a prospect which pleased her for reasons entirely non-scientific.

'Do we pass the parcel, then?' she enquired.

'Parcel?'

'More specifically, do we now gather up all our facts and figures, and hand them over to someone else? Special Branch, Internal Affairs, or whatever?'

Her departmental head was clearly horrified by the question.

'Hand over?' he echoed faintly. 'My dear Miss Fiske, I doubt whether you can be serious. Permit me to remind you of a few facts. This department is a new venture. It exists only at the personal wish of the Chief Minister, and we are far from popular with the other agencies. We have no staff worth speaking of, yet we have access to funds. For which, as you know, I account only to my own minister, which does nothing to enhance our relations with the older departments.'

'Then this is surely an opportunity to make them a present of a good case,' she began, but he sighed, and she stopped.

'This case, whatever it is, and if it exists at all,' he pointed out portentously, 'is likely to bear fruit at any moment. We'll make no friends by handing over a situation like this. Baxter and the rest have had weeks to plan and prepare. I should most likely simply be delivering a time-bomb, due to explode at any moment, to people with no foreknowledge of what to expect, and a totally inadequate period in which to make their own preparations. What kind of thanks would we get, or deserve? No, no, dear lady, at this time we do nothing. Tomorrow, perhaps, or the next day, things will be different. After this event happens, and everyone is running around in circles, that is when we come along and supply a few details. It's all in the timing, you see.'

She shook her head in puzzlement.

'Sorry, no. I don't see at all.'

Jameson sighed then, and looked at her with an unusually benign expression.

'You have to put yourself in the other chap's shoes. Suppose I were to give him what we have, just before the balloon goes up. His position with his superiors would be quite untenable. He would have to admit that he knew about it, and at the same time, that he couldn't prevent it. No, wait,' as Jennifer began to interrupt, 'I know you're going to say he hadn't had time. Believe me, that would be no excuse at all, not in the eyes of the powers-that-be. They deal in absolutes. Now, look at the other side of the coin. Something happens, something totally unexpected. There is an immediate uproar, and everyone's shouting for blood. While it's at its height, I quietly furnish information to whoever is in charge. "Thought you might find this useful, old boy," that kind of thing. He'll grab it up, you may be sure, like our old friend, the drowning man. He can rush off to his masters, and report enormous progress in a short space of time. He won't give us the credit, not publicly, and I should neither expect nor want him to. But he won't forget who got him out of trouble. Do you understand it better now? Same information, same people, only the timing is

158

different. If we talk too soon, we make only enemies. But if we talk at the right moment, we make friends for life. Timing, Miss Fiske.'

Miss Fiske could understand well enough, but that did nothing to make her like it any better.

'But it's not right, is it?' she offered weakly.

That was rewarded with one of his wintry smiles.

'Right and wrong are things seen clearly only when one is young,' he assured her paternally. 'After that, they become confused by such externals as politics, expediency—'

'—and timing,' she supplied acidly.

'That too,' he conceded.

'I hear you, master. So, what are we going to do? Do we call everybody off? Hardcastle could do with a break.'

Jameson paused, thinking. Even accepting that he had been wrong about the *Sunderland Lady*, he was still reluctant to abandon entirely the warlike Baxter. And what was this nonsense about Hardcastle? It couldn't surely be that Fiske, the super-brain with the detached intellect, was casting favourable eyes on that provincial roughneck? No, of course not, the idea was preposterous. He was letting this abortive scheme get him down.

'Hardcastle? He'll have to press on for a while. Drop the rest of it, but I want the surveillance maintained on Baxter's people. I haven't quite abandoned hope, not yet.'

The nod of acknowledgement from his assistant was almost absent-minded. Fortunately he was by this time accustomed to her seeming mental wanderings. In common with many boffins, Jennifer was capable of operating on two levels at once. Perfectly conscious of her surroundings, and able to take her part in whatever was going on, she also possessed the faculty of pursuing coincidentally some entirely separate line of thought, normally associated with her work.

Jameson's assumption was only half-correct. It was true that his assistant was following a mental line of her own, but it was by no means associated with her work.

Jennifer Fiske, with her new and deeply-felt attachment to Ben Hardcastle, was beginning to concentrate her thinking on ways in which he might be kept safe, not merely for

159

the present, but for all time. The direction in which her imagination was leading her was a considerable surprise even to herself. It was fortunate that her chief possessed no powers of telepathy.

Had he been able to detect the thought-patterns which were beginning to shape inside her head, he might well have decided that she was about to take leave of her senses.

At that early, formative, stage, she might even have agreed with him.

CHAPTER SIXTEEN

It was about ten p.m. when Albie Collins entered the saloon bar of the Black Duck. The public house was in full swing, with half the noisy, jostling customers trying to carry on thirty or forty different conversations, while the other half attempted to listen to the throbbing passion of the sequined group on the platform in the corner.

Collins was not a very tall man, and he had to strain his neck continually in an attempt to scan the crowd. Finally, he spotted his quarry, a tall, gangling man in a leather jacket, leaning against the bar at the far end, and seemingly oblivious to the pandemonium around him. The dreamer spotted Collins, as he pushed his way through the crowd, and beamed with pleasure.

'There you are, my old son,' he greeted, 'I was getting a bit bothered. They tell me Morrie Glassman was looking for you. You all right?'

His tone was low, as befitted the circumstances. When Glassman wanted somebody, it was always a serious matter, and, as often as not, to the great disadvantage of the person concerned. Collins bobbed his head reassuringly.

'He's all right, is Morrie. We're mates,' he announced. 'Matter of fact, he's done us a turn, Joey.'

Joey looked sceptical. When Morrie Glassman did anybody a favour, it was usually in exchange for their life savings, at the very least.

'Oh yes,' he replied.

'Straight up. Listen,' and Albie peered around him anxiously, to ensure they were not being overheard, 'he's bought two barge loads of tyres off me. What you doing on Saturday?'

'Same as always.' Joey's tone was offended. 'Gonna watch the Spurs, ain't I?'

Collins shook his head in rebuttal.

'Not tonight, Josephine,' he contradicted. 'No football for you, my son, not this week. You got to help me shift them tyres. And you have to keep stumm about it.'

'Listen,' protested Joey, 'it's a big match. Very important. We only need two points and—'

'Never mind points,' whispered Collins urgently. 'There's two ton in it for you.'

Joey's long face changed now from indignation to suspicion.

'Two hundred quid? For shifting a few tyres? There's something smelling a bit around here, and it's not old Pop's tobacco. What's going on?'

Albie swivelled his eyes around again before replying.

'You know where the old St. Augustus Dock is?'

'I know where it was. Last time I was down there, it was only two planks and a rat. What about it?'

'That's where we take the tyres,' explained Albie. 'We tie up there at seven o'clock Saturday, no later, then we scarper.'

The tall man shook his tousled head.

'What for? I mean, what's it all for? It don't make no sense to me. What does Morrie want with a load of grotty old tyres, in the first place? In the second place, nobody's been down the St. Augustus since the Crimean War.'

Collins sighed. He had expected precisely the reaction he was now getting, and was ready with his final arguments.

'It don't have to make any sense to you, Joey,' he stated firmly. 'Nor me, for that matter. You only have to understand two things. One is the two hundred sovs. The other one is Mr. Glassman. He told me to tell you he'll be very disappointed if we don't do this right, and it'll be even worse if we spread it about. You know what happens to people when Mr. Glassman is disappointed.'

Joey went pale then.

'You told him my name?'

'Had to, didn't I? He knows I couldn't shift that lot on me own. We're lucky, really. It's nothing bent, and it's good money.'

But no further persuasion was needed. The fact that the ferocious Morrie Glassman even knew his name was all the convincing that Joey required.

'What time Saturday?'

The s.s. *Sunderland Lady* was making good time.

'Doesn't talk much, your skipper.'

The speaker was the river pilot, Tom Corcoran, one of the three brothers who were the current generation of that famous family of rivermen. The Corcorans had been ushering their charges through the hazards of the Thames for more than a hundred years and the name was known to seafaring men in every corner of the globe. They knew every mudflat, every shift of tide or current. Some people claimed that a man couldn't throw an empty cigarette-packet in the river without the Corcorans knowing about it.

Tom was addressing his remark to the first mate, who didn't seem a bad sort, for a Frenchman. The captain himself, name of Kokis, had greeted the pilot in his cabin, which was a bit unusual, then handed him over to the mate. Luckily the mate spoke excellent English.

'I do not know him very well,' replied the mate. 'We only joined at Marseilles, and I have not sailed with him before. He is not feeling very good.'

Marco Leonides, in his new role as Michael Kokis, had come aboard at night, and taken command. His upright bearing, immaculate dress and, above all, his new luxuriant beard, had proved to be quite sufficient to pass the superficial scrutiny which had been possible in the half-light. He was not anxious to put it to the test in the close confinement of normal sea-going conditions. The majority of the crew knew him, and it would be foolish to risk exposure. There was a new first mate among the half-dozen replacements taken aboard at Marseilles, and the bogus Kokis had gladly handed over the running of the ship for the brief six-day journey to London. Meals, and other requirements were seen to by one of the newcomers.

They had made good time, and the trip had passed without incident. Kokis had experienced a few anxious moments in the Bay of Biscay, that turbulent stretch of water which was ever ready to test the balance of a vessel. The new tanks, charged now with oil, would have presented a hazard if the extra weight topside had not been correctly countered by the ballast in the hold, but the load had been properly assessed, and the *Lady* came through the ordeal with dignity.

Tom Corcoran was glad to be on this particular run. So many of his charges these days ended at Tilbury, with its great new deepwater quays and the grain terminal. It hadn't always been thus. In his younger days the near deserted banks they were now negotiating had been a hive of activity. There had been other great docks then. St. Catherine's, London, Surrey Commercial, all nearly finished now. Even the great India/Millwall complex was now on its last legs. There'd be nothing left in a few years, if they went on at this rate.

Corcoran grinned suddenly to himself. He was beginning to sound like his grandfather, he realised. The old man used always to be chuntering on about things not being what they were. Tom could recall how he and his brothers would exchange glances when the old man used to lead off about great wharves, now abandoned. The old St. Augustus, now looming up forward, was once full of activity, with its three- and four-masters coming in from Baltimore and the Indies. The young Corcorans had had no patience with the old boy. Progress was progress, they used to say.

Well, it was his turn now, he reflected, as the *Sunderland Lady* wended her stately way past deserted quays and wharves, and made preparation for berthing.

*   *   *

Wang Teh made the small clicking noise with his tongue which was the closest he ever came to a show of impatience. As a Stone Step Five, he exercised considerable authority, and was widely regarded as a man to be feared and respected. That was as it should be, and no more than fitting to his rank and station. But, because he was based in London, he lacked the autonomy enjoyed by his equal-ranking brothers in Birmingham and Manchester. For London was also the base for his master, whose level was that of Stone Step Two. This eminent person carried the responsibility for the whole of Europe, and was therefore, notionally, not involved in matters of routine business. Nevertheless, his physical nearness was a constant and unwelcome reminder of his existence, coupled with the fact that from time to time, and unpredictably, he would elect to interest himself in mundane matters to the discomfort of the local chieftain.

This bootlegging business was a case in point, and Stone Step Five was anxious that he should not be over-ruled.

Wang Teh, like his brother officer in Marseilles, Sammy Fong, was heavily influenced by, and acutely aware of, the advanced and sophisticated methods of his Western competitors. Envy was not a luxury he permitted himself, but there were times when his thoughts turned wistfully towards his New York based colleague. A keen student of organised crime, he read everything he could find about the great national structure in the United States, and would have given much to be able to observe it at close hand.

The problem before him at the moment had been solved many times in the past, right back in the days of prohibition. The new law gave birth to one crime, bootlegging, which in its turn spawned another, the hi-jack.

In this instance, the bootlegging was being done by others. A ship, the s.s. *Sunderland Lady*, was due in from Marseilles. In specially constructed tanks she would be carrying, not the fuel oil and diesel described on her papers, but a thousand tonnes of quality spirit, probably brandy. Wang Teh was charged with the task of acquiring this windfall, and he had posed the problem to three of his more promising recruits.

The first man had wanted to take over the ship during the night of her arrival. The attack would be swift and unexpected.

'And how do you suggest we remove the brandy?' he was asked.

The man's thinking had not progressed that far, and the question floored him. The second man, masking his amusement at his comrade's discomfiture, thought he had the answer.

'I would take the ship, as suggested by my honourable friend. I would then pump the spirit into bulk liquid containers, such as are used for petrol. The containers would of course be thoroughly cleaned first.'

Wang Teh nodded. At least this one had thought about it more deeply than the first.

'And where do you propose to obtain this equipment?'

The second man had floundered then. It had been his assumption that all items of equipment came from some vast and mysterious storehouse, known only to people senior in rank to himself.

'My brothers are known to be men of courage,' began the third recruit smoothly, 'but there are times when stealth is the better weapon. What do we want with a ship? We are not sailors. The Western devils will have planned the removal of the spirit, so why should we give ourselves that trouble? Let them proceed. When they have driven it away from the docks, that is the time for us to strike. Their forces will be scattered, possibly two men in each vehicle. Resistance will be small.'

This was what Wang Teh had intended all along, and he grunted with approval.

'The plan will require ten men,' he announced. 'Their names are on this piece of paper. The ship arrives on Friday night. These men will be ready from six o'clock on that evening. The darkness will be our friend. The attack will be quick and silent. There will be no guns. Hatchets and knives will be used. Am I understood?'

The chastened recruits nodded.

'They will be quartered at the address which is on the paper. There must be food there, and mattresses. We cannot prophesy when the foreigners will unload. The ship will be watched constantly from time of arrival. Go now, and prepare. Report completion at this time tomorrow.'

When they had left, Wang Teh stroked happily at his smooth cheek. Lucky Luciano himself could not have done better.

*   *   *

Ginger Davis poked his head inside Mallory's tent.

'Ready for me, boss?'

Joe Mallory put down the Browning 9mm automatic he had been cleaning, and waved the visitor inside.

'Ready for you, Ginger, and for that.'

Davis was carrying two metal plates from which came a nose-twitching aroma. Now he passed one to Mallory who looked at it appreciatively.

'Cookie's done it again,' he marvelled. 'What is it this time?'

'Some kind of venison pie,' he was told. 'Don't ask me how he manages it. He shouldn't be on this job, old Cookie. Ought to be at the Waldorf or somewhere.'

Mallory got busy with his fork, nodding.

'Agreed, but don't tell him. We want to keep him ourselves. Did I hear some kind of argument out there?'

Ginger swallowed before replying.

'Not really. Sparkes was pulling his leg, that's all. He said there ought to be an alternative kosher dish, just for him. Didn't stop him shovelling it down, though, I noticed. Why are we eating on our own? What's on your mind?'

Mallory, intent on eating his lunch while it was hot, did not reply for several seconds. Then he looked seriously at his companion.

'Strictly between us, yes?'

'If you say so,' agreed Davis, and he meant it. Whatever the Yank wanted, it would be all right with him.

'O.K. Well, here it is. Major Baxter is away at a briefing session, as you know. When he gets back, I guess we'll be moving out in two, maybe three days. From the moment we pack up this camp, we'll be on field discipline. Just like old times.'

Davis nodded.

'Suits me. Except I never thought I'd be doing it in me own country. Be a bit strange.'

'Let me tell you something. I've spent a lot of time thinking about this job, and I can't find any holes in it. It's my assessment that the success probability is ninety per cent plus.'

Mallory waited. He knew the value Davis put on his opinion, and gave him time to absorb the information. The listener's face crinkled into a grin.

'That's the kind of odds I like,' he returned.

'I was talking about the job itself,' continued Mallory. 'What I'm concerned about is what happens afterwards. After we get the bullion away, I mean.'

Ginger's smile faded.

'I don't follow you.'

'Major Baxter doesn't trust the people we're working with in London. He has a suspicion that there might be a double-cross once we hand over the gold. No, wait a minute,' as Davis began to interrupt, 'let me finish. None of us, you, me, the men outside, know any of the guys running this operation. We just do what we're told, collect our money and blow. The Major doesn't think they'll bother about us. He's different. He knows who they are, and that makes him a danger. They might decide to take him out.'

'Lousy bastards,' breathed Ginger.

'Agreed, but it makes good business sense, like it or not. Baxter had asked me to stay close, once we contact these people. They don't know we're around, so that gives us an edge, but we don't know what the odds are. I'll be watching his back, which they won't expect, but that leaves my back. That's where you come in, Ginger. I want you to watch out for me. Will you do it?'

'You didn't need to ask.' Davis looked almost offended. 'But why do you want to make a big secret out of it? We've got the toughest platoon in the entire world out there. One word to that lot, and they'll sort out anybody.'

Mallory had anticipated Davis's reaction, and his answer was prepared.

'No. That's more or less what I said to the Major, but he won't have it. Those men are combat soldiers. If they're warned to look out for treachery, they're liable to find some. If somebody coughs, or even looks a bit strange, they are likely to start a shooting war, just out of instinct. There's no need for that, in Baxter's estimation. He's the one at risk. All he's asking is a little extra alertness from me. And I'm asking for it from you. Do we have a deal?'

'Sure we do,' confirmed Davis vigorously, 'but I still don't see why we don't tell the lads.'

'O.K. Then let's talk it through. Look at it this way—'
Mallory began to analyse the reasoning, in low, persuasive tones.

CHAPTER SEVENTEEN

The tapping at the door became more insistent.

Baxter opened one reluctant eye, and stared at the luminous dial on his watch. It was two-fifteen in the morning, and less than ten minutes since he had climbed into bed, weary from his chase round London disposing of his hundred thousand pounds.

Now, when he was safely in the hotel room, which he'd reserved the previous day under another name, somebody was intent on disturbing him.

'Who is it?' he called, then realised he probably could not be heard through the thick door.

Scrambling out of bed, he released the safety catch on the Colt automatic which had been under the pillow, and padded to the door. Standing, out of habit, to one side of the wood-work, he spoke again.

'Who's there?'

Whatever tiredness remained in him drained away as he heard the soft reply.

'It's me, Estelle. Let me in.'

Estelle? Impossible. No-one knew where he was, no-one. It couldn't be Estelle. It was some kind of trick, that was obvious. But who could play the trick, if no-one knew how to find him?

'Estelle who?' was the best he could manage, and even he realised how ineffectual it sounded.

The light, derisive laugh from the other side of the door was well deserved, he admitted.

'You never knew before, and I'm certainly not telling you now.'

Baxter turned the key on the double-lock, and slid back the heavy chain.

'Come in,' he invited.

The door opened a fraction, as Baxter levelled his heavy weapon at stomach height. A further push, and there she was, framed in the doorway, and staring at his tense face with cool appraisal.

'My, my, we are jumpy,' she drawled, advancing into the room, and staring around.

Baxter secured the door and inspected her. Middle of the night or not, she looked like one of those impossible models he only ever saw in expensive magazines in Harley Street waiting rooms. An ankle-length dress of shimmering silver clung to her like a sheath, and, presumably to ward off the night chill, a sable wrap was draped around the rich shoulders.

He put the automatic down on the bedside table, shaking his head.

'All right,' he said resignedly. 'Just one question. How?'

She smiled, the red lips mocking him.

'How did I find you? It wasn't too difficult.' She tossed the sable negligently onto a chair, and crossed to the small refrigerator. 'Since you don't offer a lady a drink, I presume you've no objection if I take one?'

He crossed to her then, moving her aside.

'I'll get the drink,' he snapped. 'You just talk. Gin?'

'Thank you.'

There were two armchairs in the room. She glided over and sat down, the deep tan of her slender arms contrasting vividly with the pale beige of the padded leather.

'There's no great mystery,' she assured him. 'All I had to do was to follow you. I knew those idiots had reserved a hotel room in your name, naturally. But I also felt you were a man who preferred to make his own arrangements. In that respect, Baxter, we have a good deal in common.'

He had no intention of being side-tracked onto personal matters, not at this stage. If ever, he reminded himself, thinking of Gregory Ryder.

'Gin,' he announced, holding out the glass, 'and tonic. What do you mean, you followed me? From where?'

'From the time you left the meeting with Halloran and Williams,' she replied coolly. 'Thanks. You made a lot of calls. Do you realise my taxi-fare was thirty-two pounds?'

He didn't like the sound of it. If Estelle had kept a note of his various stopping places, it wouldn't be too difficult for someone to recover the cash. Especially a determined character like Williams.

'You went to a lot of trouble,' he acknowledged. 'The point is, why?'

Estelle sipped at her drink.

'I needed this, it was getting damned cold in that cab. And you got the mix right. Perhaps it's an augury. I came here to make you an offer, my friend.'

Having previously decided against taking a drink, Baxter now changed his mind and helped himself to a large scotch.

'Cheers,' he saluted. 'What's the offer?'

'Subject to certain conditions,' she replied slowly, 'it's me.'

He thought at first he must have misunderstood.

'You?' he echoed.

'Subject to certain conditions,' she repeated.

He laughed then, but without humour. Baxter had been the target for some strange offers in his time, but never before had a beautiful woman offered herself to him, unsolicited, at two-fifteen in the morning. A woman who also happened to be clearly stamped as the personal property of one of the most powerful men he'd ever encountered. It was a crazy situation, but, crazy or not, there was no mistaking the fact that Estelle was in deadly earnest.

Now, he frowned at her.

'At this hour of the night, or morning, and seeing that no-one else knows where I am, it's unlikely I shall get a better offer,' he admitted, choosing his words. 'What's this about conditions?'

Long tapered fingers drummed lightly on the chair arm.

'Let me explain the package from my side,' she began. 'In addition to me, and don't bother to deny your interest in that direction, you will also have a complete analysis of Gregory Ryder's operation. Some of it you won't be able to touch, but you will be in a position to take over a substantial portion of it. You will be made for life, with money and power you never dreamed of. Believe me, Baxter, when I tell you that I am in a position to deliver.'

The words were uttered with total conviction. Despite his enormous misgivings, Baxter realised he was in the middle of a very serious discussion. He had to know more.

'That's your side of the package, and it's a hell of a

172

contribution,' he conceded. 'But why are you so good to me? I do as well as the next man where women are concerned, but I don't deceive myself. I'm nobody's Adonis. You want more than just me, right? What, for instance?'

'Ten million pounds in gold for instance.'

Well, at least she made no bones about it, he admitted.

'You put a heavy price on yourself,' he snapped.

If he had expected to annoy her, he was to be disappointed. She merely smiled, that lazy provocative twisting of her mouth, and inclined her head.

'You forget that I bring an empire with me,' she reminded.

Her calm assurance was beginning to have its effect, and that, since he knew how wild the proposition was, served to make him irritable.

'Look, Estelle,' he suggested, 'why don't you pick up your nice fur wrap and get the hell out? Go back to Ryder, and we'll both pretend this never happened.'

There was no smile on her face when she next spoke.

'Ryder is dead.'

The words struck at his stomach like physical blows.

'Dead? When, I mean how—'

'Yesterday afternoon,' she informed him. 'At home. Quite suddenly. I killed him.'

'You—' he began, but did not finish the sentence. Instead, he swallowed the remainder of his scotch, and went at once to the refrigerator for a refill. He had conducted too many similar conversations in the past to be in any doubt about her sincerity. Ryder was dead. The planner, the master organiser behind the whole thing. And his murderess had come to offer him the throne.

'Christ, what a mess,' he muttered, as much to himself as to the composed woman who sat watching him.

'Not really,' she contradicted, 'it simply means that there will have to be some last-minute adjustments. Until this new development, you see, the plan was that Basil Williams would kill you, once the gold was safely away. Naturally, that will have to be changed now.'

'Naturally.'

So he'd been right about that, at least. He now knew for

certain what previously he had only suspected, and that meant he must now kill Williams. Then a new thought struck him, as he brought his mind more sharply to bear on all the implications.

'You're forgetting, aren't you, that the operation might be called off altogether, cancelled? As soon as Halloran and Williams find out about Ryder, they might cry quits, until they can get re-organised.'

But her head had begun to shake a negative, even while he was still speaking.

'They don't know, and they won't find out,' she stated, with utter conviction. 'Ryder is supposed to be in Washington, and the instructions are that there will be no contact between them until Tuesday of next week. The body is well hidden, and the servants were already away for a week's holiday. The only person who knows that Gregory Ryder is dead is me. And now you. So you see, Baxter, you hold all the cards. You must go for the jackpot. And I don't think you need that other drink.'

The last words flicked at him like whips of ice. She was quite right, he admitted, and set down the glass. His mind was now in full flight, assembling all known material, incorporating new developments, and re-formulating strategy.

'Question time,' he announced suddenly. 'One. Why did you kill Ryder?'

The woman in silver did not reply at once, and he was about to repeat the question when she eventually spoke, in a low voice.

'The man was totally evil. I knew I'd made a mistake, almost as soon as he bought me—oh yes, he bought me—but there was no escaping him. A very property-conscious man, our Mr. Ryder. Running away would have been easy enough, but he would have tracked me down, no matter what the cost. And so I stayed, and waited for my chance. When you came on the scene, I realised I would never get a better opportunity, but I couldn't quite bring myself to take advantage of it. Planning was one thing, but putting the plan into action was another. I lived in such mortal fear of that devil, that he'd actually sapped my willpower.'

Her voice trailed away, and Baxter had the eerie feeling

174

that she had almost forgotten he was there. The large eyes, although fixed on his face, had become somehow translucent, as if looking right through him.

'You changed your mind though,' he pointed out sharply. 'Why?'

The faraway look disappeared, and she blinked rapidly.

'No,' she denied. 'Ryder himself did it for me, when he had Papa Louie killed. He swore to me that Louie would come to no harm, and like a fool I believed him. I was the one who betrayed him, on Ryder's instructions, but I didn't know what they intended. Even after they killed him, it would have been easy to lie to me, to tell me he'd been taken back, but that wouldn't have been Ryder's style. They put the corpse in my bed, so that I'd find it waiting for me. When I found it, my mind nearly snapped. Instead, I turned revulsion into resolve. Ryder signed his own death warrant that night.'

Despite himself, Baxter grimaced at the scene she described, but he was still not entirely satisfied.

'Let's get to question number two,' he said abruptly. 'If you've been wanting to break with Ryder, what took you so long? Halloran has been around, so has Williams. Don't tell me you couldn't have got one of them to take over. Or both, for that matter.'

Estelle brought her attention back to the present.

'Oh yes, it would have been easy,' she agreed. 'But neither of them is good enough. Gregory knew what he was about when he recruited those two. They are a formidable pair. Halloran is the planner, the organiser, what you army people would call the chief of staff. Williams is the strike force. Cunning, dangerous, always alert. But neither could run things on his own.'

'And you think I could?' he questioned, with a hint of sarcasm.

The inflection in his tone was not lost on Estelle.

'If you mean by that, do I consider you the equal of those two, the answer will have to be "no",' she told him frankly. 'But you're as close as I'm likely to come, and I'm satisfied that you can do it with my help. Otherwise, you may be sure, I should not be here now.'

She didn't mince her words, thought Baxter, but in the circumstances, plain speaking was the order of the day. If it had been a straightforward question of retaining the possession of the bullion, he would have had fewer reservations. But Halloran wasn't the only one who could think ahead.

'Let's play a game,' he suggested. 'Let's pretend I'm a man who suddenly gets his hands on ten million pounds in gold. It sounds wonderful, but it's just a heap of scrap metal. I wouldn't know what to do with it. Had you thought about that?'

Her face betrayed nothing of her mental processes, but Estelle was quietly elated by the question. Baxter had delayed too long in rejecting the proposition, and was now seeking for ways to make it viable. The end was no longer in doubt.

'Luckily for you,' she replied, her tone close to banter, 'there is also a woman in the game. She is on your side, this woman, and she knows exactly where to take your scrap metal. The price will be four million, not ten, but it will be real money.'

Baxter nodded slowly, the last of his objections dissolved by the realistic response.

'If I fell in with all this,' he said stiffly, 'we must be clear about one thing. We will be partners, but when it comes to a crunch, I give the orders. I may not be Ryder, but you had better believe I'm a very nasty man to cross.'

'Oh, I know that, from your record,' she assured him. 'And you, in turn, may believe that I wouldn't have it any other way.'

The whole thing was madness, reflected Baxter, but he was unable to contain a feeling of rising conviction that he could carry it off. That they, rather, could carry it off. The circumstances were ridiculous.

It was almost three o'clock in the morning. There he stood, in his bare feet and rumpled pyjamas, in a strange hotel room, with this beautiful enigmatic woman, completely at her ease, and discussing with utmost seriousness one of the strangest criminal conspiracies ever conceived.

He laughed shortly, and with total awareness of the harsh reality behind his next words.

176

'All right Estelle, we have a deal. There's a hell of a lot to thrash out, and a lot of fine print we haven't looked at yet, but all right. It's a deal.'

She stood up, in one graceful movement, and looked softly into his eyes.

'Very well. It's a deal.'

'Then I guess we should shake hands or something.'

It was Estelle's turn to laugh.

'I'm going to like you, Baxter. You have a fine sense of the ridiculous.'

A sinuous shrug of her magnificent shoulders, and the silver dress was in a heap at her feet. She kicked it to one side, and put out a red tongue.

'Let us by all means shake hands,' she invited.

CHAPTER EIGHTEEN

'No, no. You're out of your mind,' declared Hardcastle. 'Besides, we'd never get away with it.'

It was his fourth refusal within the space of twenty minutes, each carrying less conviction than the last. Added to which, he was now considering the likelihood of achievement, a clear indication that his resolve was weakening. Jennifer stroked absently at his chest.

'What makes you think we might fail?' she murmured.

'It's all too preposterous,' he replied irritably, his mind racing.

What she was proposing was clearly out of the question, even if she was right about the gold. Jameson's decision to call off the surveillance, with the sole exception that Hardcastle should maintain his solo vigil on Baxter, had not pleased Jennifer Fiske in the least. It left her man altogether too exposed, and she was particularly concerned about leaving Williams to roam at will. At first, she entertained a few wild ideas about involving other agencies, unbeknown to her acidulous chief. An anonymous telephone call, with a few clear directions, would undoubtedly produce the extra help that was needed, but she quickly dismissed the temptation. When all the heat had died down there would be an inquest, and Hector Jameson would not for long be under any illusions about the source of the mysterious tip-off. No, any assistance she sought would have to come from some new quarter altogether, and she put her mind to the possibilities. There was Williams, to begin with. The Americans would be interested to know that he was still very much alive, and would no doubt welcome the opportunity of renewing his acquaintance. But the practical side ruled them out. They weren't likely to agree to any undercover activity such as Jennifer would propose. Why should they? They were on friendly soil, and would automatically approach the proper authorities, with the same final result that she was anxious to avoid.

Friendly soil.

The phrase stuck in her mind, worrying at her, and refusing to be dismissed. That was when she first thought of Nawabia. The department knew all about Baxter's involvement in the recent uprising in the African state, and how close that coup had been to overthrowing the present government. They might welcome an opportunity to get their hands on Major Baxter, if it could be put to them in the proper way, and their relationship with the U.K. government was in no way comparable with that of the Americans. Indeed, there was a good deal of mistrust on both sides, and it was unlikely that any formal approach for the extradition of Baxter would find any favour in Whitehall. If she could offer them a scheme which permitted them to abduct him unofficially, then they might be prepared to listen. The more Jennifer thought about the idea, the better she liked it, but first she had to know more about the nature of the basic operation.

Having long ago ruled out any political possibilities, the most likely alternative was robbery on some huge scale, but robbery of what? She had no knowledge of such matters, which were no concern of the department. For a while, Jennifer was frustrated. If her enquiry had been an official one, there would have been no problem. A request from the department to a certain planning room in New Scotland Yard would have produced detailed information on all high risk locations in the London area. It was part of the ongoing routine procedure at the Yard that such targets were logged and monitored, and it would have been easy to acquire details. But this was not a departmental matter. This was entirely private to a certain Jennifer Fiske, and must remain that way.

The simple route of a direct question being denied to her, she would have to look elsewhere for the essential information, and she knew exactly how to go about it. Expert at keying into other people's systems, she put the mighty Wurlitzer to work on searching the records of the insurance companies and security organisations. Within a short time she had concocted a list of attractive targets, which she then proceeded to whittle down, until only three remained of sufficient size to warrant the scale of the attack being

179

mounted. Two involved large deposits of precious stones, and the third was the bullion warehouse. In the end, it was the location which decided her. One of the gem hoards was three miles from Baxter's base, and the other was on the wrong side of the river. The warehouse containing the bullion was only a short distance from Baxter, with a deserted dockland area in between. It had to be the bullion, she decided, as she fed all her unauthorised print-outs into the shredder. Now the decision was made, she could turn her attention to the practicalities.

From the moment of her last interview with Hector Jameson, the computer expert had been astonished at the confusion of thinking which had come into her mind. By instinct and training, she was accustomed to channelling her thought patterns along clear and productive lines. This mental jumble was a new and unwelcome experience, and she was under no illusions about the cause. The culprit was one Ben Hardcastle, with whom she was undoubtedly in love. Blast the man. Hitherto, that side of her life had been well-ordered, almost regulated. Scientist or no, she had always derived considerable pleasure from her occasional forays into the physical world. This thing with Hardcastle was different. She had suspected early on that it might be, which was one of the reasons she had always kept him at a distance. Now it was too late to go back, even if she had wished.

It was a natural corollary of their new situation that Ben Hardcastle should remain alive. The possibility that he might come to an untimely end had been, hitherto, an integral factor of the job. Such a development was no longer acceptable, and alternative arrangements had to be made about his future, a future in which the department had no place. If he'd been a bank official, it would have been so easy. All one had to do was to hand in three months' notice. The department did not operate like that. Once a man was in, he was in, and there was no question of changing course. Perhaps, in ten years time, there might be the prospect of a desk job in some ministry, or an assistant consul post on a tropical island, always assuming he lived that long. The prospect of existing through those years on a knife-edge was more than she could face.

Instead of wailing about her fate, as so many would have done, Jennifer set herself the problem, much as though it had been an examination question, and looked for the solution. The only exit from the department was by permanent disability or death. The first alternative was out of the question, leaving only the second, which was equally unacceptable.

Those were the halves of the equation as it stood.

The trouble was that Ben Hardcastle was a valuable man, otherwise the situation would never have arisen. Jennifer smiled ruefully at her own lack of consistency. It was ridiculous for her to feel resentful. If it hadn't been for the very qualities which made him valuable, she would never have fallen for him in the first place. Then another thought struck her. Suppose for some reason he was no longer so valuable? That would be a new factor in the equation, something to weigh in the balance. But what? She couldn't take away his intelligence, nor his experience, nor his training. She couldn't suddenly discount his physical fitness, his ready adaptability, any of his personal qualities. Valuable was right. Ben Hardcastle was well equipped in every area for his secret role in the department.

His secret role.

She almost laughed aloud as the solution presented itself. Suppose she could remove the secrecy, give him a public image? Then his use to the department would be at an end. Suppose, instead of the usual faceless anonymity behind which their work was normally conducted, Hardcastle should be exposed suddenly to the full glare of publicity. Then his career within the department would terminate at the same moment.

Once she had arrived at the basic concept, her mind ranged rapidly over the means of realisation, and several alternatives presented themselves in quick succession. Then she decided she was trying to project too far ahead. She had her answer—publicity. The method of its achievement would have to await developments. First, she would have the predictably difficult task of selling the scheme to Hardcastle himself.

His initial and expected refusal was now beginning to show signs of lessening.

'We'd never get away with it,' he repeated. 'What chance would we have, just the two of us, against a gang of professionals like that? We'd need an army of our own.'

That ought to shut her up, he thought smugly. It was clearly of no avail to argue the ethics, but she couldn't close her eyes to the practicalities. They were just one man and one woman, and the sheer size of the opposition put her idea out of court.

'I can get an army,' she returned quietly. 'Next question?'

He sat bolt upright in bed, staring down at her, but there was no laughter in her eyes. She was clearly serious.

'Where?' he demanded.

'Never mind that now. Just assume we can get all the help we need. What other objections have you?'

Forced now to concentrate, he thought rapidly.

'I should be betraying the department,' he pointed out. 'I don't want to sound like a flag-waver, but treachery is not quite in my line. You can imagine what the newspapers would do with it. Secret department exposed, all that stuff.'

Jennifer chuckled.

'All this sex is sapping your mental powers,' she scoffed. 'You don't belong to any secret department. You are a Senior Assistant at the ministry, with a desk and an office to prove it. Nothing secret about what you do. The job's not even classified.'

That was true enough, he admitted. His cover job was sound enough.

'Jameson would never stand for it,' he muttered.

'Stand for what? It won't be your fault,' she wheedled. 'You'll be unlucky, that's all. The spotlight will suddenly be on you, and you'll have to put up the best yarn you can, off the top of your head. If we do it right, little Hector will be quite proud of the way you come through. It'll be the end of your undercover career, naturally, sorry old boy, and all that, but he might even be grateful to you. Anyway,' she started stroking thoughtfully at his stomach, 'do I take it from the tenor of these questions that we begin to have the basis of an understanding?'

'No,' he denied, 'no, that would be putting it too strongly. There are about four hundred more points to take up.'

There is always a stage reached in an argument where one of the protagonists can sense that the other is ready for the kill. Jennifer grinned inwardly, and pulled him down beside her.

'That's quite a lot of points. Suppose we take them one at a time?'

CHAPTER NINETEEN

On the second Saturday in May the sun rose at five-seventeen a.m. The overnight rain had gone, and the clouds with it. The day dawned bright and clear, as the sun began its slow upward climb, and its warming rays edged their welcome way along the river.

In the narrow terms of the statistician and the geographer, the Thames is not a big river. Her two hundred odd miles' cannot bear comparison with the mighty waterways of the world. The Nile, the Amazon, the Missouri and the others, with their thousands of miles' length, would dwarf her in any such league-table. Turn instead to the historians, with their wider terms of reference, and the position alters. Every yard, every foot of her winding length is steeped in historical incident, and mellowed by two thousand recorded years of drama, from the Roman invaders onwards.

Invasion, treason, plague and war. Triumph, despair, prosperity, starvation. Heat waves, floods, even icebergs. There was no device of man or nature which had not been watched, felt and absorbed by those wise old waters, lapping now with calm confidence at the time-worn banks.

Here came the familiar sun, under which there was nothing new. Nothing, that is, until that second Saturday in May. For, on that day, an event was to occur which would add a new page to the turbulent history of the Thames. An occurrence which, if foreseen, might have occasioned a flutter of alarm, even in her unruffled depths.

For the first time ever, she was to be set on fire.

*   *   *

Captain Michael Kokis, né Marco Leonides, was up betimes. The paltry little retirement ceremony in Marseilles had not touched him in any personal sense. It had been no more than an incident in the play-acting, which would lead ultimately to his comfortable old age. Today was wholly different. Today was the real thing, his last appearance as a

184

sea-going man, and the full realisation of it was not lost on him. He knew how the day must end, and he would play his part when the time came, but that was many hours away. In the meantime, he was still a ship's captain, with close to half a century of seafaring contained in his gnarled frame, and a captain he would be, for every remaining minute.

There would be no idling aboard the s.s. *Sunderland Lady*, berthed or no. She, too, was at the end of her road, and, by God, she would go out proudly, and in fine style. Swinging his feet to the floor, he inspected the snowy linen and the immaculately pressed best uniform which awaited him. Not yet. First there was his bath and shave. He poured himself a tot of rum, toasted his outer self, where it hung ready for him, and lit one of his special cigars. Yes, he mused, this Captain Kokis might be a bit of a mystery to all the crew, who had scarcely seen him on the voyage, but, by damn, they'd know he was a real sailor before this day was out. And the sooner, the better.

'Coffee!' he roared.

*   *   *

Wang Teh had passed a restless night, expecting at any moment to be summoned to the docks, but there had been no call. Clearly, the Westerners had missed their opportunity for siphoning off their illicit load, since it was not something which could safely be carried out in the light of day. They must now wait again for nightfall, as must his own men. The strengthening sunlight was now filling the room, highlighting the sparseness of his way of life, which befitted a man of his dedication. The sun could not reach beneath the floorboards, where a canvas bag secreted passbooks for three major banks. The entries in those books spoke of another Wang Teh, a person of considerable substance, but the time was not yet ripe for him to be revealed. Soon now, perhaps one more year, and the old Wang Teh would disappear, but not yet. At the moment, his whole attention must be centred on brotherhood matters.

Why had the brandy not been moved?

The logical thing was to have unloaded in the safety of the

night hours, and yet this had not been done. Why? The question nagged at him, as his bowl of tea grew cold. Then, a most unpalatable explanation presented itself.

Official bandits.

What if the bandits had discovered the contraband? The ones they called Customs, or dock police, or any one of those meddlesome roving bands with uniforms, all intent on preventing men of honour from following their natural pursuits. It was a chilling thought, and Wang Teh could not put it from his mind. The point was, how did a man learn of these matters? It was not a subject for casual questions, and the ship could not be studied closely at her berth. The *Sunderland Lady*, moored at her wharf, was effectively cut off from the public gaze by hundreds of yards of dockside buildings, and the advent of an inquisitive Oriental would scarcely pass without notice.

The river.

The ship could be seen close up from the river itself. A passing launch would attract no attention, and, driven slowly, it would provide ample opportunity for scrutiny. If there was trouble with the officials, then someone would be standing guard over the cargo, someone in a uniform.

Although not anxious to have his suspicions confirmed, Wang Teh was grateful for the prospect of some positive action. Here was something he could organise, something he could do, and he put his mind to it gladly.

There were several wealthy members of the Chinese community who owned rivercraft of various kinds, and who would be glad of the opportunity to display their high regard for Wang Teh and those he represented.

The thing was to decide on the type of boat most suitable for the work in hand.

*   *   *

Cookie McLeish whistled cheerfully as he went about his preparations for breakfast. Although he had enjoyed the challenge of the training camp, it had placed quite a strain on his ingenuity, in trying to produce varied and interesting meals under primitive conditions. Here, in this vast ware-

186

house, there was comparative luxury. A portable cooker, with an oven and three burners, ample room to spread out his utensils on empty packing cases, and no threat of sudden rain or heavy wind. To a lesser man the arrangements may have looked primitive, but to McLeish it was the equivalent of the kitchens at the Ritz itself.

The others were stirring now, wandering in and out of his protected zone to refill their mugs, but no more. Hardened veterans of a dozen campaigns they might be, but no-one was tempted to steal a tidbit no matter how appetizing the food looked or smelled.

'Breakfast is nearly ready,' announced Mallory, setting down a mug of tea beside the seated Baxter. 'Smells good.'

Baxter felt his own insides growl in agreement as the fragrance of frying bacon floated over to him.

'Who's up on top?' he queried.

'Porter is there, until seven. Then Oz Graham goes up.'

There was a rickety wooden ladder fixed to the wall of the warehouse, and running forty feet straight up from the ground to a catwalk which surrounded the interior. From one corner it was possible to maintain surveillance on the bullion shed and the river beyond. The men took it in turns to spend one hour crouched on the narrow wooden ledge, with binoculars trained on the target. It was Baxter's estimation that one hour was sufficient in that awkward position. The last thing he wanted was for one of them to develop cramp and come hurtling down.

'The O'Rourkes are excused that duty,' he decided. 'Once breakfast is out of the way, I want every available minute spent on rehearsal with that beauty.'

He pointed to the fire engine.

Baxter had anticipated all kinds of difficulties in laying hands on a genuine fire engine. It was such a specialised vehicle, so highly distinctive, that there could be no question of a casual theft, as in the case of any ordinary piece of transport. He had visions of being compelled to buy one from the manufacturers as the representative of some foreign government or other.

It had been the O'Rourkes who set him straight on that.

'Easy as pie,' scoffed Des. 'You can pick one up anywhere

for a few hundred quid. They sell 'em, you see. They have this replacement programme every few years. As soon as the new one turns up, they flog the old one. No problem.'

'But who'd buy them?' queried Baxter. 'They must be clapped out, surely?'

'Not at all,' he was assured. 'Just a bit old, that's all. That's where the works fire brigades get their appliances from. Will you want the H.P.?'

Hire Purchase? What was O'Rourke talking about?

'Certainly not,' snapped Baxter. 'I shall pay cash, naturally.'

The Irishman laughed.

'Not that kind of H.P. Major, darling. 'Tis the hydraulic platform I'm meaning. If we're going on any roofs, we'll need one. Shaun and me know how to operate it.'

Baxter congratulated himself on his foresight in recruiting the O'Rourkes. They had been invaluable in familiarising the men with the equipment they would carry, and already they had lost their sense of strangeness inside the uniforms. During the next few hours, they would all be kept busy with the machine itself. Except the platform. Only the O'Rourkes were safe with that.

Mallory sipped at his tea, put it on to a packing case, and lit a cigarette.

'There's nothing more we could have done,' he began, 'but I sure as hell hope everybody else knows what they're doing. It's kind of like relying on an air-strike or artillery support. You never know whether it'll be there when you want it.'

Baxter could understand his apprehension, and sympathised with the reasons for it. How many infantry assaults had failed because of lack of the proper support? In a military situation, these matters had to be taken largely on trust, but in this particular exercise they were better placed, and he set himself to explain.

'I've looked at the terrain,' he began. 'We are relying on three outside events. One is the ship. She's the key to the whole thing, of course. If she doesn't arrive, or fails to get the fire going, then we have a washout. Operation cancelled. That's the first point to have clear, no problem there.

The second diversion is the road accident at the end of Rope Street. I've had a look at it, and it's perfect. There's a pub on the corner, the Twiner's Arms, and the road itself is only eighteen feet wide. A couple of big waggons jammed up there, and especially with this petrol fire risk, there's no way the emergency services can get it clear for hours.'

'How about that petrol?' queried Mallory. 'Do you trust these people not to set it off? I wouldn't like it if a lot of kids got burned.'

'Nor me,' agreed Baxter, 'but it won't happen. Oh, I don't mean they won't set her off. In fact, knowing that sadistic bastard Williams, I wouldn't be surprised if he did it, just for fun. But it's all non-residential, the whole block, just little shops and most of them empty. So that leaves us with the big hole in the road at Chandlers Way. That's even narrower than Rope Street, just sixteen feet from side to side, so progress down there will be damned slow, if it's possible at all. And,' he'd been saving up his trump card for the end, 'there's this.'

Mallory had speculated about the contents of the small grey side-pack which Baxter had been carrying, but decided it probably contained a few personal items. Now, as the major unbuckled the flap and pulled it clear, he could see that it was a small but powerful two-way radio. Baxter tapped at it, grinning.

'Nothing on here at the moment but good old radio,' he explained. 'Party time is twelve noon. The boys outside will establish contact, and report progress. So will we. After that, it's silence until eighteen hundred, and from there, we'll use it as needed. So you see, Joe, we don't have to worry ourselves about air support or artillery. If everything is not firing on all cylinders, we don't go. Satisfied?'

The American nodded. He would have gone ahead in any case, just on Baxter's say-so. But to have all these additional safeguards made him feel that they couldn't possibly fail.

'Let's get to breakfast before those wolves eat it all,' he suggested.

*   *   *

189

The Land-Rover pulled to a halt, twenty yards clear of the great steel doors of the bullion shed. Inside were the six relief guards who had come to take over the next shift. The senior man spoke into a small hand microphone.

'Shift Two booking in. Are you ready, please?'

'Ready and waiting,' crackled the radio. 'Please dismount for visual check.'

The shift boss nodded, and they all climbed out of the Land-Rover, walking bareheaded to the entrance, where they could be easily scrutinised.

'Thank you,' said a voice above their heads. 'I am requesting clearance.'

There was an interval of thirty seconds, while the man inside confirmed clearance with the distant offices of the security company, and then the doors moved fractionally aside, leaving a gap sufficiently wide for one man to pass through. The first man stepped inside, and, when he was in, another man emerged, moving to one side. The second man followed, and the man he was replacing then came out. In this fashion, the whole shift changed over, but at no one time were there less than six guards inside. When the exchange was completed, the senior relief officer took his place at the small control desk inside the doors, closing them instantly.

'Thank you Number One Shift, it's all ours.'

The men who had been relieved walked thankfully across to the Land-Rover, and climbed inside, driving away. They were not due to return now for twenty hours, or three a.m. on Sunday. The three to ten on Sunday morning was the most unpopular and boring of all the shifts, and they did not relish the thought.

They had no way of knowing it was to be the least boring appointment they had ever kept. Or, rather, failed to keep.

*　　*　　*

Albie Collins walked up and down the towpath, muttering to himself. A punctual man by nature, he had little patience with people who were late, no matter what their excuse. In the distance, he caught the glint of sunlight on metal, and there was the lanky figure of Joey, trundling along on his bicycle as though time was the last thing on his mind.

'Morning,' greeted Joey cheerfully, ignoring Albie's thunderous expression. 'Beautiful day innit?'

'Beautiful buggery,' snapped Collins. 'Do you know what time it is? Twenty past bleeding eight, that's what. You was supposed to be here at eight.'

'Didn't hear the alarm, did I?' returned his unrepentant assistant. 'No harm done. We got plenty of time.'

Albie turned, and led the way into the ramshackle structure he called the yard, where worn and useless car tyres were piled in great ungainly heaps.

'Take us four hours to load this lot,' he grumbled. 'Then we got four hours on the water, at least. That's eight hours, that is, could be nine. I hate to be rushed, you know that.'

'Nobody's got to rush,' soothed Joey. 'Keep your shirt on, Albie. We've got to be at the St. Augustus wharf, Gawd knows why, by seven o'clock tonight. That's ten and a half hours, that is. All the time in the world.'

Albie glowered at him.

'Barring accidents,' he reminded glumly, 'barring accidents. Always want to allow plenty of time on a job like this. Never know what might go wrong.'

Joey locked his bicycle carefully, although there was no one else within miles.

'Don't see what,' he argued. 'Straightforward job, as I see it. 'Ere, Albie, what does Morrie Glassman want with two loads of old tyres? Did you find out?'

Albie Collins fixed him with his ferrety eyes.

'You must be orf your skull,' he said slowly. 'Me? Ask Morrie Glassman questions? Me? Shall I tell him you was asking, then?'

The good humour disappeared from Joey's face.

'Christ, no,' he muttered. 'You wouldn't do that, would you?'

Albie was a firm believer in kicking a man when he was down.

'I might, and I'll tell you this. If we're late at that wharf tonight, Morrie's going to know who's responsible. So let's have less of the talk, and a bit more do. Sharp, now.'

191

Joey grabbed a handbarrow and walked to the nearest pile.

*   *   *

Basil Williams tooted impatiently on the carhorn. Halloran emerged from the house, pulling the door carefully shut, and walked calmly over to him.

'It's only ten to,' he greeted. 'We said nine o'clock.'

Williams grinned.

'You know me, George. Always get there ahead of time. You never can tell what the other chap might be up to.'

Halloran snorted and walked to the rear, opening the boot and tossing his small suitcase inside. Then he went around to the passenger door, and got in.

'Where did you get this revolting old wreck?' he demanded.

'Now, now, George, don't be so fussy,' reproved Williams. 'It wouldn't do for us to arrive in a Daimler, not where we're going. This old banger will attract no attention. It'll sort of blend into the scenery, as you might say. Did you bring the gun?'

Halloran was, like so many people, a man of curious contradictions when it came to violence. He recognised the need for it, on occasions, and would apply it without hesitation, through a third party. He preferred to leave such matters to others, mainly in his absence, as though the lack of his physical presence absolved him in some way from responsibility.

'It's in the bag,' he replied shortly.

Williams nodded approval.

'Hope it's clean. You probably won't need it—'

'I should hope not!'

'—but if you do, it wouldn't be too healthy if it jammed on you. Better let me take a look when we get there.'

It was a fine spring morning, and Halloran did not choose to think about the heavy black revolver in his case, and especially he preferred not to think ahead to the moment when he might find himself compelled to use it.

'It's only a precaution,' he reminded. 'If everything goes

192

according to the book, I shouldn't have any need of it.'

The corners of Williams' mouth quirked into a shape of derision. According to the book, eh? That was typical of old George, that simplistic view. If A did his part, and B was on time, and C came up to requirements, everything would go like clockwork. That was what it said in the book, and, therefore, that was what should happen. Him and his book. Halloran always seemed to forget that A might lose his nerve, B could easily get held up at the traffic lights, and C might demand more money at the last minute. That was where he, Williams, came into his own. Checking, following up, pressurising. You worked according to the book, up until the actual operation. Then you threw it away, and handed over to someone like himself. Up until today it had all been a fascinating theoretical exercise. Today was different.

Today they were going to steal ten million pounds.

But not yet, he reminded himself, as he carefully negotiated the morning traffic. There were people to be seen, last minute checks to be made, a hundred and one details to be polished. The next few hours were going to be very busy.

'Pity about Baxter, in some ways.'

Halloran's change of subject cut into his thoughts.

'How d'you mean?'

'I mean he's a valuable man, and we might have been able to use him again. Don't misunderstand me, Basil, I know he has to go, but it's rather a waste.'

'I agree,' intoned Williams, to his companion's surprise.

'My sort of chap, that. Not just a muscle-man either. That business with the confession was a nice little touch. Put the frighteners on me, to start with. If it hadn't been for the governor's foresight, he might have had us going there.'

Gregory Ryder was, first and foremost, a meticulous planner. His trip to Washington D.C. was no anonymous, private affair. He would be visiting the United States as a distinguished man of affairs, following a timetable of consultation with officials of various government departments. Accompanying him, as part of a small entourage of experts and advisers, would be George Halloran and Basil Williams.

The men who were to carry out these impersonations had been carefully selected, months earlier. They were by no means doubles of the original pair, but bore sufficient physical characteristics to carry off their roles. On the night of the actual robbery, they would be among the hundred or so guests at a small reception given by no less a personage than the British Ambassador.

Ryder had taken all these precautions from the outset, not because he anticipated treachery from any particular quarter, but in order that his two chief lieutenants were aware of the comfort of his protection, even while he was three thousand miles away. All they needed to do was to maintain a low profile on the home front, and their security was assured.

With half the United States Senate, not to mention His Excellency, prepared to testify as to their whereabouts at the time of the great bullion robbery, Halloran and Williams had little to fear from any statements made by a dead and self-confessed thief, such as Philip Baxter. The Director of Public Prosecutions would probably apologise to them personally for any embarrassment caused.

'I still don't see,' announced Williams, as they waited at a red traffic light, 'why you're letting that man Leonides go. He could be a danger to us at some time.'

Halloran watched the little knot of pedestrians passing in front of the bonnet. This was an area where he often found himself in conflict with the man beside him. Williams' philosophy was very simple, too simple. Seek out possible danger spots and eradicate. To what extent his reasoning was prompted by an elementary logic, as compared to his natural joy in human destruction, Halloran had never entirely fathomed.

'Captain Leonides is a man with a long history,' he replied slowly. 'Over the years, he has developed a habit of conspiracy, of keeping his own counsel. More than one government would have been embarrassed if that man had chosen to talk. He has proved himself reliable, time and time again, over affairs of more significance than ours. All he wants now is a quiet life. A few old cronies, a chair in some harbour, a comfortable bed. He is no threat to us, and cheap at fifty thousand. On top of which, he is a valuable asset.'

He added the last part, almost as an afterthought, knowing that it would carry more weight with Williams than any sentiment about the benefits of retirement. His companion rose to the bait.

'Asset? In what way?'

'Israeli security people have long memories,' continued Halloran. 'Our interests are wide, Basil. It could be that one day we need to do business with the Mossad. How handy for us if we have a tasty extra up our sleeves, such as the whereabouts of one of the masterminds behind that Naples armaments hi-jack. That could buy us a lot of good will.'

Williams grinned, although his argument was lost. Cunning old sod, was George. Always thinking two jumps ahead, and he was right in his assessment. It could be useful to have Leonides tucked away, against such an eventuality. Let the old pirate go, then.

'Love fifteen,' he conceded, as they moved away.

* * *

Estelle made a final check around the room, and closed her suitcase carefully, locking it, and carrying it over to where its twin stood waiting by the door. That was the bulk of it done, she reflected. There now remained the vital matter of the sling bag she intended to carry with her.

Sitting on the bed, she tipped out the contents in a heap. Then she restored each item individually, ticking it off on a mental check-list. The more intimate pieces were quickly dealt with. Make-up, hairbrush, comb, etc. A small bunch of four keys made her thoughtful for a moment, then she thrust them inside. Finally, she was left with a small purse, an alligator wallet, and an envelope. The purse contained twenty pounds in notes of small denomination and a handful of coins, and would be used for various cash purchases during the day. The wallet was for later use. There was six hundred pounds inside it, plus credit cards, and this she placed into a special compartment inside the sling bag which had an independent zip. Only the envelope remained, and she opened it with care, although there was

195

nothing fragile about the contents. Her passport came out first. It was new, and she was secretly not displeased by the small photograph, which was a great improvement on some she had carried in the past. The name, too, was new, and had a certain ring to it. Estelle had a long history of passports, issued by various European governments, and always with a different name displayed. According to this one she was Estelle Hope-Amesbury, British Subject, and Citizen of the United Kingdom and Colonies. She had been born in London, was thirty years of age, one point seven metres in height, and her occupation was that of writer. Well, why not?

Next to the passport were two airline tickets for the following day, Sunday, destination Rio de Janeiro. This was no time for daydreaming, she reminded herself, and slipped them into the small pouch, along with the wallet, zipping it carefully. Then she stood up, slipped into the duffel coat which lay ready, and patted at the pocket where the gun rested.

Along with everyone else concerned, on that second Saturday in May, Estelle was ready to move.

*　　*　　*

In a telephone booth outside a public house in near-deserted dockland, a nondescript looking man spoke quietly into the mouthpiece.

'Our two friends are now together,' he reported. 'They're inside that vehicle repair firm which friend A visited earlier in the week. The place is empty, but for them. They were carrying two heavy-looking suitcases, and it's my guess they'll be staying for a while. Do I carry on?'

At the other end, Jennifer Fiske thought rapidly. Everything seemed to be coming together now, and the last thing they wanted was to have people from other departments anywhere on the scene. The decision would have to be hers, and it would have to be right.

She took a deep breath.

'Thank you, no. The department has no further interest in those people. Our thanks to your chief are in the pipeline.

196

Please discontinue as of now. Out.'

At the other end, the man heard the click of dismissal and shrugged, replacing the receiver.

Bloody amateurs, he reflected, wasting so much valuable time and manpower. James Bond had a lot to answer for. Still, and he cheered up at the prospect, at least he'd be able to watch *Match of the Day*.

CHAPTER TWENTY

Captain Michael Kokis was mildly concerned. He had expected that at some time during the day he would receive a sign from his employers, some small indication that all was well. Yet here it was four bells, just two hours away from zero hour, and nothing had happened. He stood on the bridge alone, staring pridefully at the spotless appearance of the *Sunderland Lady*. She couldn't have looked in much better trim on the day she was first launched. All that was lacking was the bunting, and the portly figure of some dignitary's wife swinging a bottle of champagne against her.

He stroked affectionately at the gleaming rail and went below. There were only a few people aboard now, in addition to himself. The mate, Rambert, and the five taciturn men who had accompanied him aboard at Marseilles. In his cabin, he poured himself a drink. There was a tap at the door, and the mate entered.

'It won't be long now,' greeted Kokis. 'Drink?'

Rambert shook his head.

'Thank you, no. I am to give you this.'

'This' was an envelope, which he now extended. Kokis took it, looked at the visitor thoughtfully, then slit it open. Inside was a banker's draft, made out to Marco Leonides, in the sum of fifty thousand pounds, and dated the previous day, Friday.

'I don't understand,' he frowned. 'Where did you get this?'

'I brought it aboard with me at Marseilles,' was the answer. 'My instructions were to hand it to you at this time, and assume command.'

'Assume—d'you mean you're kicking me off my own ship?' spluttered the captain.

'Certainly not,' Rambert assured him. 'You have done a splendid job, Captain, but it is finished. We now go into action, and our employers do not wish you to be exposed to the problems of the next few hours. You will leave the

Sunderland Lady with all ceremony, for a well-earned retirement.'

Although the man's tone was placatory, there was no mistaking the finality of his words. Ah well, so be it. On the whole, it was perhaps better this way. At least he would not have to witness the final degradation of the *Lady*. He would be able to remember her as she was at this moment, the late evening sun reflecting from every shiny surface.

Ten minutes later, he stood on the wharfside, staring up at her for the last time. From the rail Rambert saluted him, and without mockery.

Captain Kokis, né Marco Leonides, marched stiffly away to his retirement.

*   *   *

At two minutes to seven, Baxter called Mallory over to one corner of the warehouse, and tuned in the two-way radio.

'I want you to hear this.'

At precisely seven o'clock, Basil Williams' distinctive tones came from the tiny speaker.

'Station announcer,' he said briskly. 'Engineering check.'

'Go ahead, station,' replied Baxter. 'Engineers listening.'

'There will be no programme changes this evening. Repeat. No programme changes.'

'Thank you, station. Engineering works will proceed.'

Baxter switched off, and grinned at the American.

'Well, you heard him. Everything is at "Go". Call the men together, Joe, and we'll go through it with them.'

While Mallory gathered up the others, Baxter pinned up a rough drawing on the side of a wooden packing case. Up until that moment of final clearance, he had deliberately withheld the total picture from the men. Their main task had been to learn their own vital part in the scheme, and all briefing had been towards that end. It was now time for them to hear the whole plan, and for him to answer at last the many questions which had naturally arisen during the training period.

They stood around in a group, paying careful attention.

*   *   *

Albie Collins clucked with impatience as Joey hopped nimbly from the leading barge, and began to tie up. Ten to bleeding seven already, and they'd only just about scraped home, despite all his assistant's morning confidence.

'D'you know what?'

Joey's voice came clearly across the calm water.

'What? Nothing wrong is there?'

Please don't let there be anything wrong, he prayed. Morrie Glassman was not a man who understood about other people's misfortunes.

'It's these mooring rings,' came the reply. 'They're brand new.'

'Well, there you are then.'

Brand new, eh? There was something coming off here, all right, and Albie was anxious to know nothing whatever about it. Obviously Mr. Glassman, or somebody else, had foreseen the possibility that the gear on the old St. Augustus wharf would be rotted and rusted. It was important, for some reason, that the barges should not drift away. Well, they needn't worry about that. Them barges would be tied up tighter than a chicken's backside. The only drifting away was going to be done by a certain Albert Collins and his stupid assistant. And the sooner the better. Albie grabbed at the coil of rope up forward.

''Ere,' he shouted. 'Catch.'

*   *   *

'That's funny.'

Flynn, seated in a little recreation room at the top of the bullion building, looked up from his newspaper, to where Page was staring out of a window.

'What's funny?' he demanded.

'Down there,' said Page, pointing. 'There's a couple of barges tying up. Full of old tyres, by the look of 'em. What d'you suppose they're up to?'

Flynn sighed and got up. Might as well take a look. Anything was a break from the endless monotony of the

200

shift. He stared across to where two men were busily making a couple of ancient barges secure.

'How do I know?' he grunted. 'Just knocking off for the day, I expect.'

'Bit rum, though. I mean, nothing's ever tied up there before. I think the chief ought to know.'

'Suit yourself.'

The shift foreman, a man named Hoskins, reported the arrival of the barges to security headquarters as a matter of routine. The information was duly logged and forgotten. What could possibly be significant about a heap of old tyres?

*   *   *

The motor launch, reluctant donation of a certain fat restaurateur, had proved to be a runaway success. It had fulfilled its prime purpose, which was that of checking on the *Sunderland Lady* for outward and visible signs of official restraint, but it had done more. It had given Wang Teh's men an added interest in their task of routine surveillance. It was infinitely more rewarding to ride up and down the river in a powerful craft than to sit for hours at the window of a dingy rooming-house, with binoculars trained on the wharf exits. Wang Teh prided himself on his adaptability to changed circumstances, and on an innate skill in utilising all available resources. As soon as he witnessed the effect on his men of their small river-trip, he was quick to organise similar inspections at two-hourly intervals. The new patrols added a welcome spice to the day's routine, enabling the hours to pass more pleasantly.

The man from the last of these jaunts had reported seeing someone of importance leaving the *Sunderland Lady*, possibly even the captain himself. Well, if it was the captain, mused Wang Teh, they could be confident that nothing would happen in his absence. It would be a foolish chieftain indeed, who left matters of such delicacy to the blundering fingers of subordinates. If the captain was really ashore, then the brandy would remain where it was until he returned.

But Wang Teh, man of prudence that he was, kept his

201

own counsel in this matter, and vigilance was maintained at peak level.

* * *

At eight o'clock that evening, the sun was on the wane, shooting great blood-red fingers along the peaceful Thames. First Officer Paul Rambert, acting captain of the s.s. *Sunderland Lady*, checked his watch. It was time to start the engines. He gave the order calmly, and was rewarded at once by the sensation of deep, rhythmic throbbing below his feet. He would now allow a few minutes of warm-up, although it was not strictly necessary. It was his intention to spend the time in last-minute checks on each of his men, and their equipment. There were three men on deck, awaiting his instructions. The other two were below.

He strolled towards the little group unhurriedly. It was essential in an operation of this kind that there should be no appearance of haste. Everyone's nerves were keyed up, which was as it should be, but there was a fine edge between a state of high preparedness and panic action. Rambert had dealt with this kind of situation many times in the past, and knew how to handle it.

He addressed the men by numbers, combat style.

'One and Two!' he barked.

One spoke for them both.

'On the command we will open the aft tanks. When they are half empty, we will open the forward tanks. Then—'

'Wait!' Rambert turned to the third man.

'Three?'

'While tanks are unloading, Three, Four and Five will launch the small boat.'

'Having first done what?' snapped the mate.

'After checking that the petrol cans and flame-throwers are aboard,' said a crestfallen Three.

Rambert glowered at him and turned back to the others. 'Continue.'

'When forward tanks are almost empty, we take up positions in the dinghy.'

The interrogation continued until every last point had

been covered. Finally, Rambert nodded his satisfaction.

'All right, lads. Stand to. I'm taking her out.'

To the east, there were already signs of the gathering darkness as it closed snugly around the murmuring river, while to the west, the great red orb was throwing its final sky-patterns as it sank slowly beyond the far horizon.

In the recreation room Security Guard Page was still seated at the window, never tiring of his beloved Thames. It had been quite interesting, that evening. First of all there had been those two geezers with their barges full of rubbish, then that launch-load of Chinese, chasing up and down. They didn't seem to go very far each time, and Page could see no point to it. Must be some kind of Chinky holiday, he decided, although he had some vague notion they always used fire-crackers. Now here came this ship, a regular ocean-goer, but a bit closer to the banks than he was used to seeing them. Hallo, she seemed to be stopping. Could she be in some kind of trouble, he wondered? It was hard to see clearly in the diminishing light, but it looked as though something was pouring out of the sides of her. Yes. There must be some trouble. They were lowering a boat down the side.

'Here, take a look at this,' he said urgently. 'I think those blokes have got some kind of emergency. Call the chief up.'

Rambert leaned over the side, watching the diesel as it roared unhampered from the forward tanks to settle on top of the heavy crude which was already a great black pool on the surface of the water. He waved a hand, and One and Two clambered over the side to join their comrades in the dinghy. Criminal or not, Rambert was basically a man of the sea, and he hated this ultimate betrayal of an honest vessel.

'Go with God,' he muttered, and swung over the side.

One and Two were ready with their flame-throwers, and awaiting the final order.

'Take us round to starboard,' clipped Rambert.

This was the tricky part. Any fool could start a fire. Getting away from one in safety was an entirely different kettle of fish.

*　　　*　　　*

203

'The ship, master, it is gone.'

Wang Teh stared at the breathless man in front of him, his voice jerking out the words. What was this fool telling him?

'Gone?' he repeated.

'Gone. I have run all the way here.'

She could not be gone. It was not possible. There was Western trickery here, for was not the fire-wine still aboard? The *Sunderland Lady* was moving, yes, but only to a new rendezvous, where fellow-conspirators would be waiting. Well, she was slow, but the launch was fast.

'Into the car at once. Everyone.'

They raced to the tiny harbour, where the launch bobbed gently on the evening tide. Only one of his men was capable of taking the helm, and that inexpertly. Now they edged their cautious way out into the darkening river, for Wang Teh dare not risk any lights. Then he gave the order to proceed, with everyone gathered on the port side, straining their eyes into the gloom, their progress seeming intolerably slow. Minutes ticked away.

'There,' said one man urgently, pointing.

Everyone concentrated on the direction indicated by his stabbing finger. There was a shape, yes, something. A ship, definitely a ship, but not moving. The question was, what ship? One looked like another to their untrained eyes. They needed positive identification, and the only way was to get in close. The launch slowed, and nosed inward.

Rambert had heard the powerful launch minutes earlier, and was now puzzled by the absence of lights, and the sudden throttling down of the engine. River police?

'Rambert, look.'

He and his men were now acclimatised to the poor light, and he could clearly make out the prow of a fast launch, heading for the *Sunderland Lady*. This could not be any official craft, he realised. There would be lights and loud-hailers, not this creeping anonymity. Whoever it was, they must be warned off, and quickly. Already they were at the edge of the spreading oil, and this was no time for lengthy explanations.

Rambert drew his revolver, aimed slightly to the side of

the advancing intruder and fired once, twice. It was a heavy calibre weapon, and the shots boomed resoundingly in the still evening air. His men, ready to move into their planned action, watched the dark outline with impatience.

Wang Teh had spotted the dinghy seconds before, and was puzzling as to what it could mean. Then he saw orange flashes coming from one of the standing figures, and there was no mistaking the familiar sound of gunfire. He was under attack, and must decide at once what was to be done. The time for stealth was past. He must either withdraw immediately, or fight. Fifteen yards of water separated the two craft, and he had no guns. Prudence dictated retreat, but that would cause him loss of face with the puzzled and angry men around him. Worse would follow, when he was called upon to explain the failure to achieve the prized objective. The launch was four times the size of the small boat containing the enemy, and would crush it like a beetle underfoot.

'Aim for that boat,' he ordered, and the helmsman turned the wheel slightly. 'Everyone lie flat, until we are close. You, Chang, send them our greetings.'

Chang pulled off his shirt, to give full play to the rippling muscles of his chest and arms, and tossed the gleaming hatchet from hand to hand while his feet gained a proper grip on the floorboards of the launch. Then he swayed from side to side, leaned back, and flung the weapon towards the approaching enemy with enormous strength and unerring direction.

Rambert thought he heard a faint whistling sound in the darkness, then there was a sudden flash of metal, and a sickening, crunching sound. His Number Four man gave a thin animal wail and took a step back. The others turned to him in alarm, in time to see the hatchet hanging from his chest like some alien growth. Four pivoted on one foot, then pitched headlong over the side.

Two, standing ready with his flame-thrower, waited for no instruction now. Setting the nozzle control to the full position, he directed a stream of fire directly at the launch. She caught at once, and there were screams of agony from the target. Rambert was astonished to see several Chinese faces lit up by that unholy illumination, but there was no time now for speculation. The dinghy was already floating on the crude oil, and the diesel was no more than ten yards away, and spreading. The diesel would catch quickly, generating enough heat to set off the crude, but there would be those few precious seconds which would be their escape line.

'Forget them,' he ordered. 'Fire the oil as far away as possible. Engine, full steam.'

Two angled the weapon, and a second stream of fire disappeared into the blackness. There was a dull boom, and a great sheet of flame rose suddenly from the water, lighting up the hull of the *Sunderland Lady*, and the burning outline of the mystery launch. Rambert saw two blazing figures leap from the intruder into what they imagined to be the river, changing instantly into two pointing pillars of fire as they broke the surface. Wang Teh beat his blazing arms against the wheelhouse, just as the engine exploded, and the holocaust engulfed them all. Intermingled with the smoke was the new and appalling smell of burning flesh.

Then the dinghy was round the lee of the *Lady*, and heading for the river bank. Those few yards seemed to take an interminable time to cover and then there was the joyous feeling of the nose bumping, and they leaped thankfully ashore.

One bent double, and vomited.

'Those poor bastards,' he moaned.

There was no time for chatter of that kind.

'The barges,' shouted Rambert. 'Lively now.'

Five grabbed up his five gallon can of petrol and trotted to the nearest barge. Rambert clacked with annoyance. Why wasn't the other barge being dealt with? Where the hell—ah yes. That had been Four's assignment, and Four was now dead, floating face down in that creeping inferno at the other side of the *Lady*. Rambert snatched up the waiting can himself and ran off towards the leading barge, where he poured the contents over the heaped tyres. Then he ran back to the others.

'Smoke masks,' he ordered, putting on his own at the same time.

206

A quick check to see that the men had followed suit, and he tapped One on the shoulder, nodding. At the same time, he waved the others back. One directed his flame-thrower at the first barge and discharged fire at it. A great yellow sheet of flame leaped high in the air, and One gave his attention to the second target, which erupted even more violently than the first.

'Weapons away!' shouted Rambert.

One and Two leaned back, like discus-throwers at an athletic event, and the two flame-throwers sailed away in a high arc, to splash in the oily waters around the stern of the *Lady*.

'That's it,' barked the mate, and the five figures trotted away into the night, and a waiting van.

It was eight-thirty-one p.m.

From the observation window of the bullion warehouse, men stared down in horror at the inferno below. From their isolated perch it was hard to appreciate that what they were seeing was real. Everything had happened in a matter of seconds. First, the fire-streak from the ship's dinghy, illuminating and then setting ablaze a larger vessel which the watching men had not realised was there. An explosion, as the flaming figures of living men were tossed into the air like rag dolls, then a second, deeper sound, as the river itself erupted in a raging wall of fire. The shift foreman, Hoskins, did not witness the final act, as the two barges were put to the torch. He was already on his way to the control room to summon the emergency services. The operator responded immediately.

'Which service, please?'

'All of 'em,' he shouted hoarsely. Then, more calmly, 'Start with the fire brigade.'

CHAPTER TWENTY-ONE

The headquarters of the London Fire Brigade is located on the Albert Embankment, and is the nerve centre for all six hundred and ten square miles of the Greater London area. Operationally, this vast complex is split into three control areas, dealing with more than two thousand emergency calls per week. Constantly at the alert condition is one of the celebrated fireboats, with its special river service trained crewmen.

The jerky and emotional message from foreman Hoskins was received at central control, and transferred smoothly into immediate response from the control room at Stratford, in F Division. The call received an initial classification as an 'A' risk, requiring three pumping appliances, plus a hydraulic platform, with automatic back-up from the fireboat.

From the leading appliance, Station Officer Porter could already make out the billowing smoke column against the late evening sky, as they sped down Chandlers Way, slowing at the excavation, and taking care to avoid the barrier lamps. Then they could see the fire itself, as they came out of the road and negotiated their careful way among the rusted machinery and potholes of the abandoned dock workings, towards the roaring river and the flame-lit outline of the *Sunderland Lady*.

Porter took in the whole scene with keen professional eyes, and realised thankfully that there was virtually no danger of spread. The nearest building was the big warehouse away to his left, which must be at least a hundred and fifty yards clear of the seat of the fire. In the same instant he realised something else, something less comforting. There was no sign of life on ship or shore, and that made no sense. The *Sunderland Lady* had no right to be where she was, and must have been under steam when the fire broke out. Porter knew that a ship of that size would have a crew of probably two dozen men or more, so where were they? It looked as if he might be facing a major disaster, with considerable loss of life. And what the devil were those barges doing there?

The first appliance was already in action now, using its own five hundred gallon load, while crewmen located and connected up to hydrants. The smoke was a real hazard, thick and oily, and any shift in the wind would necessitate the donning of breathing apparatus. Porter was anxious to delay that order as long as possible. The life support in the compressed air cylinders was less than one hour's duration, and he knew from long experience that this particular outbreak would take many hours to control. The fireboat would be on its way, but even flat out it could not reach the scene for another forty minutes.

Meantime, there was this mystery of the missing crew.

He switched on his radio and began to transmit.

'Hallo Control, this is Foxtrot Two Three . . .'

*   *   *

Thirty yards from the junction in Rope Street, the huge petrol bowser squatted against the kerb like some giant insect. The driver was staring out of the cab window, fascinated by the thirty foot flames licking at the sky from the direction of the river. Must be a big warehouse or something, he reflected. Four gleaming fire engines had already passed the end of the street and by the look of that lot, more would be needed. Well, if they wanted to go down Rope Street, they'd better get a move on. There was going to be a nasty accident there at any minute. He looked at his watch. Eight-forty-four. About time he got the signal. He turned away from the red sky and stared straight ahead. Come on, come on. Ah, there it was. Three rapid blinks of distant headlights. The other man was ready for him.

Reaching over, he switched on the heavy engine, and rolled gently forward. The other lights were moving now, and approaching steadily. At the entrance to Rope Street, the bowser turned gently to the right, then slowed to a snail's pace. The other vehicle was coming fast now. At this rate he ought to hit the bowser smack in the middle. Straddling the T-junction, the big container stopped, and the driver jumped clear, almost missing his footing in the blackness of the street. No bloody street lights, he reflected.

209

Typical.

There was no time for further thinking because the great lowloader was almost at the junction. At the last second, the other driver slammed on his brakes and swerved, as though to avoid a collision. The effect was that the cab slewed around to the right, but the great container, skidding hopelessly out of control, smashed against the metal body of the bowser, crushing it inwards.

The bowser driver rushed to the scene of the impact and turned a stopcock, then another, stepping quickly out of the way as petrol poured in two great streams to the cobbled surface of the road.

The doors of the public house were opening now, and people hurrying out to see what all the noise was about. There were shouts of alarm at the sight of the two giant transporters locked as if in mortal combat, followed quickly by fear at the unmistakable sharp smell of petrol.

'Put that fag out, for Christ's sake.'

'Somebody get the fire-brigade.'

'Where's the driver? See if the driver's all right.'

It was now eight forty-five p.m.

*   *   *

By ten minutes to nine the only way remaining to the site of the disaster was down Chandlers Way, and already it was beginning to jam with traffic. A long narrow street, and pitch dark, through some mysterious failure of the street lights, it would not have been an ideal thoroughfare under any circumstances. As things were, with half the width of the road dug up, it was close to a nightmare. People seemed to be pouring in from all sides to get a close view of the great blaze on the river, adding their private cars to the stream of emergency vehicles, television crews and newsmen from every agency in the capital. And now, some idiot had broken down alongside the cavernous hole, delaying everything.

The man in the safety hat was only one of many helmeted figures jostling on the pavement, yelling instructions and contradictions at each other and the crawling traffic. Melting into the shadows at the extreme edge of the hole, the man dropped down and was lost to view. No-one was interested in him, anyway. He picked his way carefully along, thankful for the careful survey he had made earlier in the day. He soon found what he wanted, a large diameter pipe of rusted metal. Beneath it, and carefully covered with loose earth, was a fourteen-pound hammer, which he quickly freed. There was something else, too; an oddly shaped lump of concrete, with a curved base which would enable it to sit over the pipe. In the centre of this block was an inch-wide hole. He took a cold chisel from his pocket and positioned it with care in the aperture of the concrete mould. Only two inches of the chisel protruded.

He looked quickly upwards and around, to ensure that he was not being observed. Then he hefted the hammer, swung it high above his head. One blow was sufficient, and the metal sank into the pipe. A second blow, sideways now, and the concrete shattered, knocking the chisel clear at the same time. There was a ragged hole in the pipe, but he could not see it clearly, and so he inserted two fingers into the torn metal to satisfy himself.

Good enough.

With no sign of haste, he walked back along the wide trench, and heaved himself up to street level. There, he went across to where a police inspector was speaking rapidly into a walkie-talkie.

'You in charge?' he demanded.

'Not now sir, I'm busy,' snapped the officer.

'You'll be busier in a minute,' was the calm reply. 'There's gas coming out of that hole.'

The inspector stopped speaking then, and stared at him. 'Gas?'

Others nearby had heard the exchange.

'What's all this about gas? Where? What gas?'

'Did he say gas?'

There was excitement in the hurried questions, but there was also something else, more urgent. There was fear.

The inspector gazed at the traffic-packed street, and something akin to despair began to gnaw at him. The first thing, of course, was to check the facts, but his informant

211

was gone, caught up in an unruly crowd which had rushed to the excavation, to find out for themselves.

'Quickstep One,' whispered the inspector urgently. 'Advise Gas Board of suspected major leak on Chandlers Way now. I say now. And I need gas masks down here. Seal off entrance. No further traffic down Chandlers Way—'

There was shouting now, up in the darkness by the excavation. A woman screamed.

It was eight fifty-five p.m.

*   *   *

In the warehouse, a feeling of unreality was beginning to permeate through the security guards. Not a hundred yards away, brave men were battling against a gigantic fire, hampered by the ever-thickening blanket of menacing smoke which poured first from the bargeloads of tyres, and now, seemingly, from the river itself. There was no longer the vivid clarity of those first awful minutes. The scene was now illuminated only in sudden flashes from the heart of the fire, obscured at once by the evil swirling clouds. Out there, men had died, and perhaps others were dying as they watched, but inside, everything seemed normal. Even the sound was denied to them, owing to the heavy protection of the sheath of the building and the triple glazing at the windows.

They experienced a common feeling of helplessness, in their hermetically-sealed cage, a sense of isolation from the outer reality. It was Flynn who put it into words.

'Makes you feel so bleeding useless,' he remarked sadly.

No-one replied, but they all knew what he meant. It just didn't seem fair that they should be tucked safely away in their private world, while all hell was breaking loose outside. No harm could come to them, because there was no possibility of the fire spreading as far as the warehouse. The planners had seen to that, by ensuring there was no building of any description within a sizeable radius. Even the smoke presented no threat. It was already close, and would get closer, but it was of no importance. Even if it enveloped the whole building, they would be immune from harm, in their private bubble. They were safe, they were secure, they were comfortable. Even so, Flynn had hit the nail on the head, as they all privately agreed.

They felt so bleeding useless.

*   *   *

Baxter listened to the calm tones on the radio, and grinned.

'Roger,' he acknowledged. 'Engineers out, and packing up now.'

He switched off, and turned to the expectant Mallory, nodding.

'Chandlers Way is now sealed off,' he confirmed. 'We should be the last vehicles to have got through. Your time?'

Mallory inspected his watch. It was exactly nine o'clock.

'Twenty-one hundred.'

'Check.'

Baxter looked around at the waiting convoy.

The O'Rourkes sat ready in the cab of the shining red hydraulic platform. In the ambulances, the white-coated figures of McLeish, Graham, Judd and Ginger Davis sat watching him. Sparkes and Gloomy Porter, dressed in their firemen uniforms, stood waiting by the doors of the warehouse. Baxter waved to them, then swung aboard the tender, followed by Mallory.

'Let's go,' he shouted.

The gleaming tender roared into life as the great wooden doors pivoted slowly open, then she rolled easily forward and out into the blackness of the night, Sparkes and Porter jumping aboard at the last second.

They approached the bullion warehouse from the blind side, and there was no-one to observe their arrival, or to take any particular notice if they had. The little armada was arriving from the general direction of Chandlers Way, and would excite no special interest.

As soon as the tender was in position, the O'Rourkes took command of the fire-fighters, including Mallory. Baxter jumped to the ground, directing the ambulances to their rehearsed positions below the central windows of the tall structure, rear doors open, and facing the wall. The whole convoy was now screened from the site of the fire. The

213

drivers leaped out and ran to the rear, each climbing inside his own vehicle, removing the short-barrelled rifle which was clipped to the roof, and fixing a gas-shell into position. Baxter stood with his back to the wall, a position from which he could see each man as he dropped into a crouched stance, ready to fire, rifle angled up towards the windows. He raised his arm, held it upright for a few seconds, then dropped it. There was a single cracking sound, as the four men fired in unison, and, above their heads, four holes appeared in the warehouse windows. The marksmen re-loaded at once, and a second volley followed the first. The shells contained the latest riot-control gas used by the inter-national peace-keeping forces, and would render the men inside unconscious within seconds. After a few hours, they would recover their senses, with nothing more serious than a raging headache to cope with.

On the extension ladder, Desmond O'Rourke stood in the railed platform, grim-faced, waiting for the signal. His brother Shaun waited by the platform controls.

Inside the warehouse, the three guards who were on the ground level heard the unwelcome sound of breaking glass, and checked around for the source. They were still gaping in astonishment at the regularly spaced holes, when the second volley came crashing through, and ended all specu-lation. Thin grey clouds were already rising from the first shells, and they looked at each other in alarm.

'Bombs,' yelled one. 'We're being bombed.'

But one man had had some military experience, and he knew better.

'No,' he shouted. 'It's gas. We need the smoke-masks.'

They all rushed to the control room, where their chief, Hoskins, was keeping in touch with security headquarters, and had just learned of the closing of Chandlers Way. Being inside the cubicle, he had not heard the disturbance, and stared in astonishment at the white-faced men who now burst in.

'We're being gassed,' ejaculated one. 'Smoke-masks, quick.'

Above their heads he could now see the wreathing va-pour rising from several directions, and wasted no time on

214

discussion. Rising at once, he opened the emergency cupboard and removed the masks from their pegs, tossing one
to each man in turn, and swiftly donning one himself.

'Where are the others?' he demanded.

One of the men pointed towards the ceiling with his
finger, indicating that Page and Flynn were still up in the
recreation room. He thrust two more masks into the hands
of the nearest man, who understood at once, and raced
away.

Control, thought Hoskins, they must be told. Hurriedly
he made contact, reluctant to remove his mouth from the
protecting mask, even for a few seconds.

'Gas,' he reported briefly. 'We are being gassed. No further messages. Help us.'

Thankfully, he pushed the facepiece back into position,
and concentrated on this new development. Clearly this
was the first step in a robbery. There was no point in attacking them, except to obtain the bullion, but the point was,
how did they hope to get in? The doors were invulnerable,
the windows too high, and there was no weak point anywhere. Except perhaps—

The roof.

A helicopter could land on the roof. He remembered
raising the point once, long ago, but the answer had been
simple.

'Yes it could. A dozen men could land, and overcome you
in a few minutes. But to what point? It would take ages to
shift the gold, and we'd have the place swarming with
policemen inside fifteen minutes.'

A good answer, and a true one, but not valid in these
circumstances. Nobody was going to come swarming from
anywhere, now that Chandlers Way, the last access road,
had been closed. They were alone. Right. They weren't
going to be trapped down here like rats. There was air up on
the roof, and these invaders, whoever they were, were
going to have a fight on their hands.

Waving at the others to follow, Hoskins stormed out of
the cubicle and into the main area, where the gas was still
spreading from the hissing shells. He dashed through it, the
rest close behind, heading for the metal stairway in the

215

corner. There was a figure lying at the foot of it. It was Smith, the man who had taken the extra masks for Page and Flynn. Must have tripped, thought Hoskins. Then he noticed that Smith didn't seem to be touching the ground at all. He was floating above it in a kind of dance. Around him, the steel shelves were swaying as if to some hidden music. The roof was reaching down towards him, and then pulling away just as he was about to grasp at it. Hoskins stopped to ponder these new phenomena, just as a yellow fog passed in front of his eyes. No, wait. Not in front. The fog was inside his eyes. How do you suppose that got there? He'd be able to think better on his knees, he decided. Yes, that would be the thing. He ought to tell the others. After all, three could think better than one, but they had already anticipated him, he found. They'd gone one better, and were lying flat on the concrete, thinking. There was a stinging now, at his nose and eyes, as he crumpled slowly to the ground. Have to complain at the next security conference. These smoke-masks, they didn't seem to be any bloody—

In the recreation room Page turned his eyes reluctantly away from the great drama on the river bank. He'd been lucky, really, to have had it all happen during his break, but he'd have to leave it now. Somebody else's turn.

'Come on Flynnie, time's up.'

There was an urgent banging at the emergency fire door leading to the roof. The two guards looked at each other in astonishment. It wasn't possible for anyone to be on the roof. It just wasn't possible. The hammering was repeated. Page went to the small window, little larger than a ship's porthole, which looked out onto the roof. Outside, in the dirty smoke, a fireman stood waiting, another behind him. They waved urgently at the staring man inside, pointing to their military-seeming gas-masks.

'It's the bleeding fire-brigade,' he reported, his voice unbelieving. 'Something about gas.'

'Well, don't stand there,' shouted Flynn. 'Let 'em in. It's not a social call.'

Even then, Page hesitated. No admission to anyone under any circumstances, this was the rule, the inviolable rule, and his limbs refused to carry out the half-hearted instruction from his brain. There was an impatient snort beside him, and Flynn was at the door, shifting the heavy levers. The thick door swung open and the masked firemen entered quickly. Swiftly they scanned the room, then Des O'Rourke nodded to the man behind him, and struck out at the unsuspecting Page. At the same moment, Sparkes dealt Flynn a savage blow to the head, and both guards lay on the floor. O'Rourke went forward to check on the situation in the warehouse below.

The riot gas had levelled off at a height of ten feet from the ground level, and the effect was similar to that of looking down on a fog from a low-flying aircraft. There was no sign of activity down there, as he began his descent, to check on the remaining four guards.

Sparkes was already advancing along the catwalk on the blind side of the building, and freeing his axe, in readiness for the task of knocking out the remaining glass in the broken windows. Behind him, Joe Mallory, Shaun O'Rourke and Gloomy Porter had already reached the roof, and were hauling up the square plastic bundles of the escape chutes.

These had been Mallory's idea. The physical task of removing the two-kilo gold blocks had to be reduced to the least possible effort both within and without. Apart from the exertion required, there was the element of time, plus the ever present danger of someone from the real emergency services arriving on the scene. It was no part of the plan to waste precious time fighting a ground-battle with those people and Mallory's suggestion covered all the requirements.

'Escape chutes,' he had said.

Baxter was not quite clear as to what he meant.

'I don't get it,' he admitted.

'Simple. We take in escape chutes, the ones they use to evacuate the passengers if an aircraft is in trouble on the ground. You know the things, they're like giant sausage skins. The passengers roll down inside, and the rescue boys are waiting at the bottom. We run them straight from the windows to the rear of the ambulances. The drivers only have to move the bars about six or seven feet, to stack them.

217

If anybody comes along, the chutes are there to evacuate the guards.'

And now there was Mallory himself, framed in an empty window space, and tossing out the first of the heavy plastic skins, to the roar of compressed air as it assumed its tunnel shape. Cookie McLeish was ready and waiting for its arrival and quickly made the necessary adjustments. Jimmy Sparkes was already in position at the next window, with Oz Graham ready behind his ambulance.

Des O'Rourke had satisfied himself that there would be no complications from the unconscious men on the warehouse floor, and now gave his attention to the stacks of gold bars. He had expected to be overwhelmed by the sight of so much gold, but in fact there was a sense of almost anticlimax. One bar, all by itself, would have prompted lively imaginings of wealth and high living, financial independence for life. But to see hundreds of them, stacked in rows as they were, was to strip them of all imagery. They were now a load which had to be shifted, and for all the excitement they roused in him, they might just as well have been bricks on a building site. Well, not quite, he realised as he picked up the first one. No builder's brick ever weighed like this beauty.

Outside, Baxter watched anxiously as the masked figure above waved. This was the first one, and the point was, would the weight prove too much for the fabric, tough as it was? The chutes were constructed to take far heavier loads, but those loads were people. Soft, resilient bodies, which would bounce gently from one position to the next. These blocks had corners, which could conceivably dig and tear at the inside of the plastic tunnels. They would soon know.

Joe Mallory placed the block carefully in position, then slid it gently forward. Owing to the sharpness of the angle, the heavy gold did not tip, but gathered impetus rapidly on the way down, slowing as the angle levelled out, and finally coming to a halt a few feet away from the waiting hands of Cookie McLeish.

Baxter stared at it thankfully. It was going to work. Now he walked along to the other ambulances, holding up his thumbs to the silhouetted figures above, and the transfer began in earnest.

The clearance work at the collision site at the entrance to Rope Street was still hampered by the crush of traffic. With the closing of Chandlers Way, the tailback had increased rapidly, with the result that heavy equipment, essential for the road-clearance job, was held fast in the queue, some quarter of a mile off.

A Chief Superintendent of Police strode grimly past the impatient queue, heading for Rope Street. Summoned from his home by an alert duty officer, he had visited the emergency operations room at the local station, and quickly understood the need for his presence. The urgent radio messages coming in from all sides painted a picture which was not unlike the nuclear attack rehearsals with which he was all too familiar.

First there was this extraordinary fire on the river itself, with some cargo ship ablaze, plus a lot of unconfirmed reports about several people having died. Thank God some of the emergency people had managed to reach the site before access had been cut off, but they would have to go it alone for the present. Then there was this major collision at Rope Street, with thousands of gallons of petrol splashing around. To top it all off, the next road, which presented the only other way of reaching the blaze on the river, was effectively sealed by a major leakage of gas. Some road engineer was going to be castrated for that one. Meantime, everything seemed to have ground to a halt. The fire brigade back-up was blocked, and by being blocked, was preventing the approach of the heavy-rescue equipment, which in turn was delaying the Gas Board emergency crew. On top of it all was the ever-present risk of fire, from the petrol in Rope Street and the gas in Chandlers Way. The final touch was added by the apparent failure in the local electricity supply. The Chief Super was not a man to sit in a control room, drinking coffee, with all that pandemonium out on the street. He had to go and see for himself, to get the feel of the situation on site, and he was getting it now. Looking at coloured pins stuck on a plan was no substitute for on-site inspection. Now, as he walked past the worried, straining faces on all sides, he could feel the enormous frustration in the air. It just didn't seem possible, he reflected, for so many routine disasters to come together in one place, and at one time. It was as bad as anything he'd seen on the emergency committee mock-ups. A man could almost think some lunatic had planned it.

*　　*　　*

There were normally a dozen or more vehicles in various stages of repair in the body shop, but tonight it was almost empty. The owner had treated the whole staff to a weekend in France, the only condition being that there must be no unfinished jobs outstanding. As a result, all the work had been completed. The men had had an anxious moment when a decrepit five-ton lorry had arrived a few minutes before knocking-off time. It was from a brickyard, and needed a complete overhaul, which would have taken several hours. But the boss had given a philosophical shrug, and accepted that they could not do the impossible. The lorry could wait, but the ferry-boat to France could not, and everyone left on time.

George Halloran and Basil Williams sat in the foreman's office, a powerful radio on the table between them. There was nothing for them to do now but wait. Outside in the night, months of careful planning was now being put in to dramatic practice, and, so far, everything was working well. Careful monitoring of the low-frequency transmissions had kept them abreast of each development among the standby services, and there had been nothing which they had not foreseen. They would be receiving their first live report at any moment now, when the Frenchmen arrived.

Right on cue, a red light flashed on the wall, indicating that someone was outside the steel roller-doors. Halloran pushed the button on the panel below the light, and the shutters clattered upwards. A small dark van drove in to the empty shop, and the shutters closed behind it.

Halloran and Williams went out to meet the men from the s.s. *Sunderland Lady*. There were only five of them, which was odd. The two groups stared at each other.

'Which one is Rambert?'

'At your service, monsieur. You are the paymaster?'

A grim-faced man stepped forward, his eyes unnaturally bright among the soot-streaked features. Halloran didn't like the look of him, nor of the silent group behind him. Neither did Williams, who kept a hand in his jacket pocket.

'I am,' agreed Halloran. 'Where is the sixth man?'

'He is dead. Murdered,' was the response.

It was the very flatness of the man's tone which gave the words more dramatic impact than any outburst of excitement would have achieved.

'Murdered?' echoed Williams, drawing in his breath. 'I don't understand that. Murdered by whom?'

'By the yellow ones.'

Rambert did not explain further. He was watching the faces of the two Englishmen for signs of treachery. This job had gone badly wrong. It was all supposed to have been straightforward, no complications, and the question of violence had never arisen. The most he had expected was that they might have had to deal with a couple of unarmed policemen, and that would not have called for murder. The intervention of the Chinese had changed all that. One of his men was dead, and, but for their quick response, the rest of them would have joined him in the blazing river. Instead, they were multiple murderers, with five or more dead Chinamen to answer for. There would be repercussions in Marseilles for this, where the state of truce with the yellow gangsters was always uneasy. The question now in Rambert's mind was, did these Englishmen know?

Halloran and Williams exchanged a quick glance, but neither could explain what the Frenchman was driving at.

'Yellow ones?' queried Williams. 'Do you mean Chinamen? What the devil have they got to do with this?'

Halloran was puzzled too, but his mind was racing away. There must be some connection between what Rambert was saying and the Chinese workers who had fitted those extra tanks on the *Sunderland Lady*. But what?

'Did you speak with them?' he demanded.

Rambert smiled, making his face more wolfish than ever.

'There was no time,' he replied. 'They are all dead. Five, six, perhaps more.'

'Jesus.'

Williams' solitary expletive did more to convince Rambert than any flurry of words. That, and the stricken expression on both faces looking at him. It was Halloran who finally broke the silence.

'Monsieur, we cannot explain this. It simply makes no sense. We have no quarrel with any Chinese people, indeed, we have no dealings with them at all. Five or six dead, you say? This is appalling.'

He was not referring to the fact of death. With an operation of this magnitude, the possibility of a few people having to die was ever present, and an acceptable consequence. His concern was that an armed force of Chinese should be involved in the affair at all. Halloran was fully aware of the international scale on which those people worked, and their unwelcome intervention was entirely unexpected.

'You realise, monsieur, that the position is now changed.'

It was not a question, but a statement of fact. Williams tightened his grip on the gun in his pocket. He didn't like the look of these johnnies at all. There were five of them to their two, and the five had already killed as many men that night.

'Changed?' His voice was ugly. 'How do you mean, changed?'

Rambert had known, from the first confrontation, that Williams was the danger-man of the two. The hand, so firmly entrenched in the Englishman's pocket, was not clutching a tobacco-pouch.

'A man is dead. There will be the matter of compensation,' pointed out the first mate. 'Also, there is the question of the yellow ones. They have many friends in Marseilles, and The Club may face unforeseen difficulties. These things were not in the agreement, and The Club will be an angry man.'

What he was saying was no more than the plain truth, and both the listeners knew it. Jean Pagnol was not a man to be taken lightly, if he felt there had been any betrayal. The more urgent question was what these menacing Frenchmen proposed to do next. Halloran, fearing that Williams might

222

take a belligerent attitude, spoke quickly.

'What you say is true,' he conceded, 'and all we can do is to assure you this whole affair is as much a surprise to us as it has been to you. Naturally, we shall have to explain the position to M. Pagnol.'

Rambert hesitated, uncertain as to whether there was betrayal here. His instinct was to kill these people, but this was not some ordinary dockside war. The Englishmen owed money to The Club, and the quick satisfaction of their deaths would be no compensation for their boss's anger if he was not paid. Some kind of compromise solution was needed.

He nodded his head.

'Very well, it shall be as you say. You, monsieur, will come with us to explain.'

The words were addressed to Halloran, but his eyes were on the tense figure of Williams. Halloran too looked now at his partner. Williams' mind was working rapidly, but in directions which would have surprised everyone present. This was a showdown, and he had never been a man to break away. From the moment he learned that something had gone wrong, he had been working out the odds. It was his estimate that he could probably kill three of the Frenchmen before he went down. This new proposal put an alternative which he had not considered. The idea of the men from Marseilles taking Halloran with them when they left was almost too good to be true. They would be doing his job for him, because Williams had plans of his own for the gold, once delivered. Those plans did not involve George Halloran, and now he was being offered the answer to his disposal on a plate. But he must not grab at it too quickly, or he might arouse suspicion. When he spoke, his words were slow, the words of a man who had not yet made up his mind.

'I don't know. What do you think, George?'

Halloran was relieved that Williams' response had not been to start shooting immediately. At the same time, he had no relish for the thought of going alone to Marseilles.

'We could telephone M. Pagnol,' he suggested. 'Explain what has happened. I'm sure—'

223

'No.' Rambert's interruption was final. 'The Club wants no telephone calls from England tonight. There must be no way for anyone to connect us with this business.'

'That makes sense,' said Williams reasonably. 'There are only two answers here, George. Either we shoot it out, or we'll have to agree. I'll leave it to you.'

It sounded genuine enough, he thought, but in fact he was giving Halloran no alternative. The odds against them were too heavy, and his partner would always rather talk than fight.

Halloran expelled a long deep sigh.

'Very well,' he agreed. 'I shall go with you.'

'Before you do, I want to make something very clear,' Williams' tone was cold, and his eyes fixed steadily on Rambert's face. 'We have not double-crossed your people, and we don't intend to. But I tell you this, Rambert, and you had better tell Pagnol every word I say. If anything should happen to my partner here, no money will be paid. Not one sou. Plus, your friend The Club will have a war on his hands like he never experienced before. You can tell him those words came from me. He knows I do not make idle threats.'

Rambert, despite his numerical superiority, felt a twinge of unease in the icy presence of Williams. This was the one Pagnol had spoken of, and he could feel the cold evil in the man.

'The arrangement was for six men to return,' he announced, changing the subject abruptly. 'We shall be six, after all. When you are ready, monsieur?'

Two minutes later they were gone, and the empty garage echoed to a strange sound.

Somewhere, a lone man was laughing.

*   *   *

The s.s. *Sunderland Lady* was now ablaze from stem to stern. Her brave new paintwork, which she had flaunted so triumphantly on the journey from Marseilles, was now curled and blackened. The shiny metal, too, was twisted and crumpling, as the superstructure sagged increasingly, in readiness for its final collapse into the inferno of the hold.

In mid-river, the fireboat was directing a steady stream of foam at the holocaust, as close as she dared to come, while one man kept a vigilant eye on the surface of the water. As yet, they knew nothing of what had happened to the launch and its occupants, but they had seen creeping oil before, and were fully alert to its danger. The searchlight on the roof of the wheel-house roved incessantly over the placid river, watching for the tell-tale dark streaks which would follow the slightest shift of wind or current.

'Hold it!'

An urgent shout from the lee-side quarter caused the swinging light beam to freeze.

'What is it, Ted?'

'Something there. Looks like a body.'

The officer in charge hurried down to see for himself, straining his eyes against the drifting smoke. There was something there all right, bobbing gently just above the surface and a few feet clear of the licking flames. A sudden puff of wind cleared the air for a few seconds, and there, in the cold outline of the searchlight beam, was the blackened travesty of a human figure. No, not one, there were two.

'God help us.'

There was no question of life-saving here. Those people, men or women, were past all human aid. As such, they came automatically within the jurisdiction of the river police, whose unenviable task it would be to lift them from the water.

'Keep an eye on them, Ted. If they get close enough, haul them alongside until the patrol boat gets here.'

The officer switched on his walkie-talkie.

'This is Bravo Two Two, fireboat Firehawk. I have located two persons in the water, presumed dead. Repeat. I have located—'

*   *   *

Inside the warehouse, tiring men were carrying the last of the bullion blocks to the escape chutes. The heavy uniforms, coupled with the essential helmets and gas masks, had made the physical task an increasing burden. The rigorous training programme of the previous week was now proving its worth, as they staggered thankfully upwards for the last time. The rest of the planning, and the careful programming, would all have come to naught in the hands of ordinary thieves. In the final analysis only men in peak condition could have coped with the sheer physical effort involved, and even they were almost at the end of their tether.

'Sir.'

Cookie McLeish's shout reached Baxter on his incessant patrol from one end of the line to the other. He hurried over to number one ambulance, where the grinning Glaswegian stood pointing at the open mouth of the chute. There, lying on one side, was a fireman's helmet. It was the signal that the last of the gold had been sent down. The men would be the next to arrive.

'Fish it out, Cookie,' instructed Baxter, 'otherwise one of your mates will land on it.'

He ran quickly to the other vehicles, warning the unloaders.

The first down was Ginger Davis, as planned. He would make the first leap to demonstrate to the others that there was nothing to fear. Mallory would be the last out, to ensure there were no last-minute hitches.

Davis emerged, bumping and sliding his way down to the waiting McLeish, who helped him quickly to his feet, and clear. Des O'Rourke was next, followed at thirty-second intervals by the others. Joe Mallory straightened up, and went to the expectant Baxter, holding up his thumbs. Baxter nodded and waved his arms. Working now in teams, the drivers and the firemen pulled the escape chutes clear of the vehicles, and locked up the rear doors. Then they climbed aboard and waited for the signal. Baxter and Mallory would leave in number one, with McLeish at the wheel. There would only be one man in the second ambulance, with two in numbers three and four.

The O'Rourkes would bring the hydraulic platform.

So far, so good, but they were by no means finished yet. The journey to the car-repair shop was not much more than half a mile, but there was no proper road. The route was tortuous, involving a careful threading between ramshackle buildings, sudden stretches of broken fencing, occasional large holes where valuable machinery had been removed from concrete foundations. There was rusted rail-track to be negotiated and, at one point, a vast rectangular excavation, the size of a swimming pool, the former site of a large chemical bath. Baxter could not risk the use of headlights, and they proceeded at a snail's pace, straining their eyes ahead in the scant illumination offered by the sidelights. The rest of them used no lights at all, following almost bumper to bumper, like a procession of snails. They were approaching the repair shop from the waterfront side, and would have to negotiate their way to the entrance at the far end of the building.

Basil Williams had been alone in the place for over two hours, and the strain of inaction was beginning to play on his nerves. The first half hour had passed quickly enough. He had needed that time in which to replan his movements when the gold was delivered. The action of Rambert and his men, in taking George Halloran away, had solved for him the problem of Halloran's disposal, but it left another problem in its place. Instead of there being two pairs of eyes to supervise the shifting of the blocks of bullion, there would now be only himself, and he would have to be extra watchful. When the work was done, and the men had dispersed, Baxter would be eliminated. It was a pity, in Williams' opinion, because he disliked waste, and Baxter was unquestionably a valuable man. But Estelle was right. Now that Ryder was dead, there was room for only one man to take his place. The others, Halloran and Baxter, knew nothing yet of the change in the situation, but when they found out, they were not the types to accept that Williams should take charge. More especially, they were going to require a redistribution of the profits. Each, in his own way, was dangerous, and there was only one way to deal with dangerous men.

The radio was a valued companion in the empty silence of the huge shed, and he was able to keep in close touch with developments as on-the-spot reporters interrupted the endless music with news flashes. Mostly, these were confined

227

to the enormous traffic jam which was blocking the entire area, but one man had actually witnessed the robbery in progress. A news helicopter had braved its way down into the dense black smoke-clouds, and in a moment of visual clarity, caused by a slight wind-shift, there had been a quick sighting of the bullion warehouse. The reporter gabbled excitedly about the rescue operation, where he could just make out the yellow escape chutes and the waiting ambulances, before the smoke obscured the view once again, and the chopper pilot had to gain height for their own safety. Williams had been unable to contain a gratified smile as he listened. It wasn't every day that a robbery was witnessed and described in such heroic terms. He looked at his watch for the umpteenth time, and frowned. Where the devil were Baxter and his crew? Ah.

The red light flashed, and he pressed the button which would roll up the shuttered doors. He commanded a good view of the entrance, and his heavy Luger was trained on that dark oblong, ready for any emergency. The first of the ambulances rolled in, followed by the rest of the fleet, and forming a neat line. At once he closed the heavy doors, and went out to greet the arrivals.

Baxter was already out of the first vehicle, along with another man, a stranger, also dressed as a fireman.

'No trouble?' greeted Williams.

'No. It's all here,' was the curt response.

'Mind if I take a look?'

Without waiting for a reply, Williams hurried to the rear, and opened the doors, peering inside. Then he took a deep breath, as he inspected the neat rows of gold bricks, reflecting a dull glow in the half-light.

'Did you ever see anything so beautiful?' he muttered.

The other men had all gathered now in a group, and were waiting. There was a tension emanating from them which was almost palpable. Williams had seen it before, and recognised it. This was the emotional reaction which was usual at the half-way stage of an operation. The objective had been achieved, which brought with it a flood of relief, but at the same time, their getaway was not yet complete, and they were in a jittery kind of emotional limbo. At such times men could be very volatile in their reactions. They needed firm directions.

'Right,' snapped Williams. 'There are clothes over there. You'll all find something that'll fit. First job is to get changed, and then bring all the uniforms back here. They will go into one of the ambulances.'

No-one moved, and for a fraction of a second, Williams suspected treachery. His hand tightened on the gun in his pocket. Then, Baxter's voice cleared the air.

'All right, lads. Let's get on with it.'

The moment he spoke, the group dispersed. Baxter strolled up to the frowning Williams, and grinned.

'You forget, old chum, these are my men. Let's go into the office and talk.'

Basil nodded grimly, and they went into the foreman's little room.

'Where's George Halloran?' asked Baxter casually.

'He's halfway to France by now,' was the curt reply. 'You and I will finish this business.'

'I don't see any cars. There are supposed to be three cars for my men.' Baxter made no attempt to hide the suspicion in his tone.

'Ready and waiting,' came the assurance. 'Pub down the road, The Slavers, with a big car park. All they do is to drive all your vehicles down there, dump them, get in the cars, and away.'

'Fair enough,' Baxter eyed him narrowly. 'Do they leave the gold inside, as well?'

'Naturally not,' said Williams tersely. 'See that lorry over there? There are bricks under those tarpaulins. House-bricks. I want your chaps to stack the bullion on there. All we do then is to cover it over with ordinary bricks, and drive out in public like honest men.'

The idea was good, admitted Baxter, but there seemed to him to be a major flaw from Williams' viewpoint.

'This doesn't feel right,' he objected. 'There are ten of us here, and you're just one man. I don't underestimate you, let me say that straight off, but you can't cope with ten men. What's to stop us from loading up, and just leaving you out of it? There's got to be a catch.'

Williams responded with one of his unlovely thin smiles.

'Think back to the beginning, Major. You got this job because you're a soldier, a fighting man. Your men are all the same. You're mercenaries, not crooks. What you say is quite true. You could kill me and steal the stuff, but what then? What would you do with it? Knock on people's doors? Got some nice bullion outside, going cheap. For you a special price. Or a discreet ad. in *The Sunday Times* perhaps, with a box number, naturally. No, Baxter, we thought of that right at the outset, and that's one important reason why we didn't hire criminals. They might have known where to go, but you don't. That stuff out there happens to be gold bullion, but it might just as well be waste paper, for all the good it is to you.'

It was perfectly true, and Baxter nodded.

'O.K. That makes sense. So we load up, collect our money, and go, is that it?'

Again, that humourless smile.

'If you like,' agreed Williams, 'but I was rather hoping you might stay behind after the others have gone. There is a certain proposition I'd like to put to you. But it's very private, just for us.'

Ah, thought Baxter, now it comes.

'What kind of proposition? A double-cross, you mean?'

Williams spread his hands in deprecation.

'Let us rather say, a slight shift in emphasis. I could manage without you, but I won't deny you would be a useful man to have. Well?'

Baxter nodded briefly.

'I'll stay. Now I'll go and get the men to work.'

Outside, the firemen and ambulance drivers had been replaced by a motley-looking crew, in an assortment of pullovers and wind-cheaters. Baxter explained the task to them, and, after a few grumbles, they set to work, transferring the gold blocks from the ambulances and onto the waiting lorry.

Baxter walked to one side, beckoning Joe Mallory to follow. From the window of the foreman's office, Basil Williams stared out at the final scene in the drama. There was the end product of months of careful planning and painstaking attention to detail. He felt a sense almost of anti-climax, instead of jubilation. There was no feeling of triumph in the air, no atmosphere of achievement. Instead, he was looking at a crowd of grimy labourers, their faces soot-streaked and hands blackened, as they unceremoni-ously manhandled dull yellow bricks onto the back of a filthy old lorry. Many men had already died because of those bricks, and he found it difficult to summon any sense of elation as he watched them disappear gradually beneath the carefully arranged workaday red of the bricklayer's craft. Against such a background, it was not easy to realise that what he was watching represented ten million pounds. The chap that Baxter was talking to must be his Number Two, the American who was to receive double pay.

At the thought of money, he turned away, and opened the old suitcase in which he had brought the cash necessary to meet the payroll. There were ten bundles of notes inside, each containing ten thousand pounds. Eight of the men would each receive one bundle, and the ninth man, the American, two.

'Ah, you're all ready I see.'

Baxter spoke from the doorway, and Williams nodded.

'Thought you might like to do this. They're your chaps, after all.'

A small courtesy, which Baxter recognised and acknowledged.

'Right. I'll fetch them in, one at a time.'

It was quickly done, and soon they were all back outside, grinning now, and awaiting the order to disperse. Baxter shook hands with each man, and had a final congratulatory word. Then Mallory, Davis and McLeish climbed into the leading ambulance, and the others followed suit with the remaining vehicles. Baxter stood by the door, and gave the signal. Williams switched off the interior lights before roll-ing up the steel shutters. The darkness at first was Stygian, but gradually it became possible to make out the vague outlines of the waiting vehicles. The first engine sprang to life, and the small convoy moved out. Williams allowed them time to get clear, then pushed the 'close' button, and the doors rolled down again. When the noise ceased he flicked on the lights.

Baxter was walking back across the floor of the shed. Williams removed the gun from his pocket, and rested it on the table. It would be so easy to kill his man now, but that wasn't Williams' way. The simple act of murder gave him no pleasure, unless it was refined by conversation with the victim. The verbal by-play, the gradual building-up to the final act, this was the real achievement. In one sense it was like making love to a woman, a complicated ritual requiring the gradual acquiescence of the person involved, so that the ultimate moment, when it came, was a shared experience. For Williams, a straightforward execution was uncivilised, an act tantamount to rape, and repellent to any man of sensitivity. He watched Baxter almost fondly, as he walked, unsuspecting, into his appointed place of death.

'Well, that's that. Now we can—ah.'

The standing man broke off in mid-sentence as he saw the heavy weapon pointing at him.

'I'm afraid our business is concluded,' Williams informed him. 'There appears to be a gun tucked in your belt, at the back. Would you be good enough to turn around, and remove it for me? With your left hand, please.'

He tensed, as Baxter made no attempt to follow instructions. Then the victim shrugged, and did as he was told. The Colt clattered to the floor. Without waiting to be told, Baxter kicked it clear.

Williams relaxed.

'There now, that's better,' he said, almost jovially. 'Do smoke, if you wish.'

Baxter sneered.

'What, no hearty breakfast?' he complained. 'I must say you disappoint me, Williams. Or rather, I should say, Ryder disappoints me. To bump off a good officer, for what amounts to about one per cent of the haul, doesn't have the mark of class. It's more like the back street thinking of some cheap hoodlum.'

Williams flushed, then shook his head.

'It isn't like that,' he denied. 'You don't understand, my dear fellow. Ryder is dead, and that changes things.'

'Dead?'

232

Baxter's surprise was not feigned. He had been expecting that Williams would try to kill him, but the fact that he knew about Ryder came as a real shock. There was only one person who could have told him that.

'Yes, I'm afraid so. Oh, you needn't look like that. I wasn't responsible. Much of a surprise to me as it is to you, but one has to adapt. With Ryder gone, someone has to scoop the pot. There are only three candidates. Halloran, me and you.'

Baxter inclined his head, understanding.

'I see. You've eliminated Halloran, and that leaves only me. Why didn't you just give me my money, and let me go? I wouldn't have been any the wiser.'

'Not today, no. But tomorrow, next week, who knows? The death of Gregory Ryder will be in the newspapers. You couldn't fail to spot it, and you might have felt you needed a bigger share, after all. You're a brave man, Baxter, and resourceful. I really couldn't go through life looking over my shoulder, to see if you were about to catch up with me. So now you understand the position.'

Almost with regret, he lifted his gun-arm free of the table, and lined it up on Baxter's stomach. Baxter yelled aloud, and flung himself sideways. From the darkness beside the brick lorry, there was a loud report and a spurt of orange flame. The window of the little office shattered into a thousand fragments, as a steel-jacketed bullet tore through and smashed its way into Williams' right shoulder. The force of the impact knocked him sprawling to the ground, his chair overturning, and the gun spinning uselessly away across the concrete floor. Baxter rolled quickly over, and picked it up. He was getting to his feet, as a grim-faced Joe Mallory appeared in the doorway, staring down at the wounded man. Behind him was the silent figure of Ginger Davis.

'I still think we ought to finish him off,' growled Mallory. 'It's the only way with double-crossers.'

Baxter had set the chair back on its legs, and was now hauling a cursing Williams to his feet, and pushing him on to the chair.

'Finish him off? Oh, we'll do that all right. But not with a bullet. It's too quick. There's no pain, no real suffering.'

'What're you going to do?' demanded Williams. He was in a good deal of agony from his ruined shoulder, but his eyes were watchful. 'Why don't you kill me, dammit?'

Baxter shook his head.

'Too easy, Basil. The police are going to catch you. We'll just leave you here for them to find. You'll get at least ten years for this little lot, perhaps more. You'll be able to sit in your cell and think of me, swanning around South America with all the gold. Plus Estelle, of course.'

At the mention of the woman, Williams' face changed.

'Estelle?' he blurted. 'What the devil do you mean?'

Baxter grinned, an unpleasant wolfish baring of the even teeth.

'Oh, didn't you know? She set this whole thing up. Smart girl, that. She knew, with Ryder dead, there could only be one top dog, but she wasn't sure which of us was the better man. So she made a separate deal with each of us. The one who survived would be the winner. He stands before you, as the saying goes. I must say, as a long-term partner, that lady worries me a bit.'

Williams' face was now grey with pain, but twin spots of colour appeared in his cheeks as he digested this new information.

'Don't believe you,' he rejected.

'Really? I'm meeting her at Heathrow at ten o'clock this morning. We're off to Rio de Janeiro. What time were you meeting her?'

The wounded man collapsed into silence, at this final proof of the woman's treachery. Well, he wasn't finished yet. It would take more than a bullet in the shoulder to put him out of the game. Once these two were out of the way, he'd find a solution to all this, and by God—

There was a loud report from the other side of the desk, and Williams yelled in surprise pain as a second bullet ripped into his undamaged left arm.

'Just a precaution,' explained Baxter, conversationally. 'You're a tough egg, Williams. No telling what you might have got up to, even with only one arm. Now, you haven't any arms at all. That ought to hold you, until the police get here. Meantime, I'm going to make a little telephone call, using your name. Hope you won't mind, but I have this passion for tidiness. Oh, and we're going to leave you this, so there's no possibility of error.'

Joe Mallory placed something heavy on the desk. Basil Williams forced open his eyes, staring through a red haze, to see what was going on. There, glinting in the light from the overhead lamp, was a block of pure gold. It would sit there, waiting to be discovered by the police, the conclusive and damning link with the robbery, and there was nothing he could do but wait for the inevitable.

'Your share,' Baxter informed him. 'Don't spend it all at once.'

CHAPTER TWENTY-TWO

Ben Hardcastle eased his cramped muscles and grunted. He felt as though he had been waiting for days, although in fact it had been only a few hours.

'Getting stiff, Mr. Hardcastle?'

The voice beside him was mocking. Turning his head, he saw that his companion's black face was split into a grin. Captain Ngumo was clearly enjoying his discomfort. The man's obvious good humour was infectious, and Hardcastle smiled ruefully.

'I hadn't bargained on all this hanging about,' he admitted. 'I rather thought there'd be a bit more action before now.'

Ngumo motioned towards the surrounding darkness with a pink-palmed hand.

'It is your decision,' he reminded. 'My men are ready to move whenever you say.'

Hardcastle nodded. They had twenty armed men commanding the entire rear area of the repair shop. If he gave the word, they would close in, to join battle with Baxter and his team. With their numerical superiority, plus the surprise element, they would probably succeed, but many lives would be lost, and without point. They had not come to look for some kind of military victory. Their purpose was to acquire the stolen gold, and the fewer people who died the better, so far as he was concerned.

'Not yet,' he replied. 'They can't just stay where they are, it's too risky. I'm gambling that they must shift the bullion before daylight. Once they're on the move, that's when we'll hit them. That depot is too easy to defend, and I don't want your chaps getting themselves killed unnecessarily.'

Ngumo acknowledged this with a slight nod of the head, and they lapsed into silence again.

When Jennifer Fiske had said she could provide an army, Hardcastle had been sceptical, but she had been as good as her word. Nawabia would have a special interest in her proposal, because of the involvement of Major Baxter. As a result of his audacious planning, the government had come very close to defeat in the uprising of a few months previously, a matter which they would dearly love to discuss with him. The strong man at the embassy, inevitably described as the political adviser, had been quick to show interest in her proposal. At the same time, he was wary of her motives. She was clearly, by birth and inclination, a product of the higher orders of society. In addition, she was a trusted Government employee.

On the face of it, there was no reason why she should need to approach him at all. The domestic law enforcement agencies were well-equipped to deal with this situation, without involving a foreign embassy. If she had been intending to steal the bullion for herself, that would have made sense, but she had made it quite clear that it would be returned to its rightful owners. What then? Was there perhaps some deep-rooted political motive, as yet undeclared? In the area of politics, one could never be certain, particularly with these upper-class types.

'Frankly Miss Fiske, you puzzle me. As to my interest in Major Baxter, yes, I make no secret of that. That man has information my government needs badly, and I would go to some lengths to make him available. My concern is with yourself. You are a stranger to me, and to my country, so why should you offer me this favour? In short, Miss Fiske, what is in it for you?'

Jennifer stared straight into the enquiring brown eyes.

'There is a man,' she replied simply.

'Ah, yes.'

A man, of course. It was the one answer which would meet the situation. The politician made no claim to the understanding of women, or their motives, but the evidence of history made one fact quite clear. For the right man, a woman would do the most unpredictable things.

'Yes,' he repeated, 'I see. I think I would like to hear a little more about this man, and who knows? Perhaps we could then take another look at this bizarre scheme of yours, Miss Fiske.'

And now, in the darkness of the night, grim-faced men waited for the instruction to bring the scheme to life. Outside the depot, one of Ngumo's men stood with his face pressed to a gap in the dilapidated corrugated iron sheeting. His line of vision was narrow and restricted, but he could see men carrying heavy brick-like objects, and stacking them on the back of a ramshackle lorry. Several different faces appeared in the frame, each concentrated in serious purpose. This was something for the captain to know. The watching man ran silently over to where Hardcastle and Ngumo were crouched, reporting in the staccato dialect of the Nau people. The captain listened, nodded, then sent the man back to his post. Hardcastle waited impatiently.

'I don't understand this, but perhaps you will,' whispered the captain. 'My man says they are apparently loading bricks onto a lorry.'

A sudden feeling of exultation came over Hardcastle, and he grinned widely. This was the final confirmation he needed. Ngumo's men had not been briefed with any details of the night exercise, and the blocks of bullion could be mistaken for bricks under the poor lighting inside the depot. Clearly the raiders, having arrived with each carrying a small load, were in the process of transferring the haul to the lorry.

'Next to Major Baxter, that lorry is now our target,' he decided. 'Nothing else matters.'

Ngumo shrugged.

'If you say so,' he conceded. 'What happens next?'

'We wait.'

The waiting was short-lived. Soon there came a mechanical rattling sound, as the metal shutters of the depot rolled upwards. Engines were switched into life, and the convoy was clearly about to move out. Timing was everything to the waiting ambushers, and Hardcastle hoped fervently that there would be no premature attack.

'Wait,' he ordered urgently. 'We must wait for the lorry.'

'And Major Baxter,' reminded Ngumo. He had strong personal reasons for renewing his acquaintance with that gentleman.

'Agreed,' said Hardcastle. 'It's my bet that he will stay with the lorry until it gets to its destination. The others are of no importance.'

Without further discussion, Captain Ngumo melted away into the darkness to issue orders. There was a sudden change in the engine noise, and an ambulance emerged slowly from the depot, using side-lights only, and picking its careful way along the dilapidated road. A second vehicle followed, then a third. Ngumo slipped back into place beside Hardcastle, clicking his teeth in annoyance. It would be such an easy matter to destroy the little convoy, and his military instincts rebelled at being denied such a plum target. But, and he had to remind himself again, this was not a war situation. Tonight his men were not soldiers, but brigands, and this white man Hardcastle gave the orders.

Inside the ambulances, men were whistling and telling jokes, in joyous relief from the previous tension, and blissful unawareness of the watching eyes of armed and determined men.

Hardcastle kept his eyes firmly on the depot entrance, waiting for the lorry to emerge. The last of the ambulances rolled slowly past, and then, to his surprise, the shuttered doors slid down into place again, and chinks of light appeared from the various gaps in the depot walls. Beside him, Ngumo snorted.

'What now?' he demanded. 'There can't be more than four or five men left inside, at the most. Plus this important lorry. We surely can't delay any longer? For all we know, they might be in there for days.'

It was true, and Hardcastle nodded.

'All right, we'll move in. But quietly, captain. It's my ambition to take back all your men alive. I want the man with the gas-bombs beside me, please. No heroics.'

He ran easily across to the shuttered doors, followed by Ngumo. Men appeared from their hiding places, awaiting the signal to strike. Suddenly, from inside, came the unmistakable sound of a shot. Hardcastle threw up his arm in a signal of restraint. If the remaining raiders were going to fight among themselves, so much the better. Ngumo, at his shoulder, whispered softly.

'What do you think?'

'Somebody doesn't like his share, by the sound of it. We'll give it two more minutes.'

Almost as he spoke, there was a second shot, then a muffled roar as an engine sprang to life. The soldier who had been peering through the spyhole ran to his captain, speaking rapidly.

'It is the lorry,' reported Ngumo. 'Two men in the cab, plus one outside.'

'We'll take them as they come out. You on the far side, Captain. I'll deal with the driver. Don't forget, your people want Baxter alive.'

Inside the lorry Baxter waved a hand. Ginger Davis pushed a button, and the shutters lifted clear of the ground. At the same moment, he switched off the interior lights. The lorry, heavy now with its golden cargo, rumbled slowly out into the darkness, stopping as soon as it was clear, so that Davis could close the shutters and take his place in the cab. Joe Mallory held the door open ready, and Baxter was facing towards the left, when he heard the door behind him open quickly. The fool was getting in on the wrong side. Turning savagely, he saw the soot-streaked face of a stranger, with a dozen armed men behind him.

'Good evening, Major.'

CHAPTER TWENTY-THREE

Estelle looked at the slim platinum watch on her wrist. Nine forty. Plenty of time yet for him to arrive. She felt a cool amusement, not unmingled with anticipatory pleasure, at the thought that she had no idea who would be keeping the appointment. Each of them was dangerous, although their methods were different, and whoever turned up in the first-class lounge at Heathrow would have demonstrated that he was the better of the two. That was as it should be. With a prize of this dimension, it was only fitting that it should go to the best man. What a time they would have, she reflected. Unlimited money, no-one left alive who knew anything about them, and the whole world available for nothing but their personal pleasure. Yes, he would have earned his prize, whoever he was, and she would see that he enjoyed every moment of it.

Not for ever, naturally. Nothing lasts forever. The time would come when she would have to consider a more permanent future, but there was no need to dwell on that now. This was the time for abandonment to nothing but the pleasures of life and she was looking forward to every second.

The men in the lounge were intrigued by the darkly-beautiful woman who sat alone. She was obviously one of those wealthy South American ladies, of old Spanish or Portuguese stock, although her English, when she addressed the hovering waiter, was flawless and unaccented.

'Just coffee, thank you. Black.'

Then she resumed her reading, idly turning the pages of a glossy magazine, but finding little to hold her attention.

'Excuse me, madam.'

She looked up, to see a tall good-looking man standing before her. He wore a black uniform with gold buttons, and there were two thick gold bands on his sleeves.

'Yes?'

She half-smiled at him, in puzzled enquiry. He swallowed.

241

'There seems to have been some incompetence on our part with the luggage arrangements. Your bags were misdirected to another flight, and the mistake only spotted at the last moment. I have them in the office here now, and I regret I must ask you to identify them as your property, before they can be re-directed to your own flight.'

'But they have my labels on them,' she pointed out.

'Quite so, madam, but labels can be transferred. We would be happier to have your personal confirmation.'

'Very well. If I must.'

She rose reluctantly to her feet, and followed him to the end of the lounge, where he held the door wide, bowing her inside. Except for the two men who stood watching her entrance, the room was empty. No furniture, and, more particularly, no luggage. Estelle felt the first twinge of unease.

'Where is my luggage?' she demanded.

'All in good time, madam,' replied the first man. 'You are Estelle Hope-Amesbury, are you not? May I see your passport, please?'

Estelle hesitated. She didn't like the man's cold politeness, and she cared even less for his request. After a moment's hesitation, she shrugged, and passed it over. The man took it, inspected it quickly and handed it to his companion. Then he spoke again.

'Do you know Mr. Gregory Ryder, the financier?'

She had to summon all her skills to prevent any reaction from showing on her face.

'It is possible,' she replied slowly. 'One meets so many people.'

'Indeed yes,' he agreed smoothly. 'We have a rather embarrassing situation on our hands, madam, and you may be able to assist us in clearing it up. Señor?'

He turned to the man beside him, who nodded briefly.

'My name is Estaban Garcia, señora. I am an attaché from the Spanish Embassy. During the night we received a strange telephone message. According to the caller, Mr. Ryder had been murdered, and his body would be found at a certain house in Majorca. With a man of such prominence, we had no alternative but to check. The information proved

242

to be correct.'

He paused and waited. Estelle's initial unease was now turning to alarm, but still she retained a passive exterior.

'I don't see what that has to do with me,' she said evenly.

'There is more. According to the caller, you were present at the house when Mr. Ryder met his death. The name you were using at the time was not the name which appears on here.'

He held up the passport. Estelle shook her head, thinking furiously.

'This is utter nonsense,' she protested.

'Possibly. If so, my government will offer its most profound apologies. However, these things must be looked into, señora. If what the man Williams says is true, there will be fingerprints in plenty at the house. I see no reason why you cannot be eliminated from these enquiries within a few hours at most. You should be able to catch the evening flight.'

Estelle had been unable to restrain her reaction of quick shock at the mention of Basil Williams. It was clear what had happened. He had managed to kill Halloran and Baxter, and was now holding the bullion himself. His final act of treachery was to hand her over to the authorities, and she felt a deep and burning hatred for his betrayal, which would be handsomely repaid. For the moment, however, she must bluff it out.

She gave a light laugh.

'I don't know that I have ever before heard so much nonsense. Your government, señor, will need to find something rather better than apology for this outrageous inconvenience.'

She looked magnificently dismissive, as she stood in that bare room, and the uniformed man fingered nervously at his tie. Then there was a tap at the door, and a small neatly-dressed man entered. He went quickly to the English policeman, or whatever he was, and whispered urgently. The man nodded, and his face went hard.

'Your passport details have now been checked with the issuing authorities,' he informed her coldly. 'They have no record of it. It is therefore false, and you are under arrest, madam. You will be detained on that charge by the British police, pending Señor Garcia's investigation of the allegations against you in Majorca. Have you anything to say?'

'Most certainly.' Estelle drew herself up in her most regal pose. 'This whole affair is a disgraceful miscarriage of justice, and I shall see to it that each and every one of you is held personally responsible.'

The Englishman nodded, looking almost bored.

'You do that, madam. Meantime, if you will come along with us, there is a car waiting outside.'

She could scarcely believe it was happening. It was a few minutes before ten o'clock, and at any moment the cool voice on the public address system would be instructing all first-class passengers to report to their embarkation point for the flight to Rio de Janeiro. As though on cue, there was a crackle from the loudspeaker in the lounge behind her.

'Attention please—'

A door was opened and Estelle moved automatically forward, flanked by Garcia and the Englishman. They proceeded down a narrow corridor, well away from the public areas, and came to a side door, which was guarded by a bored-looking man in a blue uniform. He opened the door for them to emerge at the side of the terminal building. Behind them came the distant crackle of the tannoy.

'—please have your boarding passes ready.'

Outside, in the gathering morning sun, a man sat on a low wall, eating a sandwich. He watched the little procession emerge, the beautiful wealthy-looking woman, and the grim-faced men who accompanied her. There was a black Ford parked on the double yellow lines, and they all climbed inside.

Joe Mallory dropped his half-eaten sandwich into a wastebin and watched, as the car threaded its anonymous way through the airport traffic. It had been his first and only glimpse of the beautiful woman who had remained in the background of the raid. Having seen her, he could well understand how she had been able to manipulate Baxter and that man Williams. Well, they had both lost in the end. Williams would be locked up in some prison hospital by now, and as for Baxter—Mallory sighed and got to his feet.

There was no point in dwelling on what had happened. It was simply the fortunes of war, and he'd lived with those for too long to lose any sleep over them now. The thing to do was to look on the raid as a military operation, and in that context he'd been lucky. He'd come out of it in one piece, and there had been nothing he could do to help Baxter. Those Africans had held all the cards, and could have killed himself and Ginger Davis out of hand if they'd chosen. As it was, he had simply been told that he was of no interest to them, and they had turned him loose, after a brief discussion between their leader and some white man he'd never seen before. They hadn't even stolen his money, so he was richer by twenty thousand pounds. As he stood with Davis, watching the bullion lorry drive into the darkness, he could hear Baxter's final calm words.

'Estelle. Ten o'clock, Terminal Three, Heathrow. Don't let her get away with it.'

The anonymous tip-off had been the only course he could follow without danger to himself. The decision to use Basil Williams' name had been a nice touch, he thought complacently.

Both Williams and Estelle had been busy double-crossing everyone in sight, and there was a delightful irony in leaving them each to think they had been betrayed by the other.

Mallory walked to a car, where Ginger Davis sat waiting.

'I think we've squared things for the major,' he announced. 'The lady's on her way to the hoosegow.'

'Good,' grunted Davis. 'What now?'

The American climbed into the car and stretched.

'I think we're due a vacation, Ginger. Somewhere sunny, with plenty of action.'

Davis switched on the engine, grinning.

'You must have been reading my mail.'

245

CHAPTER TWENTY-FOUR

Hector Jameson threaded his brisk way through the early sightseers on Piccadilly. It was a bright Spring day, and his conservative dark suit stood out in contrast to the bright colours of the casually dressed crowds. Turning into a side' street, he fingered thoughtfully at his tie, before entering the dark portals of The Club. Jameson had suffered a sleepless weekend, owing to the disappearance of Ben Hardcastle, and the last thing he needed was this early morning summons to a private meeting with the minister. Not that there could be any connection between the two things, he reminded himself. All the same, he might not find it easy to withhold from the minister that one of his key men was missing.

Marching up the broad modern staircase, he knocked at the door of one of the private rooms, and went in. The minister was sitting in one of the high-backed leather chairs, beneath a gloomy painting of an early prime minister.

'Come in Jameson, and sit down.'

'Morning, Minister.'

He parked in another chair, the twin of the one opposite, grateful for the sudden cool of the dark red armrests. The Right Honourable Edward Appleby waited for him to settle before opening the interview.

'Ever heard of a man named Baxter, Philip Ralph Baxter?'

It was totally unexpected, and even Jameson's impassive features registered a flicker of surprise. It was quickly gone, but not so fast that it was missed by the watching minister.

'Why yes, sir. He's a well-known mercenary. Matter of fact, I've been keeping an eye on him recently, hoping he might lead us to some of the key people behind these overseas disturbances.'

Appleby nodded.

'Yes, I know.'

A bad beginning. How could he possibly know?

'I've had a most extraordinary conversation this morning,' continued the minister. 'Chap from the Nawabian

Embassy, called himself the political attaché. That usually means some kind of gangster, as you well know, and what he told me certainly seems to bear that out. It appears that your friend Baxter is rather badly wanted in Nawabia. He had a lot to do with that rebellion recently, and they've been looking for him ever since.'

'I knew about that, sir,' Jameson assured him. 'That's what decided us to watch him.'

Appleby nodded absently, and began to stuff tobacco into an ancient meerschaum.

'Then it will probably come as no surprise if I tell you that Baxter was the man behind this bullion raid on Saturday.'

If he had been apprehensive before, Jameson was now decidedly uncomfortable.

'I had suspected that, sir.'

'H'm.' Appleby puffed carefully at his pipe, tamping down the glowing tobacco until he was satisfied. 'Clever piece of work, that. Well organised. Baxter would have got clean away, but for these Nawabian people. They've got him, and the bullion, so they tell me.'

'Good Lord,' muttered the shaken Jameson.

The minister's calm announcement had shattered his defences completely. This, then, was the explanation for Hardcastle's disappearance. There must have been some kind of a scrap, and he was probably—

'In addition,' continued Appleby, cutting across his thoughts, 'they would appear to have swept up your man Hardcastle. He's an embarrassment to them, and that's why they came to me.'

Despite the coolness of the room, Jameson pulled out a snowy square of linen and mopped at his brow. Hardcastle? Swept up? This meant that the department was blown, and his career at an end. Everything was at an end. What was that last part? Something about embarrassment.

'Hardcastle hasn't reported since Saturday,' he confirmed weakly. 'I was beginning to think Baxter had got him. What do these people want from us, sir?'

The minister was well aware of his discomfiture, and considered it thoroughly well deserved. A valuable man like Hardcastle ought never to have been engaged in this shoddy enterprise, and perhaps Jameson would learn from this experience. The department had not been established for the purpose of playing cops and robbers, and it was fortunate for them all that there was a way out of the shambles.

'I must say your chap gets full marks,' he replied. 'Kept his head very well. Insisted that he had stumbled into the whole business by accident. Writing a book, he told them. History of Dockland, or some such rubbish. Spends all his spare time roaming about the old warehouses, and simply got nosy when he saw a fleet of ambulances turn up from nowhere.'

'Ah yes, the ambulances.'

The news media had given vast coverage of the robbery, and the part played by the ambulances was now well known to everyone. Perhaps there was hope yet.

'Pretty thin story, sir,' suggested Jameson.

'Yes it is, but damned good on the spur of the moment,' grunted his chief. 'Reason they waited until this morning was because they wanted to check that he really does have a Whitehall job. The head of his department confirms that there were two telephone calls, both asking for Hardcastle. Poor man was very puzzled, because no-one has ever tried to contact him before, but it was simply the embassy people checking up. Now they at least know that Hardcastle really does work there. But they couldn't just let him go, you see. They can't have him rushing to the press, screaming bloody murder. That's why they contacted me.'

'Ah.'

Jameson's natural resilience was beginning to assert itself. It had been reasonable to assume that the minister had become involved because he was the head of Department G. As it now appeared, the Nawabians had approached him in his capacity as head of the Ministry in which Hardcastle occupied his nominal post. A very much more healthy situation altogether.

'If I understand you sir, they think they've kidnapped one of your clerks by mistake, and they're looking for a way out. What do they have in mind?'

The minister stared at him coldly, displeased at his obvious relief.

'What they are suggesting,' he replied venomously, 'is that friend Hardcastle is made into a hero. A public hero. Civil Servant Foils Robbers, that kind of thing. He turns up with the bullion, hands it over to the authorities. No reference to Baxter, and, in particular, no reference to Nawabia.'

It was a possible solution, and one that Jameson was quick to recognise.

'Means we shall lose him, of course,' he muttered.

'Lose him?' echoed Appleby, with some asperity. 'Great God in Heaven, man, you ought to get down on your knees and thank him. If he hadn't bluffed it out with these people, you'd be out of a job. As to what the chief would have done to me, if the Department had been blown, I don't choose to think about it.'

Jameson nodded stiffly. The minister was quite right, and there was no denying that Hardcastle had saved them all a great deal of embarrassment, to say the least.

'Quite, sir. This yarn he told them, about how he came to be down in the docks, do you think they believe it?'

Appleby rested his pipe on a heavy ashtray, and pressed the tips of his fingers together.

'As to that, I've no idea, and it doesn't matter. It suits them to believe it, and that does matter. The Department is in the clear. You'd better start thinking about a replacement.'

Jameson pursed his lips. It seemed to be his time for replacements. Only the previous day, during the anxious vigil they had maintained, in the hope of hearing from the missing Hardcastle, Jennifer Fiske had announced that she would be leaving during the next few weeks. In the ordinary way, he would have rejected the suggestion, but she had played the ultimate female card, and one to which he had no counter. The Fiske was pregnant, and that was that. Now he was losing Hardcastle as well. The man's face would be on every television screen, plus huge press coverage, once his recovery of the bullion was made public. The recollection of that empty Sunday prompted another line of thought.

'There's a flaw in this solution sir,' he suggested. 'If

Hardcastle is supposed to have done a Bulldog Drummond act, why didn't he just go straight to the nearest police station? What's his excuse for laying low for over twenty-four hours?'

The minister gave one of his brief smiles.

'That, my dear Jameson, is the most convincing part of his entire story. He will say he kept away out of greed. Once he was clear with the gold, he started thinking about the reward. There's always a big reward in these cases. This all took place in the middle of the night, remember, and Saturday night, to boot. No-one had yet got around to thinking that far, and it was all too late for the Sunday papers. Hardcastle decided that any reward that was posted was due to him, and he wasn't going to put himself in a position where he might be done out of it. He waited until today, when the insurance people would have made a clear statement, something no-one could wriggle out of. Five per cent is the offer, half a million pounds, and it looks as though friend Hardcastle is about to be the beneficiary. They won't like him, but they'll pay him. Oh, he'll get away with it, all right. People might question other motives. Loyalty, patriotism, doing the decent thing, all these are a bit too lofty for most people. Show them a greedy man, a man who says, "where's mine?", and they understand him at once.'

The truth of that was too self-evident to require any comment from Jameson, who simply inclined his head.

'That's it then, sir? As of now, I forget about Hardcastle?'

'You never even heard the name until today.'

'And you're letting them keep Baxter?' he pressed.

'Baxter?' Appleby affected a look of mild surprise. 'There is a mercenary by that name. My people were keeping half an eye on him at one time, but he seems to have slipped the net. It's my guess he'll turn up overseas somewhere, but you can never be absolutely certain with these chaps. Well, I mustn't detain you, Jameson, I'm sure you've a lot to do.'

Five minutes later a smartly-dressed military-looking man turned the corner into Piccadilly. A newsvendor sat behind his stand, enjoying the sunshine.

'*Standard*. Get your *Standard*. Read all about it. *Standard*, guvnor?'

Jameson stared at the poster. Bullion Raid. Huge Reward. Then he took coins from his pocket, and placed them in the tin tray. The newsman folded a paper neatly in half, and handed it to him.

'Ta, guv.'

The customer placed the paper firmly under his arm, and was soon lost in the crowds.